LOST YOU

Also by Haylen Beck

Here and Gone

LOST YOU

Haylen Beck

Harvill *Secker*

LONDON

1 3 5 7 9 10 8 6 4 2

Harvill Secker, an imprint of Vintage,
20 Vauxhall Bridge Road,
London SW1V 2SA

Harvill Secker is part of the Penguin Random House group of companies
whose addresses can be found at global.penguinrandomhouse.com

Penguin
Random House
UK

First published by Harvill Secker in 2019

A CIP catalogue record for this book is available from the British Library

penguin.co.uk/vintage

ISBN 9781911215615 (hardback)
ISBN 9781911215608 (trade paperback)

Printed and bound in Great Britain by Clays Ltd, Elcograf S.p.A.

Penguin Random House is committed to a sustainable future for
our business, our readers and our planet. This book is made
from Forest Stewardship Council® certified paper.

For my fellow Fun Lovin' Crime Writers,
Chris, Doug, Luca, Mark, and Val

1

NOW

SHE CLIMBS UP ONTO THE LOW WALL THAT BORDERS THE ROOF, even as the police officers yell at her to stop. The brickwork scrapes her knees, but she doesn't care. Ethan squirms in her arms as she gets to her feet, her soles raw from running. The weight of him almost takes her balance. Her toes curl over the edge. She hoists Ethan up, wraps her arms tight around him.

"It's okay, baby," she says.

He cries, wrestles in her grasp, his feet kicking against her thighs, his small hands grabbing at her clothes.

"Look," she says. "Isn't it beautiful?"

The moon is reflected on the black mirror of the Gulf of Mexico. Between the terrace and the sea, the infinity pool surrounded by palm trees, its water calm and glassy. She imagines it now, the cool of it swallowing her whole. The calm soaking into her.

"You want to go swimming?" she asks.

He becomes still in her arms.

"You wanna?"

He nods, his head moving against her shoulder. "Yeah, go swimming," he says, his voice so small and soft it brings heat to her eyes, a thickness to her throat.

"We'll go swimming," she says. "I promise. Just you and me."

The police officers have stopped shouting. She hears them approaching all around, their feet on the loose stones that cover the

1

hotel's roof. Somewhere far away, she hears a woman weep and call the child's name.

Below, someone catches sight of her. A cry of alarm, a rising clamor of voices, chairs and tables scraping on the tiled terrace, audible above the easy music of the lounge band that plays there every night. More voices join the choir. The band's singer falters then stops the song, his gasp amplified through the microphone, *Dios mío!* The music stutters and halts.

She looks down for the first time.

Seven stories.

The people below back away as they stare up at her. Their voices bounce between the walls and balconies. A tray of drinks slips from a waiter's hand, glass shattering, liquor spilling in firework patterns.

She imagines her body there, sprawled, casting her own red fireworks across the tiles.

And Ethan's.

Someone says her name. She doesn't turn her head to see him, but she hears his voice, soft and easy, like the world isn't about to end.

"Listen," he says, taking slow steps, drawing closer. "Just wait and talk to me. Whatever you're going through, whatever's driven you to this, it can be fixed. I promise you. Will you talk to me?"

She spares him a glance. It's the security guard from downstairs.

"I didn't mean it," she says.

"You didn't mean what?" the security guard asks.

"To end this way."

"It's not the end," the security guard says. "Not if you don't want it to be. Why does it have to be the end?"

"Because I did a terrible thing and I can't take it back."

The security guard comes closer, slow, creeping. She sees him in her peripheral vision, turns her head to see him better. He has light-brown skin and kind eyes, gray in his hair.

"Maybe you can't take it back," he says. "That doesn't mean you can't put it right. My mother always told me, there's nothing ever been broken that can't be fixed."

She looks away, back toward the sea, the glittering blackness of it.

"I know what you're doing," she says.

"What am I doing?"

"You're trying to get me talking, to make me come down."

"Ma'am, I'm not trying to do anything. Sure, that's what the police negotiators will do when they get here, but I ain't that smart. I'm just talking. Just having a conversation, that's all. Like people do every day. Just talking."

"Don't come any closer."

She hears the brittle edge of her own voice, and it frightens her.

"I'm not crazy," she says, and she wonders if anyone who ever spoke those words aloud spoke them truthfully.

"No, you're not," the security guard says, keeping his distance. "You are a sane and rational person, right? I know this isn't you, not really. Just like I know you won't hurt that little boy."

"He's my son."

"That's right. He's your own flesh and blood."

"Stay back," she says.

The security guard is a little more than an arm's length away. Too close. She edges farther along the brickwork. It bites at her soles.

"I'm staying right here," he says. "I'm not moving, all right? You know, I have a little girl around your boy's age, maybe a bit older."

He waits for a response, but she won't offer one.

"She's a real firecracker, like her mother. You should see her. Half Hispanic and half Irish. I swear, she's only four, and I aged ten years since she was born. Where was your boy born?"

"Pennsylvania," she says.

3

"Where in Pennsylvania? Pittsburgh? Philly?"

She doesn't answer. Everything is quiet. She gives him another glance. His face is loose, the kindness of his eyes tempered with sharp regret. He knows he asked the wrong question. He knows he's lost her. Defeat makes him desperate.

"Give me the boy," he says, the words quivering. "I swear to God I won't touch you. Just let me take him."

"I can't," she says.

"Sure you can," he says, but there is nothing sure in his voice.

"I can't. I won't give him back. Not now."

"It's not fair," he says. "Don't take him with you. Please."

"No," she says, the finality clear.

The security guard is right. It's not fair. She knows this. But it doesn't make any difference.

She kisses Ethan's damp cheek and says, "I love you."

The breeze comes in off the ocean, warm and salty.

"I'm sorry," she says. "Please forgive me."

She sees the security guard from the corner of her eye, reaching, reaching, reaching.

"God forgive me," she says, and puts one foot in front of the other.

Screaming, everywhere.

2

THEN

THE VACATION HAD NOT BEEN LIBBY'S IDEA. IT WAS HER LITER-
ary agent, Donna, who emailed her the link to the resort's
website. Casa Rosa in Naples, on Florida's Gulf Coast, seven
swimming pools across eighteen acres of gardens and palm trees.
For a modest upcharge, she could get a room with an unob-
structed sea view.

I'm not sure I can afford it, Libby had written in the reply
email. Maybe I should wait until I get the on-delivery money.

Nonsense, Donna had written back. The deal's done. Go on,
live a little. Treat you and your boy to a few days in the sun.

Libby remembered looking up from her laptop to the window.
The trees had browned already, and mild fall had begun its surrender to winter's bite. The rain had turned to icy needles, the
wind sharp and cutting. The first snowfall couldn't be far away.

The edits on her first novel were due in the next week or so,
and she had a second book that she needed to make a start on. It
was going to be a busy winter. A vacation on the other side would
be something to keep her looking ahead.

"All right," she had said aloud, feeling proud of herself for
making the decision, as if she had resolved some onerous problem, not chosen to enjoy a trip to Florida.

Her birthday fell in early March. She clicked the Book Now
button and selected the dates. The price wasn't as steep as she'd

expected. A couple of weeks earlier, over Valentine's or Presidents' Day, it was almost double, but this wasn't so bad.

One adult. One child.

Ethan had never been on a plane before. She wondered how he would cope. Was she going to be one of those parents who wants to be swallowed by their seat while their child squeals for three hours? Maybe she could load her iPad up with episodes of *Paw Patrol*, keep him glued to that for the duration. She didn't let him watch much TV, but she could make an exception for a long flight.

Libby found her purse, her MasterCard tucked away inside, and got it done. There. Five nights, standard rate. Maybe one night she could splurge on a hotel babysitter, hit the bar, possibly flirt with a handsome man or two. Dance, even.

God, it had been so long.

Mason had left when Ethan was six months old. Said he couldn't handle it. He couldn't be a part of their lives anymore. After all they'd been through to have this child, he ran away. Give a man some responsibility and see who he really is, her mother had once told her. Libby had thought Mason was many things, but a coward was not one of them.

But still, she missed him. In spite of his walking away from their son, she felt that void in her life, the cold, empty space in her bed. But she would not take him back, not even if he came crawling, begging her forgiveness. She wouldn't even take his money. Her few friends had urged to her to go after him, get the child support she was entitled to. But she didn't want anything from him. She had a good job with a decent salary, and she could manage by herself, thank you. When he came to visit their son twice a year, they were cordial with each other, but nothing remained of what they'd once had.

Besides, Ethan was a good kid. An easy baby, her friend Nadine had said with palpable envy. He had slept right through the night from almost the very start, he rarely fussed, was a good feeder. He had grown into a robust, healthy little boy, not long turned three. He'd be three and a half by the time the vacation came around. She pictured him in the water, wearing his float vest, little chunky legs kicking as she held his hands. He loved to go swimming. She took him whenever she could. More often since the book deal and the first part of the advance had come through, allowing her to cut her hours in the day job by half. It wasn't a Major Deal by *Publishers Weekly*'s measure, nor a Significant one, but what they called a Very Nice Deal. Not quit-your-job money, but at least pay-a-chunk-off-your-credit-cards money. Yes, she'd been managing since Mason fled, but this was the first time since he'd gone that she hadn't been worried about her bank balance.

She had never had the nerve to show him any of her writing. Not that there'd been much to show while they were together. It had always been scraps, a page here, a chapter there. One or two short stories. It wasn't until he left that she decided to take writing seriously. And it had been a useful pressure valve when Ethan was smaller. A way to balance her mind during those short spells of quiet between feeds and diaper changes.

The novel had taken shape over a year or so. Nothing terribly original, she had thought at the time. Mainstream fiction she had supposed, but her agent, Donna, told her different. With some minor tweaks it could be a psychological thriller, and a saleable one at that. All right, Libby thought, so I wrote a thriller. She still remembered and relished the way her heart galloped when Donna called with news of an offer from a publisher.

So maybe I deserve this, she thought.

The hotel's website said there were seven pools. They could spend all day swimming, go to a different one each morning, and still not see all of them. And, my goodness, they had a day-care center. If the guilt didn't sting too much, she could leave Ethan with them and have an hour or two to lie in the sun by herself, to swim on her back, the warmth on her face, the world muted by blue water that kissed her cheeks.

Libby snapped herself out of the daydream. All that was wonderful, yes, but she needed to get there. Flights, flights, flights . . .

She realized then that she should have checked availability—and Christ, what was the nearest airport to the resort?—before she booked the hotel. She cursed to herself and set about searching. Thirty minutes later it was all done and paid for, and instead of worrying about her word count for the day she was worrying about suitcases and swimwear, and God, could she lose twelve pounds in three months, what with Christmas right in the middle?

She lost fourteen, but put seven back on again between December 25 and January 1. The first month of the year flew by like a racehorse while she completed another round of edits on her debut novel, and the second book's word count barely rose. Then it was February, she was flying with her son to Florida in three weeks, and she didn't have a damn thing ready for the trip.

She chatted about it on Facebook with her old friend Shannon, fretting about whether she'd fit in there, if she'd look ridiculous in her swimsuit, if she'd burn in the sun. Shannon, as always, reassured her. You'll be fine, she said, just go have fun. She was a good friend, and was the only reason Libby had a Facebook account, and a private one at that, so they could stay in touch more easily after Shannon had moved away to Europe.

Next thing Libby knew, she was walking along a gangway with Ethan's hand in hers, boarding passes clutched in the other. In that moment, she felt more complete and in control and, yes, goddammit, happy, than at any other point in her life. Not even when Mason had slipped the gold band onto her finger. Not even when she first held her son in her arms. Not even when Donna called and told her the offer was for a two-book deal, seventy-five thousand dollars' advance.

"I earned this," she said aloud. "I fucking earned this."

"Excuse me?" the flight attendant asked as Libby stepped aboard.

Libby smiled and said, "Nothing," and found their seats.

3

THE FIRST TWO DAYS OF THE VACATION WERE THE BEST SHE could remember. She had gasped as the cab pulled through the resort's front gates. She couldn't help herself. Never had she seen a place like this, not even when she and Mason were still together.

A driveway lined by palm trees led to a turning circle in front of the main hotel building. A fountain gushed at the center of a courtyard, surrounded by the U-shaped frontage of the resort. A bellboy opened the cab door as it halted while another opened the trunk and retrieved the two large suitcases, her carry-on bag, and the little plastic wheeled case she had bought specially for Ethan.

The bellboy loaded them all onto a cart and, with a smile, asked her to follow him. She had a moment of embarrassing fluster as she dug in her purse for a dollar bill to tip the bellboy who'd opened the cab door for her before she realized she had forgotten to pay the driver. Once they were paid and tipped, she froze, watching her luggage being carried into the grand building.

I don't belong here, she thought. They'll know. Everyone will know.

Libby had always been this way. Even as a little girl, she had felt out of place at school. Her class had been full of middle-class kids whose parents had decent jobs with health and dental plans, who drove new or nearly new cars, who had cable subscriptions and home computers. Libby's father had worked in a lumber mill before it closed down, but by her teens, he eked out a living doing odd jobs around the town. It was always a stinging source of humiliation when she discovered he was painting the ceilings of a classmate's home, or clearing their yard, or hosing down their walls.

Since her first day of junior high, she had insisted that her father drop her off at least a block from school; she would not be seen climbing out of his rusting van. She never said it out loud, but looking back, she was certain he knew, and that it had wounded him. But he never complained or argued. He just pulled over every morning and told her he loved her long after she'd stopped saying it back.

It was Libby's mother who hammered home her position in the world. They lived in a modest house inherited from her paternal grandparents, and her mother kept it well, but the furniture was tired, the carpets worn thin. Her older brother had joined the army when he turned seventeen and although he hadn't set foot in the house since, he called home once a month. Framed photographs of him stood on every surface, and Libby's mother mourned him as if he'd died, not run away from her smothering grasp.

When Libby's art teacher sent her home one day with the advice that she seek private lessons to build on her natural talent, her mother responded that art was for the rich kids, not the likes of her. Maybe become a nurse, she said. There'll always be sick people, and they'll always need nurses. Best a young woman from her background could aspire to; a modest career, then motherhood. Raising children should be her goal in life, everything else secondary.

Always remember who you are, where you're from, her mother had said. Don't have to be ashamed, but you've nothing to be proud of. Not with a father like yours. When you're a mother, that's when you can hope to be proud, she'd said. I raised my boy right, and he served his country. That I am proud of.

What about me? Libby asked that question several times. Have I made you proud? Her mother never answered, always shrugged and looked away.

That creeping humility had followed her around ever since. She didn't become a nurse, but rather an administrative assistant at Albany City Hall. Not exciting work, but it paid okay. Nothing to be ashamed of, but nothing to be proud of. Mason was making his way up the ranks in the Budget Office there when she met him, and his salary was nearly double what she earned in the Department of Purchasing. On their first date, he took her to a fancy French restaurant, and she had a moment of panic when she read the menu. She had the unsophisticated palate of a child who ate spaghetti from cans and took peanut butter and jelly sandwiches to school.

"Is something the matter?" Mason had asked.

Libby had smiled and said, no, not at all, while she fought the urge to get up and run away from the table. She ordered the first items on the starter and entrée menus and pretended to like them when they arrived.

"Why did you do that?" Mason asked over drinks later that evening.

"Do what?" she asked, though she knew what he meant.

"You ordered food you didn't like and ate it anyway," he said. "Why?"

She considered lying but knew he would see through it. He always had that knack for mining out the truth, no matter how well hidden.

"I panicked," she said. "I didn't even know what I was ordering. Honestly, you should have taken me to Applebee's, that's about as fancy as I get."

"Okay," he said, smiling. "Maybe next time."

And there had been no question there'd be a next time. She fell in love with him quickly and utterly, and they married within twelve months.

But now, thirteen years later, she remembered that feeling, that gnawing fear. I don't belong here. I'm not good enough. They'll smell it on me and cast me out. As she watched the bellboy enter the hotel with her belongings, as the fountain whooshed and splashed, as seagulls called and whirled above, she seriously entertained the idea of getting back into the cab and asking to return to the airport.

Then Ethan took her hand, pulled, and said, "Mommy, let's go."

He hopped up and down, the soles of his sandals slapping on the courtyard's cobblestones.

"Go swimming," he said, pointing to the hotel's entrance.

"Yeah," she said, "let's go swimming."

They walked to the reception desk together, where they handed her a glass of Champagne, gave Ethan a lollipop, and called her ma'am and wished her a wonderful stay, to call night or day if she needed anything, and that feeling of not belonging, of not being good enough, faded to the background, became a distant whisper rather than an overwhelming clamor.

But it didn't go away.

It never, ever went away.

WHEN SHE'D LEFT home early that morning, it had been with all sorts of good intentions. One had been to insist Ethan have a nap as soon as they got to the hotel rather than going straight out to the pool. She knew he would be cranky by dinnertime if he didn't, but when they got to their room on the sixth floor, she went out onto the balcony and looked down. Below was just one of the resort's seven pools. Ethan stood at her side, his arms wrapped around her thigh, gazing down through the glass barrier.

"Mommy, lookit," he said.

"Yeah, lookit," she said.

The water was a perfect blue, the kind of blue you wished the sky to be. Although she felt tired, and an hour of rest would do them both a world of good, the water looked better.

"Let's get changed," she said.

Minutes later, she wore her own swimsuit covered by a light sarong, and Ethan, bare-ass naked, danced in front of her with the sort of excitement only young children know. Libby couldn't help but giggle as she tried to guide his feet into his one-piece bathing suit. It would protect him from the sun from elbows to knees and was recommended everywhere as the best rash guard for a kid his age. She always took great care in such things; every purchase she made for her son was thoroughly researched, from the clothes he wore to the toys he played with. Over-the-top, many would say, but she didn't care. She would do right by her boy in every decision she made. He was a miracle, and she treated him accordingly.

She pulled up the zipper at the back and turned him around.

"Look at you, little swimmer man."

"Let's go, Mommy, let's go, let's go, let's go."

"Nuh-uh," she said. "Sunscreen first."

Libby slathered it on every inch of exposed skin, even the tiny bit of exposed scalp at the crown of his hair. Again, it was the best, exhaustively tested and approved by dermatologists and pediatricians. Finally, she put him in his flotation vest and slipped his waterproof sandals onto his feet.

"Okay," she said, "now we can go."

She grabbed the bag and towels provided by the resort, threw in her own bits and pieces, and opened the door. "Come on," she said.

Ethan zipped past her and out into the corridor, his mouth open, his tongue out, panting like a puppy. The door had almost swung closed behind her when something occurred to her.

"Shit!" she said, and stopped it with her foot, ignoring the pain as the wood slammed into her little toe. "Ethan, baby, wait up."

She reached inside and took the keycard from the slot by the door, slipped it into the bag along with everything else. Now she let the door close.

Libby looked around for her son, but he wasn't there. A flare went off in her chest, bright and fierce.

"Ethan?"

She heard him giggle along the hall and marched in that direction, rounded the corner to the elevator bank.

"Honey, what are you—"

He stood inside the open elevator, oblivious to her, laughing as he pressed buttons and made them light up.

"Ethan, don't."

She heard a chime, and the doors began to slide closed.

"Shit," she said, and lurched forward, her arm outstretched.

The doors closed on her wrist, then opened again.

"Mommy, lookit," he said, pointing at the rows of illuminated buttons.

Libby hunkered down, seized his upper arms, her nose inches from his. "Don't *ever* run away from me like that again."

"But, but—"

"No buts, nuh-uh. If those doors closed and the elevator went away, how would I know which floor you'd gone to? Huh?"

His lower lip curled, and his head dropped, as a whine rose out of him. His face reddened and fat tears dropped from his eyes onto her bare knee. Regret clawed at her, and she pulled him close, wrapped him in her arms.

"It's okay, baby, I'm sorry. I shouldn't have gotten mad, okay? I just don't want to lose you, all right? What would Mommy do without her little man, huh?"

She wiped the tears from his cheeks.

"I'm sorry, honey. I'm sorry I yelled at you. Mommy's sorry. Okay?"

He wrapped his arms around her neck, buried his face between her jaw and her shoulder. "I'm sorry I did the buttons."

"It's okay, no harm done. You won't do it again, right?"

He nodded and sniffed.

Libby didn't know the elevator doors had closed until she heard a chime and a disembodied voice said, "Seventh floor." The doors swished open and an older couple entered. She stood upright, took Ethan's hand in hers. The couple smiled, and the wife waved at Ethan. He hid his face in Libby's sarong, and the woman awwed and cooed.

They all remained silent as the elevator stopped at every floor on the way back down. The don't-belong-not-good-enough feeling bubbled up again as Libby noted the couple's expensive clothing, the amount of gold around the woman's neck and on her fingers.

Stop it, she told herself. You have every right to be here.

Even so, the feeling followed her out through the side doors that led to the pool she'd seen from her balcony. The pool lay in its own enclave, surrounded on three sides by balconies just like hers. She looked up to the sixth floor, counted three along, and guessed that was her room. Beyond the pool, on the one clear side, lay pathways through a forest of palms that she supposed must lead to the rest of the complex. She squeezed Ethan's hand to get his attention. He looked up at her, squinting against the sun.

"You want to take a walk or swim right here?"

She knew the answer and wondered why she even bothered asking.

"Swim right here," he said, and tried to drag her to the water.

"Just a second," she said, and guided him to a pair of free sun loungers. "Sit."

Despite his protests, she made him stay put while she laid out the towels, staking out her territory. She made sure her purse and phone were buried deep in the bag, her Kindle at the top, a trashy magazine on her lounger.

"Okay," she said. "Now we swim."

They had been in the water for a gleeful thirty minutes before it occurred to Libby that Ethan was the only child here. He had been kicking and splashing and giggling and squealing as she held his hands, or put him on her back while she swam, or lifted him onto the side and let him jump into her arms.

She hoisted him onto her shoulders while he laughed, and she turned a full circle, looking at the others on their loungers. None of them looked back. Something was wrong, and she couldn't tell what. That don't-belong feeling came screaming to the surface, and she felt a small peal of panic, even though she had no idea why.

No kids here. Not little ones, anyway. The youngest were early teens. The rest were middle-aged or older. Then she realized.

"Oh God," she said quietly. "Oh no."

She lowered Ethan from her shoulders down into her arms and waded toward the steps.

"Mommy, no," Ethan said.

"It's okay, honey, we're just going to find a different pool."

She whispered, I'm sorry, I'm sorry, as she passed others on her way to the loungers she had claimed. Ethan began to kick and wriggle and she prayed he wouldn't freak out here, Oh God, please, not here.

There, right behind the damn loungers she had chosen, where it couldn't be missed, and yet she had: the sign that read QUIET POOL: PLEASE RESPECT YOUR FELLOW BATHERS AND KEEP NOISE TO A MINIMUM.

A couple, two forty-something men, watched as she put Ethan down and began to pack her things. She felt the heat on her cheeks, the stinging embarrassment of making a show of herself in front of these people.

"Something wrong, ma'am?" one of the men asked.

"I'm sorry," she said in a whisper. "I didn't realize this was the quiet pool. I'm stupid. I'm so sorry. Stupid, stupid—"

"Don't be ridiculous," the man said. "What are you doing? Put your stuff back, you don't have to go anywhere."

The other man propped himself up on his elbows, and a deeper part of Libby's mind noted the hard definition of his body.

"Yeah, you don't have to go. You weren't bothering anybody."

She gathered up a towel, rolled it into a ball, and said, "No, no, we were, we were making too much noise. I'm so sorry."

The first man, the one closer to her, reached out and touched her arm. "Hey. Stop. Cut it out. Put your things back and relax. All I heard was a kid having fun, and if that bothers anyone, then trust me, they have worse problems than a little noise."

He directed those last words at an elderly gentleman who watched from the next row of loungers. The elderly gentleman cleared his throat and looked away.

"I'm Charles," the man said, extending his hand.

Libby looked at his hand for a moment, then took it, told him her name.

"This is my husband, Gerry." He indicated the man on the far lounger, the one with the pecs and abs that glistened in the sunlight.

"Hey, Libby," Gerry said as he reached across and shook her hand.

"Now, here's what I'd like you to do," Charles said. "I'd like you to put your stuff back, lie down, get some sun, and let me order us some cocktails. How's that sound?"

Libby hesitated, then said, "I shouldn't."

"Bullshit," Charles said before looking at Ethan and covering his mouth. "Sorry. Bullpoop was what I meant to say."

Ethan grinned and said, "Bullpoop!"

Libby laughed in spite of herself, in spite of the fear and the uncertainty she felt.

"What about you, young sir?" Charles asked. "You think Mommy would let me buy you an ice cream?"

17

Ethan's grin widened, infecting them all.

"I guess that'd be okay," Libby said, and she sat down on her lounger.

Charles looked up at the cloudless sky, licked the tip of his finger, held it up to the breeze. "What do you think, Gerry? This time of day, this temperature and humidity, the wind speed. I'd say strawberry daiquiris, wouldn't you?"

"I concur," Gerry said.

"That's settled, then," Charles said. "Strawberry daiquiris all round."

As he looked for a waiter, Libby felt a glow inside, a smile on her mouth that reached way down deep inside of her.

"Thank you," she said, the last vowel choked by tears that shocked her.

Charles pretended not to notice.

4

"OH MY GOD, YOU'RE A WRITER?"

Charles's reaction made her blush. Libby had never described herself as such before.

"Well, I'm not full-time. Not yet, anyway. I still have a day job."

Charles floated on his back, his outstretched arms on the tiled edge, his legs kicking lazy circles. Libby crouched so the water lapped at her chin, Ethan within her arm's reach.

"Even so, I'm impressed. And can I tell you something? Fair warning, this might make you want to avoid me for the rest of your vacation."

"Go on," she said.

"I'm an aspiring writer too," he said. "At least, I used to be. I haven't written anything in a year, but I sold a few short stories, wrote a couple of novels that haven't seen the light of day. I could never get an agent. I got as far as one reading a full manuscript once, but he didn't bite in the end. God, I was crushed. How did you get your agent?"

"The old-fashioned way," she said. "Through the slush pile."

"I hate you," he said, his smile crooked.

Gerry came to the pool's edge and hunkered down.

"Hey, it's getting late. You want to go get ready for dinner?"

"I guess," Charles said. He looked back to Libby. "You'll join us, right?"

She felt herself blush again. "Oh, no, I couldn't."

19

"Sure you could."

She reached for Ethan's hands, guided him back toward her. "Honestly, I wouldn't impose dinner with a tired three-year-old on anyone."

"Nonsense. Please, I want to pick your brains." He looked up at Gerry. "She's a writer. Her debut comes out in the fall."

Gerry raised his eyebrows at Libby. "For real? Congratulations."

That heat in her cheeks again. She chided herself for it, even as she smiled.

"No way he's going to let you not eat with us," Gerry said. "Save yourself some trouble, just say yes."

"Okay." She hoisted Ethan up, and he wrapped his arms around her neck. "But I warn you, this boy's going to get cranky."

But he didn't.

After Libby had showered and dressed them both, she let Ethan lead her down the hall to the elevator bank. Too late, she saw that one stood open, and had to dash after him. This time, she reached the elevator before he had a chance to press anything.

"We talked about this, remember?" she said, taking his hand.

He looked up at her, suppressing a grin.

"It's not funny," she said, "so don't you dare smile at me. It's too dangerous. You're not allowed into an elevator on your own. Got it?"

"Got it," he said, but the look on his face suggested otherwise.

They met Charles and Gerry outside one of the resort's two buffet restaurants, and as soon as they had a table, Charles ordered cocktails.

"You're a bad influence," Libby said.

"God, tell me about it," Gerry said. "I just look forty, I'm actually twenty-three and have been weathered away by the lifestyle he inflicts upon me. I had a full head of hair when we met. And he wasn't gray."

"I'm not gray," Charles said.

"Three words," Gerry said, leaning in close to Libby. "Just.

For. Men. H-35, medium brown. He thinks I don't notice the Amazon orders."

Libby had become tipsy enough over dinner that she had to take care with her words, sharpening her consonants as she spoke. Ethan ate well, thankfully, not even complaining when she insisted he eat the green beans. He seemed enraptured at sharing a table with men, watching them talk, enjoying when they fussed over him.

She knew the question had to arise at some point but was no less disappointed when it did.

"So, where's Ethan's dad?" Charles asked.

It was a friendly inquiry, no discernible judgment or challenge behind it. Even so, it scratched at her, like grit on her skin.

"Mason," she said. "His name's Mason. He moved to Seattle when Ethan was six months old. We're divorced now."

"I'm sorry to hear that," Charles said. "Do you still see him? I mean, when he visits with Ethan."

"He visits Ethan twice a year. We don't have any contact other than that."

"Really? Why did you split?" He leaned in, lowered his voice. "Was he violent?"

"No, nothing like that. He just . . . couldn't handle it."

Charles placed his hand on her forearm, warm and gentle. "Was the responsibility too much for him?"

"Something like that. We went through a lot to have Ethan. It was difficult, emotionally, physically. I tell myself now, after all we had to deal with, it maybe took the will to be a parent out of him. Maybe he just didn't want it as badly as I did."

She watched her son from across the table, giggling as Gerry pulled faces.

"Listen," she said, "can we not talk about it? I don't want to be a downer."

Charles squeezed her arm. "Of course. Now tell me about your book."

By the time they'd finished dessert, Ethan had fallen asleep in his chair. Gerry offered to carry him up to her room for her, but she declined, insisting she could manage. They agreed to meet up again the following day, and Libby went to bed with a warm glow inside, perhaps encouraged by the two mojitos and two glasses of Rioja she had enjoyed with dinner.

There were two beds in the room, but she slipped in beside Ethan, gathered him in close. She rested her head on the pillow beside his, felt his rib cage rise and fall against her chest, his soft snores like a cat purring. Somewhere outside, she heard a band playing, a maddeningly familiar song, but rearranged as easy lounge music. Along with the music, the hint of chatter and laughter.

Before sleep took her, Libby kissed her son's cheek and wondered how she could ever survive without him to tether her to this world.

5

THE MORNING AND AFTERNOON OF THE SECOND DAY WERE long and easy. After breakfast, Libby and Ethan put on their swimming things and took a walk through the grounds of the resort. They visited each of the seven pools, including the infinity pool that seemed to disappear into the sea. Libby knew it was an illusion, that there was a promenade between the pool's edge and the Gulf, lined with restaurants and boutiques. They would stroll there another day, maybe go to the beach. Around noon, they found the toddler pool that was hidden in the center of the Lazy River. There, she could let Ethan splash in the knee-high water to his heart's content while she relaxed with her Kindle on one of the nearby loungers. She only had to call out to him a few times, mostly for playing with water toys that weren't his. A promise that she would buy him an inflatable of his own seemed to keep him happy. He spent a good thirty minutes playing with a little girl whose parents smiled at Libby from the other side of the shallow water.

After lunch, she found Charles and Gerry sunbathing by the northern side of the Lazy River and asked if she could join them.

"Please do," Charles said.

"Hey, Gerry," Ethan called, waving.

"Hey, buddy," Gerry said, waving back. "You want to go swimming with me?"

The two had gotten on like they were best friends since

yesterday. It felt good and right that Ethan should spend time with a man. Even so, she hesitated.

"I can't ask you to do that," Libby said. "You didn't come here to look after my kid."

"What are you talking about? It's fun."

"Please, Mommy," Ethan said, turning his cutest face up to her.

"Okay, but be good, all right?"

Ethan pulled his hand from hers and ran to Gerry.

"You all sunscreened up? You got your float vest? Your goggles? Okay, let's go."

Gerry took him by the hand, his long strides making Ethan run to keep up. She watched them enter the water, Ethan jumping on Gerry's back, Gerry laughing hard.

"We wanted to adopt," Charles said.

Libby sat down on the free lounger next to him. "Didn't work out?"

"We got close," Charles said, and she heard a sadness to his voice for the first time. "I mean, we were one signature away. Gerry was heartbroken. You think people are all on the same page these days, that the old barriers and hatreds won't be there anymore. But they are."

"I'm sorry," Libby said.

"He'd be a great father," Charles said.

She looked back to the water where Gerry threw Ethan up into the air, catching him again as he splashed down. Their laughter, high and low, rippled through the warm air.

"He would," she said. "And so would you, I think."

Charles smiled and squeezed her hand. "God bless you."

Libby settled back onto her lounger, opened her Kindle, and began to read. A book that had been recommended to her about a killer haunted by the ghosts of his victims. She was finding it hard to get through, the violence too strong, but she never liked to give up on a book once she'd started it. Without her noticing, the Kindle grew heavy in her hand, her eyelids heavier still. The sounds of the poolside, adults chatting, children laughing, distant music, all melded into a soothing murmur. Libby sank into a warm, calm sleep.

She dreamed of her mother, how she persisted in calling her Elizabeth long after everyone else had stopped.

Her mother said, Elizabeth, how long can this go on?

They sat in her mother's kitchen, all shafts of light and shadow, the smell of coffee.

Forever, Libby said. It'll go on forever.

It can't, her mother said. You know it.

It has to, Libby said.

But it can't. You can't keep it hidden forever.

And she wanted to shout at her to shut up, to stop, but the words couldn't get past her lips, her jaw locked. Her mother seized her wrists, held her in place, made her look even though she didn't want to.

Libby woke with a cry, swatting the warm hand away from her arm.

"Hey, hey, hey," Charles said, his voice soft and kind. "You were dreaming."

She looked around. The sun had sunk below the tops of the palm trees, and shadow cooled her. Ethan sat with Gerry, his Spider-Man towel wrapped around him, eating an ice cream.

"How . . . how long was I asleep?"

"Maybe ninety minutes," Charles said. "I probably should've woken you, but you looked so peaceful. Until all the moaning and groaning, that is."

She rubbed her eyes and yawned. "I guess I needed it. Gerry, I'm sorry you had to be babysitter."

"Stop," Gerry said. "I get to hang out with my buddy."

"Thank you."

"Listen," Charles said, "we're going to get ready to go out. It's date night, and Gerry's taking me to this Cuban place that's supposed to be fabulous. But after, say around eight, I insist you join us on the terrace for cocktails and dancing."

"Oh, no," Libby said. "That'll be too late for Ethan."

"He can stay up late one night, no? Even for an hour. Come on, what do you say?"

"Say yes," Gerry said. "He'll be insufferable if you don't."

She couldn't keep the smile from her face. "Okay. Thank you."

Charles stood and packed the last of his and Gerry's things away. "And I want you all gussied up, you hear? We're going to turn heads tonight, right?"

She blushed. "I'll try."

"Try nothing." He leaned down and kissed her cheek. "You're going to be a knockout."

Ethan came and sat in her lap, and they both waved goodbye. He curled up, his head against her chest as they watched Charles and Gerry leave.

"You like Gerry?" she asked.

"Yeah," Ethan said. "He's funny."

Libby felt an aching crack of loneliness then, realized how much she missed the company of others. She had never been particularly sociable, enjoyed her own space, but that didn't mean she wanted to live in isolation. The thought of dancing and laughing eased the ache.

Thank God for Charles and Gerry, she thought.

She kissed Ethan's damp hair. "You think we got time for a swim before dinner?"

He looked up at her, eyes beaming. "Yeah."

"Then let's go," she said.

LIBBY AND ETHAN got to the terrace before Charles and Gerry. It opened out from the hotel's main reception and bar area, an expanse of terracotta tiles that reached out over two levels to a stretch of lawn, then the infinity pool, then the sea. A small stage stood at the edge of the upper level, tables and chairs gathered around it. Libby found a table close by where she could watch the band and see couples dance.

The band consisted of two men and two women, all of them Latino, playing popular songs arranged as easy bossa novas and sambas. She recognized a Beatles number even though it sounded far removed from the original.

Ethan sat in her lap and gazed openmouthed at the woman who sang and played bass guitar. She winked at him and he grinned, turned, and buried his face in Libby's bosom. He had eaten well, the day's swimming having given him a fierce appetite. Libby rocked him in time to the music, whisper-sang into his ear, making up the words she could not remember: "Ethan's got a ticket to fly, Ethan's got a ticket to fly-y-y."

When the song finished, she took his hands in hers, and they clapped together.

"Well, look at you, all cute."

She turned toward the voice, saw Charles and Gerry approach, hand in hand. Both of them dressed smart-casual, light suits, open-collared shirts. Ethan squirmed out of her lap, dropped to the ground, and ran to Gerry. Gerry crouched down and gathered him up in his arms.

"There's my little man," he said, swinging Ethan around as he giggled.

Charles took Libby's hand, bent down, and placed the softest of kisses on the freckled skin. "You look wonderful," he said, and she smelled a whiff of fresh alcohol.

"Oh, stop," she said, involuntarily brushing her hair away from her forehead.

She would never admit it in a million years, but she had fussed for forty minutes over what to wear. While Ethan lay on the bed watching the Disney Channel, she had tried on the five different dresses she'd brought with her. She had posed in front of the full-length mirror with each one, checking how it hung, how it swung, how it clung, even asking Ethan's opinion. He thought all of them were pretty, leaving her none the wiser. Eventually, she settled on the sleeveless dress with the floral-on-black print, and a pair of strappy heels.

"I look good," she had told her reflection, even if she couldn't quite bring herself to believe it. And anyway, why was she dressing to impress a man who—as one of her work colleagues put it—played for the other team? Because I can, she thought. Because it's good for my soul. Because it's not for him, it's for me.

"Stop nothing," Charles said as he sat down at the table. "You look great and you know it."

She couldn't help but dip her head as she thanked him, a bashful gesture, and for some reason it made her angry at herself. So she raised her head, looked Charles in the eye, and thanked him again.

"Where's the booze?" he said, casting his gaze around. "It's flowing like mud around here."

He spotted a waiter, raised his hand, clicked his fingers.

"Take it easy," Gerry said as he negotiated his way into a chair with Ethan still clinging to him. "You've got all night to get drunk."

Charles gave him a hard look across the table, and Libby sensed the tension, that this discussion had begun earlier and was not yet over.

"Okay, Mom, don't worry, I'll order some water too." As the waiter approached the table, Charles pointed to Libby. "Negroni?"

Libby hesitated, unwilling to admit she didn't know what that was. "Sure," she said.

"And what's young sir having?"

"Apple juice would be great."

Charles turned to the waiter. "Three negronis and an apple juice, if you'd be so kind."

"And water," Gerry said.

"Yeah, and some tap water, thank you."

"Sure thing, I'll be right back with those," the waiter said, and hurried away.

Libby observed as Gerry stared at Charles, who could not meet his gaze.

"Gerry thinks I drink too much," Charles said. "Which is rich, seeing as he likes to tie one on as much as I do."

"It's not that I think you drink too much, not really," Gerry said. "It's just, there's a time and a place, you know?"

Charles stretched his hands out to indicate the world all around. "Sure, but if this isn't the time and the place, then what is?"

Gerry conceded and said, "Okay, just go easy, all right?"

Charles reached over and took his hand. "All right. Now stop worrying. Remember, we're here to show this lady a good time."

Over the next hour and a half, Libby learned two things: that she liked negronis a great deal, and that Charles was a good dancer. He'd studied a little ballroom in his younger days, he said, and he moved with a smooth grace that seemed to lend itself to Libby as she allowed him to lead. She couldn't help but giggle when he spun her around, when he dipped her back, when he pulled her in close.

The odor of alcohol had disappeared now that she was a few drinks in. Instead, she smelled his cologne, and the warm man scent of him. She sighed and rested her forehead against his shoulder, felt the coarse stubble of his cheek against hers.

"What?" he said.

She lifted her head, looked him in the eye, then away again as she laughed.

"What?"

"It's just . . ."

She laughed again, delicious ripples coursing up from her belly.

"Come on," he said. "Tell me."

"It's just, oh God, I wish you were straight."

Now he laughed, and hugged her tight. He released her, held her out at arm's length.

"You know what we're going to do?" he said.

"I'm afraid to ask," she said.

"Tomorrow night, Gerry is going to babysit Ethan. Right? And you and me are going to hit the town. And you know what we're going to do then?"

She snorted. "Oh God, what?"

"We're going to find you a man and get you laid."

"Stop." She slapped his chest. "I don't need to get laid. I mean, I do, but not that urgently. What I need is to dance, get a little drunk, and laugh. And you've got that covered, so thank you."

"My pleasure," he said, and kissed her cheek.

Gerry appeared beside them, Ethan in his arms. "Hey, young lovers, I hate to break it up, but I think someone's about done for the night."

"Oh, baby," Libby said as she slipped from Charles's embrace and took Ethan from Gerry.

"Mommy," Ethan huffed, "wan' go bed."

"Sure, honey," she said, feeling a pang of regret. "Let's go."

As she went back to their table to fetch her purse, she admonished herself for the small sting of resentment she felt at the evening being cut short. This is my life now, she thought. I don't get to stay out and drink and dance. That's the deal I made with myself in return for this miracle.

"I'll walk you over," Charles said.

She didn't argue as he put a hand around her waist and guided her back inside, through the reception area, past the bar, and toward the elevator bank. They paused there, and he kissed her cheek once more.

Libby lowered Ethan to the floor, made sure he was solidly on his feet, then took Charles in her arms.

"I've had a wonderful evening," she said. "Thank you."

"Believe me," he said, "the pleasure was all mine."

"You don't know what it means to me," she said, feeling her face redden. "It's been so long, you know? So long on our own, just me and Ethan. I love him with all my heart, but just to get a little time to have fun, grown-up fun, it means a lot. So, thank you. Really."

She kissed his cheek, but he pulled away.

Before she could ask what was wrong, he pointed over her shoulder and said, "Ethan."

Libby turned and saw him inside the open elevator, laughing as he hit one button after another. The doors hissed and began to close.

She called after him as she ran. Her left heel snapped, and she stumbled, righted herself. She reached out. The doors came together, and she saw him turn to look at her before they sealed her out. She hammered them with her fist as she called her son's name.

And then he was gone.

6

LIBBY SHOUTED HIS NAME AGAIN AS SHE STABBED AT THE ELEVA-tor call button. Too late, she heard the hum and rattle of pulleys and counterweights. She grabbed a fistful of hair in each hand and stood back, watched the floor indicator over the doors as it counted up, two, three, four.

It stopped.

"Stairs," she said, turning in a circle. "Where are the stairs?"

Charles appeared by her side and pointed to the corner beyond the elevator bank. "Over there. You take them, I'll get the next elevator."

Libby kicked off her shoes, left them lying on the marble, and ran for the stairs. Two flights per floor, she took two steps at a time. Arms churning, thighs singing with the effort, she counted off. Second floor. Third floor. Lungs heaving now, air like fire. Fourth floor.

"Ethan!" she called as she rounded the corner to the elevator bank.

No one here, she ran to the farthest elevator, looked at the numbers above it. The car had risen to the fifth floor. She sprinted back to the stairs, up two more flights, around the corner.

No one.

She called his name again, ran to the far elevator. It said seventh now. The top floor. Her legs and arms trembled as she ran once more for the stairway, lungs straining as she climbed.

"Please, please, oh God, please . . ."

She found the elevator door open on the seventh floor, the car empty.

"Ethan?"

Libby turned in a circle, looked up and down the hall. No one there. Perfectly quiet.

She closed her eyes and tried to remember the layout at this end of the building. The central section of the hotel was book-ended by two towers with courtyards at their centers. The rooms opened onto walkways that overlooked the courtyards. Her room was on the far side, on the sixth floor.

Libby walked past the elevator bank, her hand against the wall for support, and found the open arch leading out to the walkway. Soft lights glowed above each door, showing the room number. She went to the handrail and looked down into the courtyard seven stories below. At the bottom was a small garden filled with tall tropical plants, large broad leaves and fronds.

"Libby?"

She looked across, two stories down, and saw Charles looking back up at her.

"Did you find him?"

"No," she said.

"Don't worry," he said, his voice resonating in the space. "He can't have got far. I'll keep looking."

Charles disappeared from view, and Libby cast her gaze down, down into the drop that seemed to stretch in her vision, and she felt a sickly wave as her balance shifted. Could he have? Could he have climbed the barrier?

"Oh no . . ."

She ran back into the hallway, past the elevators, and into the stairwell once more. The stairs seemed to go on forever and she lost count of the flights, ignored the concerned looks from the few people she passed.

At last, she emerged onto the ground floor, the marble cool on her soles. Gerry stood there, by the elevator bank, confusion on his face.

"Libby, what's going on?" he asked.

She did not answer, ran straight past him and through the series of archways that led to the courtyard she had gazed down upon just a minute before. Her toes snared on a sprinkler hose and she crashed onto warm, damp earth. She peered through the dimness and the tangle of stems and branches.

"Ethan? Ethan!"

Libby got to her feet, pushed her way through the plants, parted the leaves with her hands, looking for a flash of yellow T-shirt or pale skin in the dark. Gerry called her name from the edge of the square patch of earth, but she ignored him. She circled it three times and found nothing. Unsure whether she felt relief or regret, she paused and looked up.

"Ethan!" Her voice echoed between the walls. "Ethan!"

A hand closed on her shoulder, made her gasp. She spun around to see a tall man, black hair going gray.

"Ma'am, you can't be in here."

She looked down and saw his white shirt and black tie, the badge, the gun at his hip. His nametag read: R. VILLALOBOS.

"I've lost my son," she said.

"Okay," he said, gently guiding her back to the archways. "Come with me to reception and we'll get this figured out, all right?"

She pulled away. "No, I need to look for him."

He took her arm again. "And I'm going to help you do that, ma'am, but first we're going to calm down and explain exactly what happened, okay?"

Libby allowed herself to be steered back into the light, through the arches, and past the elevator bank. She became conscious of the eyes on her, the other guests staring, and she felt a burning shame. The soles of her feet stung with cold and grazes, and she wondered for the smallest of moments if this was one of those dreams where she realizes she's left home without her shoes and wonders if anyone will notice.

But no, this was reality, hard and glaring.

The man brought her to a cluster of couches, Gerry following, and sat her down.

"Please, I need to go look for him."

"In a moment," he said. "Ma'am, my name is Raymond Villalobos, I am deputy head of security at the resort. Now, I want you to be calm and tell me exactly what happened."

Gerry came and stood over them both. Villalobos gave him a stern look, and Gerry took a step back.

"We were over by the elevator bank," she said, pointing, her voice quivering.

"Who was?"

"Me and Ethan," she said. "And my friend, Charles."

Villalobos looked toward Gerry.

"My husband," Gerry said.

"Then what happened?"

Libby wiped at her cheeks and her nose, tried to steady her breathing. Villalobos produced a clean tissue from his pocket and handed it to her.

"Since we got here yesterday, Ethan's been doing this thing, running ahead of me to the elevator and hitting the buttons. I told him, no, stop, but he kept doing it. Then five, ten minutes ago, I was there talking with my friend, and I didn't see him go in the elevator, and when I looked round, the doors were closing, and now he's gone and I need to find him."

Villalobos took her hand. "And I promise you we're going to do that. First, give me a description. Name, age, height, build, what was he wearing, like that."

She closed her eyes and pictured him. "Ethan. His name's

Ethan. He's three and a half, light red hair like mine, not quite three feet tall, solid build. Pale. He's wearing his yellow T-shirt with the crocodile on the front, and blue shorts."

"Thank you. Just a minute."

Villalobos stood, walked a few feet away, and unclipped a radio handset from his belt. He spoke softly, but Libby could still hear him.

"All details, listen up. We've got a lost child last seen getting into an elevator on the ground floor of the north-tower bank. Three and a half, male, red hair, about three feet, yellow T-shirt, blue shorts. I want anyone available over here right now. Jamal, you there?"

An unintelligible crackle in response.

"Usual procedure at the gates, and have any lifeguards that are still on-site do a quick check around the pools, all right?"

"Oh God," Libby said, picturing all seven pools they'd seen today, all that water.

Gerry sat down beside her, put an arm around her shoulders. "Don't worry," he said. "They'll find him."

Villalobos spoke once more into his radio. "Alejandro, you copy?"

"Yes, boss."

"Wind back the feeds on the north-tower elevator bank, all floors, say, about fifteen minutes. Start at the ground floor till you see the kid go in the elevator and take it from there."

"Yes, boss."

He came back to where Libby sat, and hunkered down in front of her.

"Ma'am, I want you to stay right here so I can bring your boy to you when I find him, okay?"

"But I want to look for him, I can't just sit—"

"Ma'am, please, I promise you we will find your son and bring him here to you." He gave her a smile, but his eyes remained hard. "I don't want to spend five minutes looking for your son, then an hour looking for you, you know?"

Libby shook her head. "I can't stay here."

"I'll wait with you," Gerry said, and she thanked him.

"Good," Villalobos said, as if Libby's words meant nothing. "I'll ask a waiter to bring you some water."

He stood upright and strode away.

Gerry stroked her shoulder and held her close. "It's going to be all right," he said.

But she knew he was wrong.

7

"I CAN'T JUST SIT HERE," LIBBY SAID. "I CAN'T."

She got to her feet, and Gerry took her hand.

"He said to wait here," he said. "I think you should do that."

"No."

Libby shook his hand away and strode back toward the elevator bank, where Villalobos huddled with three men in similar uniforms. She walked past them unnoticed and went for the stairs once more. Commanding herself to think, she worked through the possibilities. He could have stepped out of the elevator onto any of the floors from the third up. And where would he go from there?

Anywhere.

That was the only answer, and it made her sick to her stomach. So far, she had only searched the corridors and walkways adjacent to the elevator bank, but there were hallways leading back to the central block of the hotel, which in turn connected to the southern tower. And there were further wings beyond the northern and southern towers, with corridors and open doors connecting them all.

The terrible image of her son wandering lost and afraid entered her mind, and she stopped halfway up the first flight of stairs between the second and third floors. Fear threatened to overwhelm her, to bring her to her knees. But she straightened, willed herself to keep control. She kept climbing.

On the third floor, she went once more to the elevator bank.

There, she turned in a circle, took in all the possible routes Ethan could have chosen. So many, so many. How could she know where to start? She went to an open doorway that led to the central block, saw the hallway stretching away as far as she could see, doors on either side.

"Ethan?"

As she listened, a middle-aged couple emerged from one of the rooms. They both watched the barefoot woman as they approached. Libby stepped back to let them pass.

"Did you see a little boy?" she asked. "Red hair, yellow T-shirt."

They shook their heads and went for the elevator. She ran past them, back to the stairs, and up to the fourth floor. Again, she went to the doorway leading to the central block, found a hallway exactly like the one below.

"Ethan? Ethan!"

Panic edged in, promising to reduce her to a shrieking mess. She pushed it back, refused to let it take her. Libby was stronger than that. She told herself so. Everything she'd been through these last few years had toughened her. Given her a suit of armor that she could use now.

Not here, she thought. Move on.

Back to the stairs once again. She paused at the bottom of the first flight, her thighs and lungs aching at the prospect of another climb. No matter. There was no choice. She took one step after another, breathing in through her nose, out through her mouth.

As she came eye-level to the flight's top step, something made her stop. The marble steps were well lit, the surfaces glistening. The small landing between this flight and the next was the same. But there was a darkness underlying the sheen. She couldn't quite see it from this angle, so she took another step.

Red.

The marble of the landing was coated with a pool of deep red. She smelled it then, like ripe meat, cloying at the back of her throat.

"Oh God," she said.

Libby climbed the remaining few steps, already trembling. The pool of red glistened.

"Oh please God no," she said.

She reached the top and looked around the bend. A cold and selfish relief flooded her when she saw Charles lying sprawled on the landing. The relief washed away as quickly when she saw one arm folded at an impossible angle beneath his body, his legs resting on the lower steps of the second flight, and the gash that ran in an arc from above his left eye to a couple of inches above his ear.

Libby said his name and kneeled by his side, ignoring the cold wetness of his blood on the marble. She placed a hand on his cheek.

"My God, Charles."

His eyelids fluttered at the sound of his own name. His lips parted and his jaw worked as a deep grunt bubbled from his throat.

"Don't try to talk," she said. "Just lie still."

Libby looked up and down the stairwell. Somewhere below, she heard men's voices, the security guards searching for Ethan.

"Up here!" she called. "Come quick!"

Fast, heavy footsteps, growing louder, echoing up through the stairwells.

"Please, he needs help."

One man, then another rounded the turn at the bottom and climbed toward her.

"Oh shit," the first man said.

The second grabbed the radio from his belt and thumbed the button on the side. "Call 911. We're going to need a paramedic up here, and an ambulance. Looks like a head injury and a broken arm. We'll do what we can right now."

The first man took Libby by the shoulders, helped her to her feet, guided her away.

"We'll take care of him, ma'am," he said. "What's his name?"

At first, she could not answer. Her mind could hold no other thought than him falling, one arm shattered by the force of it, his head connecting with a step.

No, he didn't fall.

That idea rang clear in her mind, so hard and bright she could see nothing else.

"Ma'am, what's his name?"

The guard's hands tightened on her shoulders, brought her back to the now. She stared at him for a moment, then said, "Charles. His name is Charles."

The second guard, now kneeling where Libby had been only seconds before, used his thumb to lift one of Charles's eyelids, his other hand operating a flashlight, shining the beam into the pupil.

"Charles, can you hear me?"

Charles moaned, coughed.

"Hey, there you are. You had a fall. Don't try to move."

Libby backed away, thinking, He didn't fall. She wanted to say it out loud, but she couldn't. What if she was wrong? Probably she was. Charles had simply lost his footing at the top step, distracted by his search for Ethan. That was all. Surely, that was all, wasn't it?

No, it wasn't.

Even though logic and reason told her otherwise, she knew the moment that she'd been fearing for more than three years had finally come. As inevitably as morning follows night, the truth had found her. Perhaps the knowledge should have calmed her, but instead it sharpened her fear, brought panic back to the surface.

She stepped around the two men tending to Charles, ignoring the wetness at her soles even as she slipped on it, grabbing at the handrail to keep herself upright. Mounting the bottom step of the second flight, she called her son's name.

As she climbed, her certainties shifted and changed, then changed and shifted back again. Charles did not fall; he was pushed. He wasn't pushed; he fell. She became vaguely aware of one of the guards calling, Ma'am, where are you going? But she ignored the voice. Instead, she shouted her son's name again, and again, and once more, as she reached the next floor.

A family, two parents, two children, all well dressed, reeking of money. They waited at the elevators, stared at her as she passed, shoeless and bloody. She didn't care.

"Ethan? Ethan!"

The mother approached, her expression wary.

"Ma'am? Do you need help?"

Libby turned to her, unseeing. The woman took a step back.

"I need to find my son," Libby said.

The woman stepped closer once more, reached for Libby, touched her forearm.

"Do you want me to get security? I can go down to the—"

Libby turned away from her. "Ethan! Ethan!"

She called her son's name again and again, louder each time, until it burned her throat. And yet she kept calling, even as her voice cracked.

Charles didn't fall, she thought. And this time, the idea didn't turn on itself, it didn't change. He didn't fall, he didn't fall, he didn't fall. And Ethan isn't lost.

Oh God, Ethan isn't lost. He's been found.

Panic took her, finally, totally.

She fell to her knees, barely conscious of them cracking on the marble floor. Her son's name tore from her mouth, shredding her voice, until she could no longer shout, could only emit a strangled whisper.

Somewhere far away, the woman told her husband to get help, quick, now, go, and other voices gathering round, hands on her shoulders, but she was deaf and blind to them all.

Libby tried to scream his name, but her voice had deserted her, and his name became a long unending exhalation, taking with it all the air in the world, and then everything was quiet and black and sparkling and something cold that might have been the floor slammed into her cheek.

8

RAYMOND VILLALOBOS WALKED THE LENGTH OF THE LAZY RIVER pool, following as it looped around to form an ellipse that enclosed a rocky island, which was as fake as the artificial current that carried relaxed guests along its course. It was a favorite among the older patrons, and those with young children. One could hardly imagine a safer place to swim, but Villalobos knew better.

He could see clearly the tiled bottom lit from beneath the water, the vents, the drains. In his eight years at the hotel, he had found one body out here: a middle-aged man who had decided to go for a late swim and suffered heart failure. There had been other close calls: he once had to pull a teenage girl from the shallowest stretch and pump water from her chest.

He said a silent prayer that he would not find the boy here or in any of the other pools. The idea was a constant worry for him, that a child would wander away from his parents and into the cold blue. The lifeguards were all well trained, good at their jobs, but they weren't on duty twenty-four hours. Therefore, he always had one of his own men walking a route around the grounds, from pool to pool, looking for little explorers who'd grown too bold.

Villalobos's daughter had drowned at the age of four. He had not long retired from the Naples Police Department on medical grounds, heart trouble, and he and his wife had been renting a place with a bean-shaped swimming pool. Jess had woken early and somehow managed to unlock the sliding doors out onto the patio. He had been jarred awake by his wife's screams, and stumbled his way out, following the sound of her voice. Jess floated facedown, still in her pajamas, one of her Barbie dolls bobbing beyond the reach of her hand. When he got there, Carmel was wading through the water to her, still screaming her name.

Their marriage didn't survive the loss, and they'd drifted out of touch over the nine years since. Last he'd heard, Carmel was in Miami, managing some dive bar, keeping a heroin addiction barely under control. On the last anniversary of Jess's death, his cell phone had rung, and the number was from that city. He did not answer, and he regretted it still.

Villalobos left the Lazy River satisfied the boy was not there and followed the winding pathways leading to the infinity pool. A few of the feral cats that lived on the grounds watched him as he passed, their eyes reflecting the beam of his flashlight. Scruffy and fat, they resisted the resort staff's attempts to get rid of them because the guests were so generous with their leftovers. Villalobos didn't mind them because they kept the rodent population in check.

He came to the northern edge of the infinity pool and found Pete Corr there, still in his lifeguard's uniform.

"Anything?" Villalobos asked.

"No," Pete said. "I've been all around, and Tony went in the water, but the kid isn't here."

"Okay, good," Villalobos said. "Stick around a while longer, will you? Just keep an eye out in case you see him wandering."

"Sure," Pete said, and Villalobos thanked him.

Pete was a good kid who had dropped out of college two years ago. Villalobos knew he was a pothead, and he stayed in this job because it paid him to hang around a pool all day long, but he was conscientious, and had saved at least five lives that he was aware of.

Villalobos walked around the shallow end of the infinity pool and its artificial beach, making for the Ladon pool, the one

45

exclusively for the VIP guests who could afford the rooms that opened out directly onto it.

He was worried about the child.

No way would he say it aloud to the mother, but the length of time he'd been missing was a serious concern. In his eight years, he must have dealt with hundreds of children getting lost on the grounds. Almost every time, the child would be found within minutes. But the boy had been gone for more than half an hour now, and there were many accidents that could befall a child across a resort such as this.

The Ladon pool came into sight between the palm trees ahead. An older couple sat on their private swim-up terrace, a bottle of wine between them. With luck, they'd been there awhile and would have seen a child if he'd come near. He was about to call out to them from this side of the water when his radio crackled.

"Boss? You there?"

He unclipped it from his belt. "Yeah, who's that?"

"Carlos."

Villalobos pictured the tubby man, ex-military, who worked at least three different security jobs to support his family.

"What's up?" he asked as he turned away from the pool toward the south gate.

"Me and Tom Landry, we're in the north tower, in the public stairway, between the fourth and fifth floors. We got an injured man here, looks like he took a bad fall. He was with the mother before the kid ran away. She was here a second ago, then took off. I think you should maybe come up here. Things are getting a little crazy."

Villalobos stopped walking and cursed. "You call 911?"

"Yeah, paramedics are on the way. Shit, listen, something's going on next floor up. I gotta go."

Villalobos turned and started walking back to the north tower. "All right, I'm on my way."

Dammit, he thought. Maybe it was a coincidence, but as a

46

former cop, his belief in coincidences only stretched so far. The worry he'd felt before now deepened, creeping into fear. And part of the fear was selfish; he had no desire to deal with a missing-child incident that was worsening by the minute.

The band played on the terrace as he approached, and he noticed the mood among the guests. They knew something was wrong, that something bad had happened. No one danced, and the guests were gathered in clusters, heads close as they shared rumors.

God, please don't let it go bad.

The quiet prayer surprised him even as the words formed in his mind. He had ceased talking to God after Jess died. He still believed in a higher power, but that didn't mean he should waste a thought on a being who could kill a child for no reason at all. But there it was, a plea to the God who took his child not to take another.

He was almost at the doors leading to the lobby, and the elevators and stairs beyond, when the radio crackled again.

"Boss, you copy?"

He recognized the voice despite the distortion.

"I'm dealing with something, Alejandro, I'll come back to you later."

"Boss, you need to come down here."

"Dammit, Alejandro, I've got a situation in the north tower. It'll have to wait."

"Boss, you don't understand. I got the kid's movements on camera."

Villalobos stopped. "And?"

"You gotta come down here and see."

"Fuck," Villalobos said, no longer caring that he was cussing within earshot of the guests.

It's going bad, he thought as he turned toward the southern tower and the stairs that led to the control center.

God help that boy, he thought.

9

"I CAN'T DO THIS," MASON HAD SAID.

He said it so many times in those few months, shaking his head, staring into the dim distance. As if he had a right to opt out now that the baby was here, as if he could simply pretend this miracle hadn't occurred.

Mason's drinking increased in those first days, the wine opened earlier in the evening, the stink of it stronger in the morning. He had always taken a drink, as Libby's Irish grandfather would have said. He'd take a half 'un, that boy, the old man would say in that Derry accent. And yes, Mason would take a drink ever since she'd known him, but she'd rarely seen him sloppy drunk.

There was their wedding night. Mostly thanks to his best man, Johnny, whom they'd lost touch with since. As soon as the vows had been made, the rings placed on their fingers, Johnny had put a drink in Mason's hand, and made sure his glass had not been empty the rest of the day. As a result, Mason had fallen asleep still dressed in his suit within a minute of them retiring to their room. Libby had cried that night, feeling a sting of regret that they hadn't made love. It was all she could do to keep herself from falling into the black, that dark place where she knew she had no worth, would never be good enough for anyone or anything. She had kept that side of herself hidden from Mason so far. She didn't tell him until years later about the episodes she'd had as a teenager, the downward spirals that she was lost to for weeks at a time. When she did finally gather the courage to talk about it, he was kind and understanding, as she should have known he'd be. Either way, they made love early the next morning, and in the dawn light she admonished herself for her foolishness at being upset at such a thing.

She could count on one hand the times since then that he'd gotten drunk enough to not be in control of himself. Mason was a man who liked to be in control. Libby had learned that when they first started dating. When she asked one too many times to split the dinner bill, and he bristled, his male pride blistering. And she had liked that, in spite of herself. She liked that he took control when they bought a new car, or applied for a mortgage, or opened a bottle of liquor. Despite every shred of her being that considered herself a feminist, she enjoyed that he, ultimately, took care of her. She loved that she could relinquish control to him, and not hate herself for it.

Dear God, what her college friends would have thought. She had submitted to the patriarchy, they would have said. She had surrendered.

If she'd had the nerve, she would have countered: So what?

In the years since she'd left college, she had looked back on all those long and turgid nights, talking politics and gender, gender and politics, and realized she simply didn't care anywhere near as much as she thought she did. Within five years of graduating, Libby had reached the middle ground and found herself content there. All those things that seemed so desperately important when she was twenty faded into the background when the necessities of living took precedence. Food, rent, roof, water, power. She learned the human capacity for compromise was near limitless.

Then along came Mason.

She'd been a year in her post at the Capitol Building in Albany. Administrator was such a dull title, but it befitted the work. Requisitions, acquisitions, invoices, remittances. Her days were a smear of spreadsheets and coffee breaks. But it kept her alive, saved her from returning to her cold family home, the humiliation of having to crawl back there and withstand her mother's silent gloating.

It bothered her that all the years she spent as a child and a teenager, wishing she were an adult, no one warned her what a grinding bore adulthood would turn out to be. She supposed that was the final cruel joke the old play on the young: promise them the world, give them a shared two-bedroom apartment, an eight-year-old Hyundai, and decades of debt.

Mason, at the time, seemed like a bolt of lightning in her dull existence. Good-looking in a WASPish kind of way, his thirty-something years beginning to show around his midsection—a dad bod they called it nowadays—and the easy confidence that comes with age. He asked her out after their first department meeting, and she had done her best not to gush and giggle like a schoolgirl, said yes, and spent two whole days in raptures of agony wondering what she would wear.

He was not difficult to fall in love with. Entirely unlike the men and boys she'd known before. Everything was so easy, so simple with him. They married within a year of that first date, a low-key affair, close friends and family only. She told him she wanted to try for a baby straightaway. He asked, Can't we just enjoy being married for a few years? They had time, after all, her still in her twenties, him barely in his mid-thirties. But what if it doesn't work the first time? What if we have to keep trying and trying?

The specter of her mother's words hung over her, that she would have nothing to be proud of until she gave birth. Her higher mind knew that was nonsense, generations of inverted misogyny manifested in the imperative to breed, as if that were all she was good for. Yet she felt how deep those words had penetrated, in spite of herself. And all those difficult times, when she had become lost, they loomed in her memory. The times she had been sent home from school, her mother waiting for her, saying

50

not a word as she entered the house and went to her room, the silence that smothered their home. The bitter hatred seeping from her mother. It felt to Libby that those things would fade away in her memory if only she could do the one thing her mother deemed worthy of pride.

When she was fourteen, Libby had asked if she could start taking the pill to ease her periods. Her first had come when she was twelve, and nothing had prepared her for the pain. When she spoke to her mother about it, she was told to pull herself together, every young woman had to endure it, why should she be any different? It was only when she went to the school nurse one day for a painkiller that she discovered her periods were not the norm, that her bleeding and cramps were unusually severe. Once again she went to her mother, and once again she was told to accept the cost of her sex.

Her mother refused to take her to the doctor for a contraceptive prescription, even though Libby had read that the pills could ease the torment that struck every twenty-eight days. No daughter of mine goes on the pill when she's only fourteen, her mother said. I didn't raise a slut.

Libby withstood it another two months before she found a local Planned Parenthood clinic. Using a pay phone outside school, she made an appointment, and told her mother she was trying out for the drama club's latest production. A doctor there gave her a prescription for three months' worth of pills, and she took them home and hid them on top of the wardrobe in her room. The relief, when her next period came, was immense. She still bled, but nowhere near as much, and the cramps went from agonizing to bearable. Libby thanked God for the clinic and the kind doctor.

Then one day, when she was fourteen and a half, she came home from school and found her mother waiting for her, Libby's remaining stash of pills on the kitchen table. Her mother had seldom hit her before, and not hard; her words usually hurt more than her hands. This time, however, the beating was savage and seemed to go on forever. Looking back now, she could remember little of it, only shielding herself from the blows, her mouth filling with blood, then being dragged by her hair to the closet beneath the stairs. The door remained locked, leaving her sobbing in the darkness, until her father came home and let her out.

Years later, her fears about conceiving were proved right. It took ten years, three miscarriages, and more tears than she could count before Ethan came along. In that time, her demons returned, snapping and biting, telling her, of course she couldn't conceive, not her, why would she ever think herself capable of carrying a baby?

She spoke to her mother about it once, not long before she passed away.

It was those pills did it, her mother said, left you barren.

Libby didn't go to her mother's funeral. Nor did her brother, and her father had been long gone by that time. She imagined the lonely graveside, no one there but those who came out of pity, and in a secret part of her, Libby was glad. A month after her mother was put in the ground, her brother called. The first time she'd heard his voice in close to fifteen years. They didn't talk for long. Enough to find out he'd left the service and become a state trooper in Arizona.

We're better off without her, he said.

I know, Libby said.

She hadn't heard from him since.

There were more dark times in those years. Mason had stuck with her, supported her, kept her afloat. He reminded her that her failure to conceive was not the root of her problems; rather, it had become something for her to focus her negativity on, to obsess over. And on one level, she knew he was right, but in the blacker corners of her mind she believed she did not deserve a child. At Mason's insistence, she had one session with a therapist who did her best to convince Libby that motherhood was not the be-all of her existence, that she was loved and valued with or without a child. And Libby smiled and nodded along while sorrow festered into anger inside her.

After Ethan came, it was Mason who went to pieces. The change was so complete and so immediate that it felt like a stranger had slipped into their bed. At first, he became quiet and still, watchful, keeping to the corners and hallways. The heavy drinking took hold and he began staying up long after she'd gone to bed, then joining her hours later—if he did at all—the smell of alcohol following.

Looking back, she couldn't remember him ever giving Ethan a bottle. He seldom held the baby, she knew that, and when he did, it was as if his son were some exotic and fearful creature. When Libby tried to talk to him about it, he would simply drop whatever he was doing, walk away, and close the door. And that was what it had been: a gradual shutting down, sealing himself off from her. No shouting, no anger, only a widening distance that she could not bridge no matter how hard she tried.

He told her he was leaving as she ate breakfast. Ethan was having his morning nap, and she had stolen a few minutes for herself, a fresh pain-au-chocolat and a mug of coffee on the table in front of her. It had been weeks since she and Mason had shared a meal together, one of the casualties of their slow parting.

"Do you understand?" he asked as he sat across from her. "I can't do this. I just can't."

There had been a time when she would have begged him to stay, promised him anything to reconsider. But not now. He had proved himself unfit for the task of being their son's father.

"Then go," she said.

That moment played in her mind, like an old and familiar movie scene, as she awoke on the marble floor in front of the elevator bank. People gathered around, strange faces hovering over her, filled with concern. A security guard pushed his way through.

"Step back, please. Step back." He knelt down beside her. "Ma'am, can you hear me?"

Libby sat up despite his efforts to keep her down.

"I'm okay," she said, her voice rasping, her head still swimming. A deep ache registered beneath her right eye.

"Don't try to get up," the guard said. He turned to the people gathered around them. "Ladies and gentlemen, everything's under control, so I'd appreciate it if you'd go about your evening. Please use the elevators and not the stairs. Thank you."

The stairs? Then she remembered the blood on the marble, the gash in his scalp.

"Charles," she said. "Is he okay?"

"My colleagues are with him, they're trained in first aid, they'll take care of him until the paramedics get here. Please, stay down."

Libby tried to push his hands away, tried to shift her balance to get her legs under her, but nausea flooded her senses. She covered her mouth and swallowed bile.

The security guard's radio crackled. He brought it to his mouth and said, "Yeah?"

He listened to words Libby could not decipher, the radio now pressed to his ear. His eyes met hers, and he said, "Okay, give me a few minutes."

The guard returned the radio to his belt and asked, "Do you think you can walk?"

"I can try," Libby said. "Why?"

"My boss wants you to come to the control room," he said. "He says there's something you need to see."

10

VILLALOBOS MET HER AT THE DOOR TO THE CONTROL ROOM and guided her to a chair. He noted her bare feet and spoke to one of his underlings. "Call housekeeping, get a pair of slippers and a bathrobe sent down here."

The control room was on the southern side of the hotel's main block, one level down from reception. The guard had brought her along fluorescent-lit hallways lined with pipes and ducts to what felt like an underground bunker. The room was perhaps twenty feet square, and one side housed a computer terminal with four flat-screen displays, each subdivided into four sections showing different views of the resort.

Libby sat down, the swivel chair creaking beneath her weight. Villalobos placed a hand on her shoulder.

"I want you to know," he said, "we've already called the police. They're on their way."

"The police?" she echoed. "Why? What did you see?"

He turned to the man at the console. "Alejandro?"

Alejandro operated a tracker ball, spinning it, clicking buttons. One of the displays changed, became one large moving image. The lobby, by the elevator bank. Libby recognized herself in Charles's arms. And there, Ethan, wandering in a circle, seeing the open elevator, and running toward it.

Libby choked on a sob as she watched herself not notice her son's dash through the doors. Then Charles pulling away, pointing, her running, too late, the doors closing.

"Our elevators are getting old, almost twenty years," Villalobos said. "Newer systems sense the weight of the passengers. A boy this size, the system would cancel the calls and the car wouldn't move. But not these, I'm sorry to say."

Alejandro clicked, turned the ball. The image shrunk, was replaced by another. In white superimposed letters it said N EL BANK 3.

"Third floor," Alejandro said.

The elevator doors opened. Just visible inside, Ethan still hitting buttons, then the doors closed again. The image was replaced once more. N EL BANK 4.

"Fourth floor," Alejandro said.

This time, Ethan stood still in the elevator, went to step out, but the doors closed before he could.

"Little man," Libby whispered, one hand clutching at her stomach.

"Fifth floor," Alejandro said.

The doors opened and Ethan stepped out, his hands raised up to his chest, his fingers twined together, the way they did when he was scared. His lips moved, and Libby knew he said, Mommy.

"Oh baby," she said, unable to hold back her tears.

The elevator doors closed. Ethan turned to look at them before wandering in a slow circle, his gaze going in all directions. His face creasing, the fear written on his features.

"Oh no," Libby said, reaching for the display.

Part of her wanted to scream at them to turn it off, she couldn't watch, but she knew she had no choice but to see her little boy take slow, frightened steps along the hallway until he disappeared from view.

"Where did he go?" she asked, her voice rising. "Find him again."

Villalobos's hand tightened on her shoulder.

"Please watch," he said.

Libby wiped at her eyes, pressed the heels of her hands against them, then shook her head, fighting for clarity.

She almost missed the form of an adult running across the bottom of the screen.

"What was that?"

"Wind it back," Villalobos said.

Alejandro did as he was instructed.

A head and shoulders moved backward at double speed, then forward again. A hooded top hid the hair. Male or female, Libby couldn't tell. But there was no question the figure was following Ethan.

"And now the last feed," Villalobos said.

The image disappeared, replaced by another. A hallway, seen from one end.

"This is three minutes later," Alejandro said, pointing to the time stamp in the image's upper-left corner. "The hall leads to the south tower."

Libby watched the screen, saw nothing but a corridor lined by doors. Then a movement at the far end. An adult and a child walking hand in hand.

Her stomach lurched. "My God, someone has him."

"The police are on their way," Villalobos said. "We can hope that whoever this is, they will bring your boy to us. But these images are from thirty minutes ago. I have colleagues on every exit watching who comes in and out. If they try to leave the resort with your boy, we will stop them."

A voice came over his radio. "Boss," it said. "Cops are here."

VILLALOBOS GUIDED HER back up to the ground floor. The slippers were a poor fit, but she was glad of them all the same. She held the bathrobe tight around her body, feeling irrationally ashamed of the dress she wore.

When she reached the lobby, she saw Charles on a gurney, being wheeled toward the main doors. Gerry followed, blood on his hands, worry on his face.

Libby called his name and he came to her. "I have to go with him," he said, "but I'll be thinking of you and Ethan. They'll find him, I promise."

They embraced, then as Gerry turned to go, a uniformed police officer jogged over. "Sir, just a minute."

Gerry paused. "Yes?"

The officer carried himself differently from the others, like a man of authority. Some part of Libby's mind noted the gold bars on his collar.

"You were with the child before he disappeared, correct?" the cop asked.

"That's right."

"Then I have to ask you to stay here."

Gerry shook his head. "But my husband, I have to—"

"The paramedics and the ambulance crew will take good care of him, I assure you, but I need you to stay here."

"I can't," Gerry said.

"I'm not giving you a choice, sir."

Gerry stared at the cop for a moment, then turned his gaze to the exit, watched Charles being wheeled out into the darkness. He put a hand over his mouth as his eyes welled. His fingers left a bloody smear on his face.

A suited man approached, his cheeks flushed, breathing hard. "Officer? I'm Saul Reed, the manager here at the hotel. I've opened up the Atlantic Room for you. Would you mind setting up in there? I have the other guests to think about, and I'd like to get things back to normal as far as I can."

He opened his arms and tried to herd them away from the lobby. Libby resisted, even as he placed a hand on her arm. She shook him off.

"I'm going to look for my little boy," she said.

"Ma'am," the cop said, "it really would be better if you came with me. Let my people do their jobs."

Gerry put an arm around her shoulders. "Come on."

They followed the manager past reception, through a set of doors that led to the concierge desk, and then to a corridor lined with double doors labeled with ocean names. The Pacific Room, the Mediterranean Room, the Adriatic Room. At the far end, the Atlantic Room. Reed used a keycard to open the doors and stood back to let them enter.

"Maybe you could have someone bring us some water?" the cop said.

"Of course," the manager said, and scurried away.

The room contained a group of tables arranged into a U shape, chairs along each side. The policeman indicated that Libby and Gerry should sit.

"I guess I should introduce myself," he said. "I'm Lieutenant Michael Cole, Naples Police Department, Child Protection Unit. Ma'am, we're going to get your son back."

Libby had to force herself to sit down. The nervous energy that crackled through her body fought with the weariness in her head. She could barely hold a thought in her mind other than the need to look for Ethan. Gerry sat beside her and held her hand. She didn't care about Charles's blood on his fingers; she already had it on her feet, her knees, her clothes.

A memory crashed in on her, one that had remained buried for years, maybe decades. A fight in the schoolyard. Over what, she couldn't remember. What she did recall was scratching another girl's face, hard, drawing blood. She remembered the red trickling lines, the shock in the girl's eyes, the squealing of the other kids.

The parents had insisted on involving the police. An officer with a weary face and a quiet voice had spoken with her in the principal's office. He convinced the parents to let it drop if he drove her home and talked to her mother. When the officer left

59

her house, her mother upturned the table and the cups of instant coffee, then smashed the one framed photograph of Libby against the wall.

Cole took a seat opposite as he spoke, fetching a small notepad and pen from his breast pocket. "I'm going to ask you both some questions. I warn you, some may be personal in nature, and you may not be comfortable answering them. But the more honest you are with me now, the quicker we'll find Ethan. Right now, we're still treating this as a lost-child case, not an abduction. Is there any reason we should think otherwise?"

"What do you mean?" Libby asked.

"Well, for example, the boy's father. Where's he?"

"He left when Ethan was around six months old. He lives in Seattle now."

"Any contact?"

"He visits twice a year."

"Any reason to think he'd come around now?"

Libby shook her head. "He didn't care enough to stick around three years ago. I don't see why he'd be interested now."

Cole scribbled something on his notepad. "You arrived yesterday, early afternoon, correct?"

"That's right."

"You notice anyone hanging around, anyone paying attention to you and your boy?"

"No one."

"What have you been doing since you got here? Hanging by the pool?"

"Mostly," she said. "We hadn't even left the grounds. We spent some time with Gerry and Charles. Ethan really likes Gerry."

Cole turned his attention to the man beside her. "And what exactly was your interest in the boy?"

Gerry tilted his head. "Excuse me?"

"Why were you so keen to spend time with the boy?" Cole

asked, meeting Gerry's hard stare. "He and his mother were strangers to you yesterday. I'm just curious why you and your boyfriend would take up with a single mother and her son."

"What exactly are you insinuating, Officer? If you have an accusation to make, please go ahead and make it."

Cole smiled an icy smile. "I'm not insinuating anything. No accusations. I'm just asking a question. What age are you? Thirty-five, something like that?"

"I'm forty," Gerry said. "Forty-one next month."

"Well, see, I'm just wondering why a forty-year-old man wants to go swimming with a three-year-old boy that isn't his."

Gerry stared for a few moments longer, then got to his feet. "I'm not a lawyer, but I think I'm right in believing I'm not obliged to sit here and take this bullshit from you."

"Not unless I place you under arrest."

"Then I'm done here."

He walked toward the door.

"All right," Cole said. "But don't leave this hotel."

"I want to go to the hospital," Gerry said, his voice trembling with anger. "I want to see my husband."

"If you try to leave these grounds, then I *will* have you arrested."

"You can't do that."

"I guess we'll find out."

Gerry turned to Libby. "I'm going to help look for Ethan. You have my number. Call me if you need me."

"Thank you," she said, and Gerry left the room. She looked at Cole. "There was no need to talk to him like that. He's a good man. Him and Charles both."

"I'm sure," Cole said, "but I'm not interested in being nice. I'm interested in finding your son. Now, how much did you have to drink this evening?"

"I don't see why that matters."

"Please answer the question."

"I had two glasses of wine with dinner, I think, and two cocktails on the terrace. Maybe three."

"Would you say you were drunk?"

"No, not drunk, maybe a little tipsy, I don't—"

"A little tipsy," Cole said, writing it down. "Okay."

Libby felt anger rise through the emotions already crowded inside her. "Look, I was not neglectful."

"I didn't say you were. Do you often drink when you're looking after your child?"

She slapped the table hard enough to make him flinch. "For God's sake, I turned my back for a second, maybe two, and he ran to the elevator. What do you want from me? A confession of guilt? All right, I'm guilty, I didn't pay enough attention, and now my son's missing. Now, please, help me find him."

Cole remained quiet for a time, first watching her, then studying the few lines of notes he'd taken. The only sound in the room was Libby's angry breathing. She brought her hands together and forced herself to be calm. The cracks were lengthening and widening; she could feel them branching through her. Then he spoke again.

"Can you think of anyone who might want to take Ethan away from you? Anyone you know? Anyone that's had contact with you or him recently or in the past?"

He sees through me, she thought.

"No," she said.

Right through me, she thought.

"It's just that, in most cases of a child abduction—and I'm not saying we're dealing with an abduction, not yet—in most cases, the abductor is someone the child already knows. Is there anyone you can think of who might—"

"No," she said, too quickly, too forcefully.

Cole held her gaze.

"No one," she said.

He remained still and watchful. She had to look away.

"Ma'am, is there something you want to tell me?"

"No," she said.

And it was the truth. She didn't want to tell him anything.

11

As Villalobos emerged from the stairwell that connected the basement to the ground floor, he saw his old
colleague Mickey Cole step out of the Atlantic Room. He considered trying to slip away unseen but decided against it. He had
thought Cole to be an insufferable prick from the first time they
met on the job, more than twenty years ago. Cole was one of
those men who thought racist jokes were simply jokes, nothing
more, and anyone who was offended was just too damn sensitive.
Villalobos had taken him at face value at first, done his best to accept Cole's spic gags as if they were friendly banter, and laughed
along. Then one night, when they were both at the deep end of
a late shift, he had watched Cole beat the shit out of a black kid
because he didn't tell him his name fast enough.

But Cole had good instincts, a natural detective, with an in-
nate pig ignorance that allowed him to bulldoze his way through
a case. He might have been a racist, misogynist, homophobic asshole, but he got results. Therefore, he was worth talking to.

"Hey, Sergeant Cole," Villalobos called along the hall.

Cole looked up from his cell phone, surprise and confusion on
his face. The expression changed to recognition, and broke into
a grin.

"Well, shit, Raymond Villalobos. How you been, you greasy
spic bastard?" He pointed to the bars on his collar. "And it's Lieutenant Cole, thank you very much."

Villalobos forced a smile as he approached, shook hands, resisted the urge to wipe his fingers on his pants.

"I been good, Lieutenant, how about you?"

"Oh, getting by. And cut the Lieutenant shit. I'm still Mickey, you're still Ray, am I right? How long's it been since you got retired out? I heard about your little girl. That's gotta be rough."

"Almost ten years out of the job. We lost Jess about a year after that."

"Shit, man, I'm sorry."

They both fell silent for a moment, long enough for the idea of walking away to reoccur to Villalobos. But he had a question he needed answering.

"So, what do you think of all this?"

He tilted his head toward the Atlantic Room. Cole looked back that way, then returned his gaze to Villalobos.

"I don't know," he said. "There's something going on here. The mother, she's holding back. Damned if I know what, but there's something. You talked to her, right? What did you think?"

Villalobos lowered his voice. "I think she's scared shitless, and I think she should be. No question she's afraid for her boy, and she wants him back, but downstairs, when I showed her the video of someone leading the child away? She wasn't surprised. It was like she was expecting it."

"And you think the kid's still on the grounds?" Cole asked.

"I can't be certain, not absolutely, but I'd be willing to put money on it. There's two gates in and out of this place, one to the front, one to the rear leading down to the boardwalk and the beach. My guys didn't see anyone take a child through either of them. So unless they climbed a wall, that boy and whoever has him are still in the resort. But there's nearly a thousand rooms, eighteen acres of grounds. That's a lot of searching. And I'll tell you now, the manager's going to do everything he can to stop us going room-to-room."

"Let me worry about the manager," Cole said. "He tries to stop me doing my job, I'll shut this place down before he can open his mouth to complain."

A young uniformed cop stepped through the archway that led back to the concierge's desk. He stopped there, looking from Cole to Villalobos, nervous.

Cole stared at him for a moment, then said, "What?"

"Sorry, sir, I didn't mean to interrupt."

Cole sighed. "Officer Jameson, you tell me what you want right now or I'll stick my foot up your ass, so help me God."

"Sorry, sir, there's a lady says she seen something. Mrs. Kendrick. I thought maybe you should go talk to her."

"No shit," Cole said. "Where is she?"

JAMESON BROUGHT THEM to a cluster of couches and armchairs in the lobby. A middle-aged woman sat waiting, her knees together, her fingers entwined in her lap. Cole sat next to her while Villalobos hovered within earshot.

"Mrs. Kendrick, I understand you have something to tell me," Cole said, his voice warm and calm, his hard manner tempered for the time being.

"It's probably nothing," Mrs. Kendrick said breathlessly. She pushed her dark hair back behind her ear, showing her gray roots.

"Let me decide that," Cole said. "Now, tell me, what did you see?"

"Well, I'm on the sixth floor on this side." She pointed south. "I'm here by myself. My husband passed away before the holidays, and my friend Mary-Anne, she bought me a trip to help me rest after the fuss of the funeral and all that."

Cole placed a hand on hers. "I'm sorry for your loss, ma'am. What did you see?"

"Well, I've been here five days, and day before yesterday, a woman checked into the room across the hall from me. Not

66

directly opposite, I suppose, maybe a door or two down. Anyway, I first noticed her two days ago, and the reason I noticed her was she was on her own. I mean, she didn't have a man with her. Or a woman. Or anyone."

Cole exchanged a weary glance with Villalobos.

"I said hello to her a couple times when we passed in the hall, just to be friendly, you know? And she said hello back and all, but she wasn't exactly chatty. But that's okay, not everyone wants to be friendly, nothing wrong with that."

"Okay," Cole said, impatience sharpening his words, "so what was it you wanted to tell me?"

"Well, like I said, as far as I could tell, she was here on her own. I didn't see her with anyone else. Except for this evening, when I left my room to go to dinner, I met her in the hall, and she was in an awful hurry, and she didn't even say hello back. Thing is, what really made me wonder is that she had a little boy with her, kind of pulling him along by the hand, and I thought, that's strange, I was sure she was all alone. Then I came downstairs, and there was all these police everywhere, and I asked what was going on, and someone said to me about the little boy who'd gone missing."

Cole looked to Villalobos once again, then back to Mrs. Kendrick.

"Ma'am, can you describe the boy for me?"

She held one hand three feet off the floor. "He was about so high, kind of red, strawberry-blond hair."

Villalobos stepped closer and said, "What was he wearing?"

Mrs. Kendrick looked up at him in surprise, noted his uniform, then replied. "A yellow T-shirt, I think, and blue shorts."

"That's him," Villalobos said. "Ma'am, what's your room number?"

"Sixty-one eighty-nine," she said.

"And this other woman's room, is it to the left or right as you look out of your door?"

She thought for a moment, her hand held out in front of her, pointing first one way, then the other. "To the left, I guess," she said.

"Room sixty-one eighty-six," Villalobos said to Cole. "I have a master key."

Cole got to his feet, told Jameson to keep the woman there, and followed Villalobos to the south elevator bank. He beckoned two other officers, one male, one female, to come with them. In the elevator, Cole spoke.

"I'll knock once," he said, "then you unlock the door and step aside. I'll go in first, you two follow. We go in weapons drawn, but down, nice and easy. Fingers off triggers unless it goes to shit, understood?"

The two junior cops said, "Yes, sir."

They all fell silent as a recorded voice counted off the floors, four, five, six, then the elevator halted and the doors slid open. Cole stepped out first, then turned to Villalobos.

"This way," Villalobos said.

He crossed to the doors and the hallway beyond. Holding back, he allowed Cole and his officers to check the way ahead.

"Sixty-one eighty-six, you said?"

"That's right," Villalobos said.

They walked slowly along the hall, counting the doors. Room 6186 stood on the right, a little more than halfway along. They gathered around it, Cole and Villalobos closest. All breathing heavy, all sweating.

Ten years out of the job, and Villalobos remembered all too well the fear of the closed door. Didn't matter that it was just a kid and a woman they were looking for. Anything and anyone could be on the other side. Maybe the woman would be calm and compliant; maybe she'd be hysterical and panicked. Maybe she'd be unarmed; maybe she had a handgun aimed at the door right now, just waiting for it to open.

He checked the watch on his wrist, the one that tracked

his heart rate. One twenty-nine, goddammit. He could feel it, thrumming in his chest, and his knees felt weak. This was why he'd retired, for Christ's sake. His heart couldn't take the pressure. He breathed in through his nose, deep and slow, out through his mouth, trying to bring his pulse under control.

Cole swallowed and whispered, "We ready?"

They all nodded, drew their weapons, including Villalobos. He'd never drawn his Glock on the resort grounds in the eight years he'd been there. It felt cold and heavy in his hand.

Cole rapped the door hard with his knuckles. "Police! Open the door!"

He waited a moment, then nodded at Villalobos. Villalobos held the master key against the sensor. The lock whirred and clicked as he stepped back. Cole pushed down the handle, shoved the door open, ducked away, and waited for a shot that didn't come. He edged around the doorframe, pistol still lowered, forefinger outside the trigger guard.

"Please step out into the center of the room with your hands raised," he called inside.

No answer. No movement.

He stepped slowly inside, the other officers behind, Villalobos at the rear. Nothing in here but a lone sandal on the floor. Silently, Cole directed one cop to check the closets, the other to check the bathroom. The female officer went to the closet, pulled on the door handle. Empty, save for a small backpack on the floor. The male officer went to the open bathroom door. Lit up inside, the tiles shone harsh and bright. The glass shower screen on the bath hid nothing.

"No one here," Cole said aloud.

Villalobos glared at him, raised a finger to his lips.

Cole mouthed, *What?*

Villalobos pointed to the patio doors that opened onto the balcony. They were hidden by the drawn curtain that moved in the breeze from outside. Villalobos knew the doors couldn't be opened from the outside. You wouldn't close them from out there on the balcony or you wouldn't be able to get back in.

Cole understood, nodded. He crossed the room to the drawn curtain, the side that rippled in the currents of air. The two uniforms came to his side. Villalobos approached, raised his right hand, his fingertips grazing the edge of the heavy fabric. He looked to Cole, who nodded once more.

Villalobos grabbed a handful of curtain and voile, and pulled them back as hard and as far as he could. Quickly, Cole slipped his hand into the gap between the frame, slid the door back, exposing the balcony and the view of the main gates beyond.

Empty.

"Goddammit," Cole said.

All four of them exhaled, unsure whether to be relieved or frustrated.

"What now?" the female cop asked.

"Let's have a look around," Cole said. "We got probable cause to search."

The room had a hollow ring to it, as if it had never been occupied. Villalobos knew the casual mess of a room where someone had slept, even if housekeeping had done their job. There would always be cosmetics around the basin in the bathroom, toothbrushes in the cups, scatterings of pocket litter on the surfaces, loose bills and coins here and there. Nothing like that was visible here as they each toured the room, opening drawers, looking in trash cans, looking under the furniture.

"Just this," Cole said, pointing at the backpack that remained on the closet floor.

Villalobos reached in, grabbed it, and brought it to the bed. It weighed little, barely disturbed the blankets as he tossed it there. He unzipped the main compartment and emptied out the contents: a few pairs of underwear, one top, one pair of shorts, a clear baggie with a toothbrush and a miniature tube of toothpaste.

"Traveling light," Cole said.

70

Villalobos said nothing. He turned the backpack in his hands, feeling the three pockets. Opening the first revealed a printed ticket for a return journey by bus, Boston to Orlando and back again. Along with it, a handful of tickets and receipts for local buses and cabs. Another printout for the hotel reservation, three nights, in the name of Anna Lenihan. He handed it to Cole.

The second pocket was empty, but the third—and largest—contained something hard and rectangular. He opened it and found a small wallet inside. Dropping the backpack, he turned the wallet in his hand, undid the clasp, and unfolded it. A few weathered bills hid within, no more than thirty or forty dollars total, a couple of credit cards from the kind of companies that loaned money to those who couldn't afford more debt.

And there, a Pennsylvania driver's license, expired some weeks ago.

He slipped it from the wallet, checked the name—Anna Lenihan—and looked at the photograph. Then he looked again, just to be sure his eyes hadn't fooled him. He held it out for Cole to inspect. Cole stared openmouthed at the photo for a time, then looked at Villalobos.

"My God," he said.

12

"YOU CAN'T KEEP ME HERE," LIBBY SAID.

The police officer at the door did not reply. She stared straight ahead, impassive.

Cole had been gone at least twenty minutes. Twenty more minutes of Libby's son missing in this hotel. Gnawing worry had turned to shrieking fear and back again, over and over, and she had to cover her mouth to keep from screaming.

"What good am I doing here?" she asked. "I could be looking for him. I could be helping. Why keep me sitting around useless like this?"

The cop remained silent.

Libby shot to her feet. "Goddamn you, answer me."

The cop looked at her now. "Ma'am, please sit down," she said.

"No, I won't." Libby stepped around the desk, approached the door. "I'm leaving right now. I have rights. You can't make me stay here. I am not a prisoner. I haven't done anything wrong."

"Step back," the cop said, one hand up, the other reaching for something on her belt.

"Let me past," Libby said, moving closer.

The cop pulled something cylindrical from her belt, about the length of a pencil. With a flick of her wrist, it extended to form a baton. She didn't raise it, kept it at her thigh, but the threat was clear.

"Ma'am, I've been told to keep you in this room, and that's what I'm going to do. Now, please, sit down."

Libby locked eyes with her. "You want to keep me in this room, then you're going to have to use that."

The cop blinked, a bead of sweat running down her temple. "Please, ma'am, I don't want to—"

The sound of the door unlocking from the outside cut her off. The door opened and Lieutenant Cole entered, followed by Villalobos. They both watched Libby, a hard knowing in their eyes that frightened her.

"Sit down," Cole said, pointing at the chair she'd been in moments before.

"I don't want—"

"I said sit down, goddammit."

Something in his voice told her not to argue. She went back to the chair, lowered herself into it, her hands on the table. Her gaze shifted from Cole to Villalobos and back again. They each had the same expression, as if they were examining an insect on a pin. Her bladder filled, and her stomach loosened. She wanted to weep with fear, but she held it back.

They know, she thought. Oh God, they know.

She noticed the plastic card in Cole's right hand. For a moment, she wondered if it was the keycard for the meeting room's door, but then he placed it faceup on the table in front of her. A Pennsylvania driver's license, issued a little over four years ago to Anna Lenihan.

The urge to vomit came upon her as she read the name.

Her head went light when she saw the photograph.

It's me, she thought. Younger, maybe, but it's a picture of me.

She knew it wasn't, but still, the idea rang so loud in her mind that it drowned out every other thought.

"Who is this woman?" Cole asked.

Libby couldn't lift her gaze from the license. She could only shake her head.

Cole leaned on the table. "Ma'am, you need to start talking to me. If I didn't know different, I'd have said this was a photograph of you. A guest at the hotel saw this woman entering her room with a child that matches your son's description. Are you going to tell me that's just a coincidence?"

She closed her eyes, wished herself away from this, wished the sky to fall.

Cole slapped the table hard. "Goddammit, you tell me who this is right now, and you tell me why she took your boy."

Libby opened her eyes, opened her mouth to speak, but could find no words. She looked up at Cole as he glared back. His voice boomed.

"Talk to me, goddammit."

Villalobos put a hand on Cole's arm, told him to cool it, but Cole shook him off. He marched around the table. The cop's hands grabbed at Libby's bathrobe, hauled her up onto her feet, the chair tumbling away, pushed her back toward the wall.

"Tell me who she is," he said.

"I don't . . . I don't . . ."

Over his shoulder, she saw Villalobos approach, saw him slip an arm around Cole's chest. He dragged the cop away, and Libby struggled to keep her balance.

"Stop," Villalobos said, pushing Cole across the room.

The uniformed officer left her place by the door, the baton still in one hand, the other reaching for Villalobos. "Hey, hey, hey, let him go."

Libby noticed the door. Still open.

Move, she thought. Now.

Her legs would not obey.

"Go," she whispered. "Go now."

She lurched toward the door, her legs seeming to tangle one with the other, the ill-fitting slippers falling from her feet, the room tilting as she crossed the distance between her and the hall-way outside. She threw the door back, fell through, her knees connecting with the cold floor. She heard a shout from inside as

74

she got to her feet, voices cursing as she ran, her bare soles slapping on the marble.

The two women at the concierge desk stared wide-eyed as she passed. Her arms churned, her legs pumped, and she had no idea where she was going, what she was running toward, only that she had to get away.

"Stop!"

Cole's voice. She allowed herself a glance back, saw Cole gaining, Villalobos following with a lopsided gait.

Run, run, run, she thought, anywhere, just get away.

She emerged into the lobby, saw the elevator bank to her left, a couple stepping out of one. Without thinking, she veered toward it. People gasped, stared, pointed. She pushed past the couple into the elevator, hit a button, didn't care which floor.

"Stop her! Stop her!"

Shoe soles beating on the floor, drawing closer. The elevator doors hissed closed, and before they met, she saw Cole reaching, Villalobos coming after. Then she felt the shift in her weight as the car rose, the disembodied voice marking the passing of each floor, two, three, four, five. The panic lifted for a few moments, enough for her to wonder what the hell she was doing. She couldn't escape them, no matter how far or how fast she ran. The car slowed, rocked her on her feet, and the doors opened once more.

Libby stepped out into a familiar hallway, a mirror image of those on the northern side of the hotel. She turned in a circle, found her bearings. Can't stay here, she thought, got to move. They'll know which floor the elevator stopped at, and they'll be coming.

Got to move.

To the right of the elevator bank was the wide-open stairway like the one she'd climbed looking for Ethan, where she'd found Charles broken and bleeding. How long ago? It seemed a lifetime, but the rational part of her mind—what remained of it—told her no, it was less than two hours since her little boy had run away.

Got to move, she told herself again. But where?

She had to get off this floor, that much was clear. But not the elevator, and not those stairs. Think, think, think, she commanded. She pictured the layout on this side of the hotel, how the hallways and landings interconnected.

For no reason she could grasp, she thought of the security room, the control center with all the camera feeds. Then she pictured the narrow flight of stairs that Villalobos had brought her down to reach the basement. Yes, stairs going down, but also stairs going up. Emergency signs, EXIT-SALIDA in oversized green letters. An emergency stairwell. Did it go up this far? She made the image in her mind, the floor plan, where the stairs were in relation to the elevators.

Off to the right, nearest the corner of the block. That's it.

Libby stumbled toward the far side of the hallway, found the plain door, a bar handle halfway up. The sign said RESORT STAFF ONLY—EXCEPT FOR EMERGENCIES. Would an alarm ring if she opened it? Didn't matter. She had to try.

She pushed the bar, and the door opened inward, revealing a darkened stairwell. As she stepped onto the bare concrete landing, a light flickered into life, triggered by her presence. The door swung closed behind her. She listened, heard a distant electronic ringing. Yes, she'd set off an alarm. Move, she thought, get off the floor, don't worry about the alarm.

Libby climbed the steps, now aware of the cold, coarse concrete against her soles, but she ignored the pain. As she reached the turn of the stairs, the light below flickered off, and another came on overhead. As she reached the next landing, she found the exit door, a large figure 6 painted on it. She wrapped her fingers around the handle, ready to open it and leave the stairwell, but she heard something. A sound that tore through her like a bullet.

A child's voice. Ethan's voice. A cry echoing down from above.

She held her breath and leaned over the handrail, stared up into the dark column of air that reached all the way up from the ground floor. Above, she saw one light die, and another come to life. A hand gripping the rail as someone climbed.

Another cry.

Libby clasped a hand over her mouth to stop herself from screaming his name.

"It's okay, Little Butterfly, it's okay."

A woman's voice, soft, soothing, but frightened.

Two flights above, the light flickered out; half a story higher, another flickered on. Libby watched the hand on the rail, heard the voices move farther away.

She climbed, two steps at a time, and she could hear them, the woman and Ethan. His whimpering, her desperate cooing. They stopped somewhere up there.

"It's all right, Little Butterfly, everything's going to be all right, it's going to be all right, I promise, it'll be all right, it's going to be . . ."

The woman's voice turned into a painful whine. Then a choked sob.

Libby kept climbing, her bare feet silent on the concrete, her chest heaving. The woman's sobs resonated down, matched by Ethan's cries. Libby watched the hand on the rail as she climbed, saw the woman come into view as she reached the turn.

Ethan bucked in her arms, shouted, "Mommy!"

Anna Lenihan stopped there, halfway up the flight of steps, staring down at Libby, Ethan held tight in her arms.

13

"GIVE HIM TO ME," LIBBY SAID.

Anna remained still, staring down at her. Ethan squirmed and kicked.

"Please," Libby said. "Just let him go. You can run. I'll say I found him here alone."

Anna shook her head, her hair moving away from her face, revealing the scarring that ran from her cheek to her neck, just beneath her ear, and the imbalance of her jawline.

Libby ascended one step, then another. Anna stayed locked in place.

"It's not too late to stop this," Libby said. "Give me back my little boy and get out of here before they catch you. There's police all over the building. They know your name, they have your photograph. Get out while you can. Just let him go. Please."

She felt a strange sense of calm now. The quivering panic of the previous hours had lifted, and she felt in control of her emotions. As she came closer to Ethan, one step at a time, she grew more certain she would have him back.

"Stop," Anna said, taking one step up, then backing against the wall.

Ethan stretched his arms out, hands grasping at air. "Mommy!"

Libby paused, six steps between her and Anna. Somewhere below, she heard a door open, heavy feet on concrete.

"They're coming," Libby said, reaching. "There's no time. Give him to me and go."

Anna flattened herself against the wall, staring hard down at Libby, something terrible in her eyes, something burning hot and hateful.

"Let them come," she said, the movement of her mouth uneven, as if one side was restricted.

The calm that had settled on Libby blew away like dust.

"What?"

"Let them come," Anna said, a jagged and lopsided smile breaking. "I've got nothing to hide."

The panic came back in like a wave of ice-cold water. Libby's heart punched against her sternum, her lungs strained for air. Heat in her eyes. She looked down, over the handrail, saw the lights on the floor below, a shadow of whoever approached.

"Please don't," she said.

As tears erupted from Libby's eyes, Anna began to laugh, wheezy, edged by madness.

"Don't what? Tell them the truth?"

Libby's thighs quivered with the effort of keeping herself upright.

"Please don't do this," she said. "I beg you, don't."

She fell to her knees, the concrete biting into her skin.

"Please don't, please, I'm begging you, please don't do this."

Raymond Villalobos appeared at the turn of the stairs, his pistol drawn. He froze there, staring up at Libby and Anna both.

"Give me the boy," he said.

"No," Anna said, wrapping her arms tighter around Ethan.

"Please," Libby said, her voice thin like paper.

Villalobos holstered his pistol and came to her side, took her by the shoulders, tried to draw her away. Libby shook him off.

"Please don't do this," she said.

Villalobos stepped past her, looked from Anna to Libby and back again.

"Who are you?" he asked.

"Who am I?" Anna echoed.

She smiled and kissed Ethan's cheek.

"I'm his mother," she said.

14

FOUR YEARS AGO

"I GOTTA LET YOU GO," DEVIN SAID.

He looked genuinely sorry, but that didn't take the sting out of it for Anna Lenihan. She'd been working tables at the restaurant for nine months, making good tips, and had just about started to make a hole in her debts. Ten minutes ago, she'd been thinking how she could maybe afford to start saving some. And now this. Now it had all gone to shit.

"Why me?" she asked. "Don't I work hard enough?"

Devin had called her into the office when she arrived for her shift. The restaurant was nothing special, just another bar and grill among dozens in the area. The kind of place you could get a burger or a steak that was at least palatable, maybe some ribs, along with a decent range of local brews. Classic rock rattling over the speakers, a country band on Saturday nights and holidays.

The Flatiron Bar & Grill stood at the center of the row of stores that made up one wing of a strip mall in Superior, Pennsylvania. Superior stood an hour outside of Pittsburgh, a middle-class suburb between the city to the west and the dying mining communities to the east. The town was made up of clusters of housing developments, good homes with SUVs in their driveways, punctuated by shopping malls and schools.

Anna couldn't afford to live in Superior. Instead, she lived in a mobile-home village—a fancy name for a trailer park—over in

Lafayette. Her 1978 Revere single-wide stood on a plot among hundreds of similar homes, and she did her best to keep it presentable. She mowed the lawn, such as it was, in the summer, swept up leaves in the fall, and shoveled snow in the winter. That stubborn nub of pride in her refused to be worn away, no matter how hard life tried to grind it down.

"Why me?" she asked again. "The customers like me, especially the men."

Devin sat at the other side of the desk, an expression on his face like a man struggling to pass a turd. He held his hands out, a gesture of apology.

"Last in, first out," he said. "That's how it works. Look, I've had to let two staff go before you this month. I'm just not getting the covers to keep you on. I'm sorry. Finish tonight's shift, I'll match whatever you get in tips out of my pocket, all right? And I'll give you references. That's the best I can do for you."

Anna wanted to pick the stapler up off the desk and throw it at his head. But she needed that money, so instead she nodded and said, "Okay."

Devin smiled his sad smile and said, "Thank you. I'm glad you understand. You're a good waitress. You'll find something."

"Yeah," she said. "Of course. I'll go get ready for my shift."

She left his office, went to the kitchen, already bustling and chattering in preparation for the dinner service. Through the door in the back, past the cloakroom, to the staff restrooms. There, she locked herself in a toilet stall and cried hard.

The shift dragged by with the usual small pleasures and minor dramas. She endured a tableful of leering businessmen whose innuendos became less subtle the more they drank, knowing they'd each throw in a generous tip, not out of kindness, but to show the others how much they could afford to give away. Even when one of them placed a hand on her ass, she gently maneuvered away instead of pouring a drink over his head. They were good for fifty-five bucks and some change by the time they rolled out of the place. She watched through the window as they each got into a car—two BMWs, an Audi, and a Range Rover—and drove away, and she wished for a highway patrol stop for every one of them.

Other than that, the covers were the usual mix of bored middle-aged couples, lonesome travelers needing a meal, and a few groups of younger professionals from the tech companies that operated in Pittsburgh. It was close to midnight by the time she brought her tips to Devin's office, intending to ask him to make good on his word to match them. Of course, he'd left thirty minutes before.

"Asshole," she said to the empty room.

She hadn't been stationary for long, but long enough for the aches in her calves and lower back to make themselves known. If she had any Advil left—and God, she hoped she did—she'd swallow two and the remains of the bottle of Sauvignon Blanc that waited in her fridge back home. She knew by the time she got there, the stiffness would have set in, and she'd wait in her twelve-year-old Honda Civic until she had the nerve to endure the pain of getting out and letting herself into her trailer.

Anna turned away from Devin's office and found Betsy watching her, pity on her face. Betsy was twenty years older than Anna, and a head shorter, and had been waiting tables all her life. Her petite form made her look at least ten years younger, and she still pulled in good tips from those liquored-up men who thought a waitress's job was more about indulging their clumsy flirting than it was about serving food. We feed egos here, not stomachs, she'd said more than once.

"I heard," Betsy said. "You gonna be okay?"

"Yeah," Anna said. "I guess I'll have to be."

"Devin left you this."

Betsy took a small brown envelope from her apron pocket and handed it over. Anna opened it and found five twenty-dollar bills. Not double her tips, but better than nothing, she supposed.

"Tell him thanks," she said.

"There's not much more to do here," Betsy said. "Why don't you go on home?"

Anna almost argued, but the lure of Advil and wine was too strong. "Thank you," she said, and grabbed her coat from the rack by the office door. As she slipped it on, she said, "Stay in touch?"

The words surprised her, slipped out with no thought, which meant they were honest. She'd lost count of the friends she'd promised to stay in contact with but never had. But this time it felt like she meant it. Betsy was good people, and Jesus, she needed as many of those as she could get.

"Sure," Betsy said, and hugged her.

Anna breathed in as they embraced. The odor of fried food, old beer, and soap, but underneath, Betsy smelled clean and good.

As they parted, Betsy said, "You know what? I got tomorrow night off. What do you say I come over, bring some beer and some pizza and some trashy movies? What do you think?"

Tears came to Anna's eyes, and she wiped them away. "Sounds great."

Betsy cradled Anna's face in her hands. "You're going to be fine, sweetheart. I promise."

And Anna believed her.

SHE SLEPT TILL past eleven, held under by half a bottle of wine, and half of another, and two doses of painkillers. Harsh fall sunlight cut through the gaps in the blinds, spearing into her consciousness. She lay still for a time, flat on her back, wary of moving lest she trigger a rolling tide of pain from around her body. The layers of comforter and blanket that had shielded her from the cold during the night began to feel oppressively heavy and hot, sweat sticking her pajama bottoms to her legs.

After a count of ten, she drew her knees up, making a mountain beneath the covers, and immediately her calves cramped.

"Shit, fuck!" she hissed, grabbing a clamoring muscle in each hand and kneading the flesh, trying to get the blood moving, carrying precious oxygen to the fibers. Eight years she'd been waiting tables and still her body complained about it.

Anna had been born and raised in Massachusetts, in a nothing town west of Boston, where what little family she had still lived to this day, as far as she knew. She hadn't been back there in more than a decade, and could count on one hand the number of times she'd spoken to her mother since then. She had drifted ever since, alone but seldom lonely, bouncing from job to job, town to town, state to state.

There had been men along the way, a fling here, a full-on romance there, and two marriage proposals. She had come close to accepting one of them, but the idea of spending the rest of her life with Jonathan—a handsome, earnestly honest mechanic who worked for a car-rental firm—filled her with pitch-black dread, like staring into a bottomless pit of dinners and breakfasts and weekends and holidays all spent looking away, wondering if there was something better waiting for her elsewhere.

When she said no, he called her a cunt and slapped her hard enough to bloody her lip. As she lay on the ground in that park, as he marched away cursing, she thanked God for helping her dodge that bullet and that life.

Now, staring at the ceiling of her single-wide in Lafayette, Pennsylvania, she told herself to move, goddammit, get up. The cramps had eased to a dull throb, so she steeled herself for the shock of cold as she threw back the bedcovers. The chill bit hard, and it was only November. The long gray winter months loomed ahead like bad news. Anna missed the winters back home, real snowfall turning the world white for weeks on end. Not like here with its damp cold that seemed to creep under your clothes and next to your skin.

As goose bumps spread across her body, she sat upright and dropped her feet to the floor. The muscles of her lower back spasmed and she clenched her jaw. The urge to slide back under the blankets was strong, but she knew getting up and moving would loosen the knots back there. Besides, she had things to do. The place was a mess, and Betsy was coming over around seven. Enough time to make the place presentable.

The day passed easily. She kept the TV on for background noise as she cleared up and cleaned, one eye on talk shows and sitcom reruns as she folded laundry and wiped down surfaces. At one point in the afternoon, she stopped and ate a bowl of cereal. All the time, she considered the days and weeks ahead.

Perhaps her time would have been better spent poring over the job listings online or in the local paper, but she felt content to take a day for herself. She had enough money put aside to last a month, maybe six weeks if she was careful. Devin had promised her references, and she was a good worker, punctual, and could always fake a smile for the drunkards.

"I'll be fine," she said aloud.

Anna told herself that a dozen times more as afternoon passed into evening. Wish enough, and it'll come true, she thought.

At six o'clock, she showered, dressed in her best jeans and sparkly top, and made up her face. Part of her questioned why she went to the trouble; it was only Betsy coming over with beer and pizza, wasn't it? If I want to look good, then goddammit, I can do it just to make myself feel good. Why the hell not?

"Stop judging me," she told her reflection in the bathroom mirror.

She hummed her favorite songs as she moved around the trailer lighting the stubs of the few scented candles she owned, then she filled one bowl with peanuts and another with potato chips she'd found in the back of the cupboard. Then she sat and watched the door, waiting.

A lifetime seemed to pass before the knock came.

Anna sprang to her feet, crossed the trailer, opened the door, breathless.

"Hey, girl," Betsy said with a grin.

Using her waitressing skills, she balanced two pizza boxes and assorted containers between her left arm and her chin and held a box of Coors Light under the other. Anna had a moment to wonder how she managed to knock on the door before remembering her manners and taking the stack of food from her.

"Come on in," she said, her voice fluttering with a strange excitement. It confused her. It wasn't like she'd never had company before, but still, there it was.

She carried the stack of food to the table while Betsy closed the door and followed, depositing the jangling box of beer beside the pizzas.

"How you been today?" Betsy asked, her arms outstretched.

Anna came in for the hug, meaning to say, Good, today was just fine. But instead she felt something break and spill inside, and hot tears came, sobs choked from her throat.

Betsy held her tight. "Oh, honey, what is it?"

Anna tried to speak, but she couldn't push the words past the flood, and even then, did she know where it came from? Betsy rocked her there, a swaying motion side to side, cooing comforting whispers until finally Anna could shape the words and speak them.

"What am I going to do now?" she asked. "What am I going to do?"

15

BETSY WASHED PEPPERONI PIZZA DOWN WITH A SWIG OF Coors, burped, and said, "The world needs waitresses. I mean, who else is going to feed those assholes?"

"Yeah, I know, but around here?" Anna said. "Who's hiring?"

The tears had passed as quickly as they'd come, like a blister had been lanced inside her. Thank God for Betsy, she thought, here to shore her up and keep her right. And the beer buzz helped.

"Oh, there's places," Betsy said. "You know, you've got the looks and the figure, you're young enough, you could—"

"Nuh-uh," Anna said, shaking her head. "No way. I'm not doing Hooters or the Tilted Kilt or any of those places. God, I meet enough creeps in a regular restaurant. I don't care how good the tips are."

She helped herself to another slice of pizza, this one with BBQ chicken topping, and bit off a chunk.

"Hey, you know what?" Betsy said, her face brightening. "I saw an ad in the paper the other day, in the back with the classifieds. It said they were looking for women under thirty-five—that's me, for a start—women who wanted a money-making opportunity. Yeah, that's what it said. A money-making opportunity for healthy women."

"Strippers," Anna said. "They're looking for strippers. Or hookers. Or models."

She used air quotes for the last word.

"No, no," Betsy said, "it was nothing like that. The company name was something medical, it had the word 'clinic' in it. I bet it's one of those trial things, where they give you money to take some new pills, just to see what happens."

Anna laughed, a snorting guffaw that felt wonderful. "Yeah, a medical experiment, that's what I want to do, sign me right up. Write me a fat-enough check, and I'll have all the side effects you want."

"I'm serious," Betsy said, rapping the table with her knuckles. "Those things, they pay out thousands just to take some pills or eat something or whatever, and probably you'll get a placebo anyway, because they need, what do you call it, a control group, right? Look, do you have a copy here? You know, the *Advertiser*? The one they deliver for free."

Anna looked around the kitchen area, to the corner of the worktop where she kept her mail, then she remembered.

"I think I put it in the recycling when I was cleaning up today."

Betsy got to her feet, wavered a little. "Ooh, how many beers did I have?" She crossed to the plastic tubs in the corner. "Here? This one?"

"Yeah, but don't go rooting through my—"

Betsy paid no attention and lifted the lid from the paper-recycling box. She rummaged for a moment before giving a triumphant "Aha! Here it is."

She came back to the table carrying a folded copy of the *Superior Advertiser*. Flopping down into the chair, she pushed aside plates and cutlery and pizza boxes, spread the paper out, and opened it up. She flicked page over page, stories of dogs needing adoption, prizes won in schools, the kind of banal local chatter that fills up free newspapers that exist to sell advertising space.

"Here," she said at last, tapping a two-column ad with her fingertip. "Financial opportunity for healthy women aged twenty-one to thirty-five. Call this number 24/7 for details, or visit our website."

Anna sat back in her chair and shook her head. "Come on,

this is nuts. Like I'd let someone from a classified ad experiment on me."

"Why not call them? Just see what they want, and what they're paying. Jesus, if I thought I'd get a grand for taking some sugar pill, I'd sure as hell do it. And you need the money, right?"

"Yeah, I need the money, but not like this."

"Give me your cell," Betsy said, her hand out.

"What? No."

"Give it to me or I'll kick your ass."

Anna crossed her arms across her chest. "I'm not calling them."

Betsy cast her gaze around the trailer until she spotted Anna's cell over by the fridge. She bounced to her feet, grabbed the paper, and made a dash for it.

"No!" Anna raised herself from the chair, but didn't quite have the will to stand up. "Don't you dare," she said, but her giggling dulled the edge of the warning.

"You're twenty-nine, right?" Betsy said. "So you were born in . . ."

"Stop!" Anna said, but Betsy went ahead and entered the four digits to unlock the phone.

She squinted at the cell's screen as she thumbed out the listed number, then put it to her ear, listened for a moment. Her eyes brightened, and Anna heard the tinny sound of a recorded voice, though she couldn't make out the words.

"Anna Lenihan," Betsy said at the voice's prompt, then she recited Anna's number. Another few moments' listening, then she hung up. "There," she said. "Simple as that."

"You're a bad person," Anna scolded.

Betsy dismissed her with a wave of her hand. "Ah, get over yourself. What's the worst that can happen? They call back, you can tell them to shove their money up their ass."

She placed the phone on the table, and Anna stared at the screen while Betsy opened another round of beers.

THE CELL BUZZED with an incoming call at ten thirty-four the next morning.

Betsy had spent the night on Anna's couch and woken not long after eight, complaining about her hangover as if someone else had inflicted it upon her. Anna fixed them both some eggs, and neither mentioned the ad or the phone call as they ate. At around ten, they embraced on Anna's step while Mrs. Crane from the trailer next door watched from her window with a look of shock and horror on her face.

"I think someone got the wrong idea," Anna said, giggling.

Betsy turned and looked to the window, smiled, and waved. Mrs. Crane disappeared from view.

"What wrong idea?" Betsy said in a voice loud enough to be heard a street away. "It's been an all-night lesbian lovefest over here!"

"Stop!" Anna said, punching her arm.

They hugged again, and Betsy kissed her cheek. "You stay in touch, now. And don't worry. You'll land on your feet. I know it."

Anna watched her drive away in her Jetta, its exhaust rattling and sputtering. When she looked up, Mrs. Crane had returned to her window. Anna waved, and Mrs. Crane shook her head with disgust.

Inside, Anna began clearing up last night's mess. There was plenty of pizza left over that would do for lunch; she threw the rest of the detritus in the garbage and brought the plates to the sink. Her mind was in some distant place where money and time were plentiful when the cell vibrated on the table, startling her. She dried her hands and went to the table, checked the phone's display. Number unknown. She thumbed the green icon.

"Hello?"

"Good morning," a deep male voice said. "May I please speak with Anna Lenihan?"

A chilling unease crept up on her. "Speaking. Who's calling?"

"Good morning, Anna," the voice said, adopting a lighter tone. "My name is Mr. Kovak, and I'm calling on behalf of the Schaeffer-Holdt Clinic. You left your name and number to register your interest. If it's all right with you, I'd like to begin by asking a few questions. Would that be okay?"

Anna paused, wondered if she should hang up.

"Ma'am, are you there?"

"Yeah," Anna said. "So, what is this financial opportunity, exactly? Is it a medical experiment or something?"

"Not exactly," Mr. Kovak said. "Normally we like to get to know our candidates a little before we go into the exact nature of the arrangement."

"I don't think I should talk to you any more about this," Anna said. "Thank you for your call, but—"

"Anna," he said. "May I call you Anna? You should know that our selection process involves a one-day interview. Your fee for attending that interview would be a five-hundred-dollar cash payment, with no obligation or commitment."

Anna's mouth closed. She stared out her window, saw raindrops darken the ground where they fell, felt the temperature in the trailer fall.

"Anna, do you think I could ask you those questions now? It'll only take a few minutes."

"No obligation?" she asked.

"No obligation," he said.

"Okay," she said.

16

THREE WEEKS LATER, ANNA ENTERED THE LOBBY OF THE SHERA-
ton at Station Square, in Pittsburgh, which backed onto the
Monongahela River. The place bustled with smartly dressed men
and women attending some kind of conference. A large flat-
screen television showed a list of seminars and the rooms they
were hosted in. She felt immediately out of place among these
people with their good clothes and their ambition. Hundreds
of them giving off the reek of desperation as they tried to look
successful.

All except one.

Waiting by an ornamental fountain, he stood at least six inches
taller than any man there, with shoulders twice as wide. But not
fat. His suit was well cut and showed the proportions of his powerful body. He exuded a confidence that said he was comfortable
with his size, and how to use it. When he moved, that confidence
was carried in his stride. Anna was so transfixed by his presence
that it took a moment for her to realize he was walking toward
her. She froze in place, watching, wondering if this was what it
felt like to be prey in sight of a predator.

"Anna?" he said.

She opened her mouth to reply, but only exhaled.

He raised his eyebrows, creasing his smooth forehead. His
hair was shaved close enough to the scalp to show shining pink
skin. A deep scar perhaps an inch and a half long arced out and
down from his left eye.

"Anna Lenihan?" he asked.

"Y-yes," she said.

He extended his right hand. It swallowed hers whole. His skin was dry and hard against hers. The large and meaty hands of a workman. She fought the urge to pull away from his grasp and run for the door.

"I'm Mr. Kovak," he said. "We spoke on the telephone. I'm glad to meet you."

Anna couldn't form a reply, so instead nodded and forced a smile.

"We'll use a suite on the third floor, if that's all right?" he said. "We won't be alone, so there's no need to be concerned. Would you like to follow me?"

She did as he asked, walking two paces behind him, through the conference attendees who unconsciously parted for him. She remembered the questions he'd asked when they last spoke three weeks ago. Her date of birth, her height, her weight. Did she have any disabilities? Any hereditary conditions that required medical treatment? He had rattled off a list of diseases, asking if she had ever suffered from any of them, hepatitis, tuberculosis, syphilis, and more she'd never heard of. She had replied with a series of no, no, no, so many that she couldn't count.

The elevator door opened, and he stepped aside to let her enter first. As he followed her inside, and the door sealed them in, the fear bubbled up once more.

He pressed the button for the third floor and said, "Please don't be nervous."

She felt then that he could see through her, no, inside of her, to the place within her chest where the fear curled on itself, waiting to uncoil into panic.

"I understand this is an unusual situation. It's only natural that you'd be wary. Please be assured that you can end the interview whenever you want. You'll still be compensated for your time. Oh, speaking of which . . ."

Mr. Kovak reached inside his jacket pocket and produced a white letter-sized envelope. He held it out to her. She stared at it.

"Please," he said.

Anna took it from his hand, saw her name written on it in blue ink.

"Five hundred dollars, as agreed," he said. "You can open it if you wish."

The envelope didn't feel like it held that much money, more than she'd ever had in her hand before. She rubbed it between her fingers, felt the bills inside.

"That's okay," she said, her voice sounding ever so small in the elevator. She tucked the envelope away in her purse as the doors opened.

"This way," Mr. Kovak said as he stepped out.

Anna followed him along the hall, around one bend, through an open fire door, until they reached a door marked 3045. The desire to turn and run came at her hard, but she pushed it back. She waited as Mr. Kovak touched a keycard to a sensor, listened as the lock whirred. He depressed the handle, pushed the door open, and indicated that she should enter. She hesitated, peering inside at the furniture, like a living room in someone's house. A fancy house at that. For a moment, she wondered where the bed was, then remembered he'd said it was a suite. She'd only ever seen those on TV, never actually been in one.

"Please," he said, reaching his hand toward the room.

She forced herself to move, one foot in front of the other, inside the suite. As she entered, she saw the woman seated on the couch, blond hair turning gray, perhaps mid-fifties, maybe older. The woman smiled and stood, but said nothing. Anna heard the door close behind her.

"This is Barbara Strand," Mr. Kovak said. "She's a registered nurse. Barbara, this is Anna Lenihan."

Now the woman stepped forward and shook Anna's hand.

"Pleased to meet you," she said. "If you don't mind, we'd like to start with taking a photograph. Would that be all right?"

Anna saw the smartphone in her left hand. And the small tripod on the coffee table, facing an empty armchair.

"I guess," Anna said.

"Great," Barbara said, and pointed across the room. "Can I get you to stand with your back against that door?"

Anna followed the direction of the woman's finger, saw the door in the far wall. She supposed it opened into the bedroom, and the urge to flee rose again.

"It'll only take a moment," Barbara said, taking Anna's arm. "Please."

She guided Anna to the door, positioned her just-so, then stepped back.

"No need to smile," she said. "Just look directly into the lens. Good. Now, please turn to your left."

Anna remained still, her heart hammering.

Barbara smiled and said. "It'll only take a moment."

Anna turned, gave the woman her right profile.

"And the other side, please."

Anna did as she was asked, then Barbara guided her back to the armchair. She sat down and watched as Barbara mounted the phone on the tripod and fussed with the touchscreen.

"Are you making a video?" Anna asked.

"Yes," Barbara said. "I'm afraid it's required for the interview. Don't worry, it won't be shared with anyone outside of the clinic."

Mr. Kovak came to the couch and sat down. He lifted an iPad from the table, unlocked it, and tapped at the screen.

"Please state your full name, your date of birth, and your Social Security number," he said.

Anna recited the information, thinking only of the five hundred dollars in her purse, and how much more they might be willing to give her for whatever it was they wanted. They were both well dressed, and the smartphone and tablet must have cost something, not to mention booking the suite. Clearly, they were not lacking for cash.

She scolded herself for thinking that way. She had never been mercenary, never driven by money. And look where that got you, she thought.

Mr. Kovak went through the same series of questions she'd answered over the telephone three weeks ago. Her height, her weight, her health. She said no to the same list of diseases, illnesses, and conditions. But this time he pressed her harder on drugs, tobacco, and alcohol.

"I need you to be completely honest with me," he said, his voice kind but firm.

"I have been," Anna said.

"I know," he said, smiling. "I just want to be sure you understand the importance of candor. There's no judgment."

"Okay."

"What drugs have you used in the past?" he asked.

"A little pot when I was in high school, but not since then. That's all."

"Have you ever smoked cigarettes, real or electronic?"

"I tried it once when I was, like, fourteen or fifteen. I didn't like it."

"You said you were a social drinker. How often do you drink alcohol socially?"

"When I get a night off, maybe twice a week."

He gazed at her, a benign expression on his face, his eyes hard, seeing all.

"Please be honest with me," he said.

Anna felt a chill, her mouth drying. "Maybe more than that," she said. "I might have a glass of wine or a beer after work, just to unwind. But just one or two, and not every night."

Mr. Kovak smiled. "Thank you for your honesty. I think that's it for the questions."

"Can I ask one?" Anna said.

"Of course," Mr. Kovak said.

"What is it you want from me?"

Mr. Kovak exchanged a glance with the nurse.

"I'm sorry, I can't tell you that right now. If you're selected, you'll be fully informed of the service that will be asked of you, with no obligation to continue. Now, if you don't mind, Barbara has one last thing to attend to."

Barbara went to a table by the window and lifted a tray covered with a linen cloth. Anna hadn't noticed it before, and the sight of it troubled her. Barbara brought the tray to the coffee table. She pulled aside the linen cloth, revealing a high-sided plastic tray containing three empty vials, a small band like a belt, a sealed packet containing what she recognized as a butterfly needle, and a barrel for taking blood.

"You're taking blood samples?" Anna asked.

"I'm afraid it's a necessary step," Mr. Kovak said. "You're free to refuse, of course, but that will end the application process."

Anna looked at the needle, how thick it seemed. She hated giving blood samples. The pain was never as bad as she imagined, but she hated the idea of being pierced, even in a treatment room, let alone a hotel suite.

"I don't know," she said.

"It's entirely your decision, Anna," Mr. Kovak said. "Please don't feel under any pressure."

She looked up at Barbara, who smiled down at her.

This isn't right, Anna thought. Not right at all.

"If I pass, what will you pay me?" she asked.

Mr. Kovak shared another look with Barbara before saying, "I can't disclose the amount. But I can tell you it will be substantial."

Anna closed her eyes and made her decision. She opened them again, rolled up her sleeve, and said, "All right."

On the drive home, she stopped at the Superior Marketplace. She went to the T.J. Maxx, promising she would spend no more than one hundred of the five hundred dollars. In the end, she went over by five bucks and some change, but she got a new winter coat, along with a pair of wool-lined boots and some nice underwear.

She returned to her single-wide feeling content and convinced that even if Mr. Kovak called to say they had accepted her application to whatever the hell it was, she would tell him to shove it up his ass.

17

M R. KOVAK SAT ON THE EDGE OF THE BED, LISTENING TO THE dial tone. Checking his watch, he sighed at the knowledge that he would not be able to fly home that evening. At least not a direct flight, anyway. Barbara, the nurse, had gone home thirty minutes ago; she did these gigs on a freelance basis. It was a good day's pay for not a lot of work. He debated whether he would eat in his room or venture out. There was a Hard Rock Café just a couple of doors down; hardly fine dining, but it would do.

Eventually, Dr. Sherman answered.

"Yes, Mr. Kovak, I was just about to have dinner."

"Sorry to disturb you, Dr. Sherman."

Mr. Kovak suspected that Dr. Sherman possessed no medical qualifications, but he had long since decided not to press him on that matter.

"All right, but what is it?"

"I wondered if you'd had a chance to review today's candidates yet?"

"Just briefly. Jocelyn Mathers and Anna Lenihan seemed the standouts to me."

"Yes, Jocelyn Mathers is an excellent candidate. That she's done it before is a plus."

"True. I don't have a client match for her just now, but we'll certainly sign her up."

"Anna Lenihan, though," Mr. Kovak said.

"What about her?" Dr. Sherman asked.

"This would be her first child."

"You know I don't factor in previous pregnancies."

"Maybe we should start. It's the norm with other agencies."

Dr. Sherman audibly bristled. "The Schaeffer-Holdt Clinic is not 'other agencies.' We serve specific clients with specific needs and we must have the widest possible field of candidates. And can I remind you, Mr. Kovak, that it is not your job to set clinic policy."

"Of course," Mr. Kovak said. "But I think she's trouble. She strikes me as . . . willful."

Dr. Sherman chuckled. "Does she, now? Thing is, she's an excellent match for a client I have waiting. I mean, the resemblance is extraordinary."

"A strong resemblance won't help you if she causes problems."

"That's where you earn your money, though, isn't it, Mr. Kovak?"

"I wouldn't be doing my job if I didn't give you my honest opinion," Mr. Kovak said.

"And I do appreciate that," Dr. Sherman said. "But perhaps you should defer to my judgment on this one."

"Whatever you say, Dr. Sherman."

"Good. Now, if there's nothing else, I'd like to eat before my food gets cold."

"Nothing else," Mr. Kovak said.

They exchanged good evenings, hung up, and Mr. Kovak decided he would get drunk tonight. He would get drunk, expense it to Dr. Sherman, and just let him try to query it.

MR. KOVAK COULDN'T help but smile when the freight train came into view.

He'd taken a table right at the back of the restaurant. A middling blues-rock band played on the stage in the main dining area, but there was a separate section that overlooked the point where the Ohio River forked into the Allegheny and Mononga-hela Rivers. He had ordered a burger and fries, and he'd already killed one beer and was halfway down his second.

Mr. Kovak only drank when he traveled. Even then, he tried to stick to beer, or a glass of red if he happened to have a steak. He didn't often eat American steak, finding it too bland, the cattle having been fed on processed corn. Unless the menu boasted that the beef was grass-fed, he usually gave steak a miss. So, beer it was. A Dancing Gnome Amarillo, to be precise, and it was going down nicely.

Aside from the quiet, another reason Mr. Kovak liked to sit in back was because the train line ran past the window, between the restaurant and the water. He particularly enjoyed the freight trains because their extraordinary length was a wonder to behold. One could note the time when the engine first passed, and at least ten minutes would slip by before the final car came into view.

He looked east down the track and smiled again when he saw the light drawing closer. He checked his wristwatch as it drew level with him. Two minutes past nine, precisely.

"It'll take twelve minutes," the waitress said as she placed his food in front of him.

"Exactly?" he asked. "Or give-or-take?"

"At this speed?" She placed her hands on her hips, watching the first few cars go by. "I figure twelve minutes fifteen seconds."

"Care to make it interesting?"

"Maybe," she said. "What did you have in mind?"

"How about . . . if you're within fifteen seconds, I tip you a hundred. If not, I eat for free."

She tilted her hips, gave him a crooked smile. "Or how about, within fifteen seconds, you tip me the hundred. If not, I let you buy me a drink after my shift."

He looked up at her and said, "That doesn't seem equitable."

"Oh, it is," she said. "Depends how you look at it, of course."

"Fair enough," he said. "I'll take that bet."

She pointed to his glass and asked, "Another?"

"Please."

He thought about Anna Lenihan as he ate. His gut screamed at him not to let her sign the contract. She was trouble. He could smell it on her the moment he met her in the hotel lobby. But Dr. Sherman would have his way. It was not Mr. Kovak's place to make these decisions; he could offer advice, opinions, which he had done, but that was all.

He knew at his core that he would regret the day he ever met her.

But so be it.

Mr. Kovak finished his food, and his beer, as the last car of the freight train passed. Twelve minutes and twenty-two seconds.

He left seventy to cover the meal, and two fifties for the tip, and went looking for a dark and quiet bar where he could drink his fill.

DAWN LIGHT PIERCED the gloom of his hotel room and snapped Mr. Kovak into awareness. He found himself seated in a chair in the corner, cold and stiff through his neck and shoulders. A deep ache slithered behind his eyes. His tongue bound to the roof of his mouth, dry like coarse paper. Nausea followed.

He thought: What did I do?

His knuckles stung, with a darker underlying pain through his fingers and hands, down to his wrists. He had punched someone. Or something. He hoped it had been a wall, a bathroom stall, even a window. It took some effort to look down at himself, but he managed it, and saw the blood on his shirtfront, the spatters of it on his cuffs.

"Oh no," he whispered.

His suit jacket lay bundled on the floor. A miniature whiskey bottle on the table beside him, half of it gone. He must have helped himself to a nightcap but passed out before he could finish it.

Think, he told himself. What did you do?

Mr. Kovak remembered leaving the restaurant and walking the short distance to the Smithfield Street Bridge, which he crossed on foot, and into downtown Pittsburgh. He wandered the streets until he found a bar that wasn't too busy. He opened a tab and had his first hard liquor in a month.

After that, things became hazy. He remembered the bartender asking if he'd like some water, which he accepted. A vague recollection of a gang of college boys entering, from Duquesne, he guessed. They were egregiously loud in the way groups of young men tend to be. Like they needed to be heard, to be seen, like their presence was more important than whatever peace you'd found for yourself in whatever quiet corner.

It had to have been one of them.

The restroom. A memory hardened in his mind. Encountering one of the boys in the restroom, exchanging words, pushing the kid into the stall.

Everything after that was a blur of colors and sounds and sensations. Bright red. Gurgling, choking. The crushing of cartilage beneath his fist.

"Jesus," Mr. Kovak said, bringing his hand to his face, covering his eyes.

It had been a long time since he'd done something like this. He'd kept a lid on his rage for at least a year now. But he had slipped. Stress, maybe. The job did grind on him. Pressure building, his control scraping away until something had to give.

"No more," he said, meaning it every bit as much as he had the last time.

18

A WEEK PASSED BEFORE THE PHONE RANG.
"Anna? This is Mr. Kovak from the Schaeffer-Holdt Clinic."

She hesitated, then said, "Yes?"

"I'm calling with good news."

Her knees went weak and she sat down on the bed. It creaked beneath her weight.

"Oh?"

"Anna, your candidacy for our program was successful. I can be in Pittsburgh tomorrow to discuss further details, if you're available?"

"I . . . don't know," she said.

The five hundred dollars had blown away like dandelion fluff. Seven days earlier, she had felt in control, and now she was as scared as ever.

"There will be a further cash payment of five hundred dollars for your time and travel," Mr. Kovak said. "And, of course, no obligation to proceed."

"No obligation?" she echoed.

"None whatsoever," he said.

THE SAME HOTEL, the same suite. No nurse this time, no needles, only Mr. Kovak and his good suit and his big, meaty workman's hands. The drive into the city had been more difficult, heavier snow pelting against her windshield, slower traffic, and she had been almost thirty minutes late. Mr. Kovak didn't complain.

"Please," he said, indicating that she should sit in the same chair as before. He sat on the couch. No smartphone, no tripod, no video. She noticed small dark scabs on his knuckles, ready to peel away.

"May I have the five hundred dollars, please?" she said, blushing at her own impertinence.

Mr. Kovak smiled and said, "Of course."

He took a white envelope from his jacket pocket, just like the last, and handed it over. Anna got to her feet as she put the envelope in her purse.

"I'm sorry," she said. "I've thought it through, and I don't want to be a part of whatever this is."

She turned to the door, and he spoke, his voice firmer than she'd heard it before.

"Anna, I'd appreciate it if you listened to our proposal. I did just give you five hundred dollars."

She walked toward the door. "You said no obligation."

"That's correct, but as a matter of courtesy, I'd like you to hear us out."

"Us?" she said, turning back to him. "For a start, who the fuck is 'us'? You know, I looked up the Schaeffer-Holdt Clinic. There's no such place. It's just a shell company. I'm not some idiot you can buy with a few hundred bucks."

"Actually," Mr. Kovak said, "it's seventy-five thousand dollars in total. Five on signature, thirty-five on conception, thirty-five on delivery. Plus a generous living allowance for the term, along with accommodation somewhere more . . . salubrious than where you are now."

"What are you talking about?" she asked.

"In addition, all medical care will be provided, the very best, both pre- and post-."

Her hand went to her belly. "Pre- and post- what?"

"Anna, right now, there are couples who desperately need a surrogate mother to help them have a child, but purely because of where they live, they cannot legally get that help within their own state. What we do is act as an agent, an introduction service, if you will, for childless couples and young women who are willing and able to help them. For a fee, of course. And it's a generous fee, more than fifty percent above market rate. For the right candidate, that is. Like you."

Seventy-five thousand. The number stretched and tumbled in her mind. Gave off sparks.

"But it's illegal," she said.

"No," Mr. Kovak said, "not illegal. There is no law in the state of Pennsylvania to prevent you from offering this help. But a couple in, say, New York, can't accept it. We can, however, on their behalf. Please sit down. Please listen. No obligation."

"YOU DIDN'T SAY yes, did you?" Betsy asked, her eyes wide.

"No," Anna said.

"Did you say no?"

"No."

"Jesus, honey, you can't really be considering this, can you?"

Another box of Coors, but Chinese food this time. Anna had called Betsy and asked her to come over after her shift. It was past midnight, and weariness made the beer hit harder. Anna downed half a bottle, opened another. So far, she was two-for-one to Betsy.

"It's seventy-five grand," Anna said. "That, and two hundred a week to live on for the term, plus they'll get me out of this dump."

Betsy reached across the table, grabbed her forearm. "But you'll have to grow a baby, a human being, inside of you for nine months. Then you'll give birth. And then you'll have to just give it away. My God, sweetheart, do you know how hard that's going to be?"

"Sure, it'll be hard, I know that. But, Jesus, seventy-five thousand dollars. It could change my life. I could start a business. Make something of myself."

"What kind of business?"

"I don't know, something, anything, so long as I don't have to wait tables and live in this shithole. I need to make a change, and maybe this is what I need to do it."

Betsy took her hand, squeezed it tight.

"Honey, this isn't a palace, sure, but we've both lived in worse. And if you don't want to wait tables, then work in a store, or go back to school, whatever, just don't do this. You're going to get hurt. And this clinic, if that's really what it is, sounds shady as hell."

"I haven't said yes to anything, I'm just thinking about it. No need to get all protective. You're not my mom, you're not my big sister."

Betsy sat back in her chair, and Anna saw the wound she'd inflicted with her words. She let go of Anna's hand and got to her feet.

"I think I'm okay to drive," she said.

"Don't," Anna said, reaching for her. "I'm sorry, I didn't mean that. You've been a good friend to me, and I appreciate your advice, but . . ."

"But you don't want to take it," Betsy said.

She lifted her coat from the back of the chair and slipped it on.

"You're a grown woman," she said, "and I guess you'll do what you think is right. Whatever it is, you know where I am."

She left the trailer, closed the door behind her, but not before a blast of icy cold air cut through the place, a fine drizzle riding its currents.

Anna put her head in her hands and said, "Shit."

19

M R. KOVAK PREFERRED TO WORK FROM HOME. NOT THAT HE'D ever been given an option. There had never been a question of his having to take an office at the clinic in Brooklyn, which he had still not visited after several years of working for them. Apart from anything else, he didn't relish the idea of a daily commute from Queens. And his apartment was wonderfully quiet. Just across from the park, he could hear children playing when he opened his windows in the warmer weather.

Not today. Today was cold. Not as cold as Pittsburgh had been, but chilly enough. He had flown back yesterday, landing at La Guardia a little before midnight. As he boarded, the flight attendant had glanced at his scabbed knuckles, still healing, and again during drinks service. Mr. Kovak had pretended not to notice. Business class. The clinic always flew him business class, which was just as well, because his large frame didn't fit coach. He had a bad knee from his days in the service. Patellar tendinopathy, the doctor said, the tendon between his shin bone and his kneecap. It had gotten him a discharge after two tours of Iraq. He'd damaged the knee pulling a collapsed wall off of one of his team. The son of a bitch died anyway, and Mr. Kovak was left with a limp that he worked hard to conceal.

Mr. Kovak had not enjoyed his time in the military. His father and uncle had been soldiers, as had his elder brother who had died in Afghanistan, but Mr. Kovak had not taken to the life. In truth, the discharge had come as a relief. Battle had not been the experience he had expected. He saw little bravery in either the enemy or his own people; instead, it was mostly fanaticism met with blind terror. It turned out that when a young man came under fire, his first instinct was as often as not to shit his pants and keep his head down until it was over.

The fear got to him more than anything else. Not just the barely contained panic of combat but the tension of waiting for the next attack to come. Like a guitar string inside him and each of his brothers tuned up too high and ready to snap at any moment. It never went away, not even when he came back home. Even now, years later, he was always conscious of the tightened string.

He had attended counseling sessions at the Queens Vet Center on and off since he'd left the service, both on his own and in groups. Had they done him any good? They didn't stop the night terrors, or the jolting fear of loud, sudden noises, but he could at least function day-to-day, even with the constant tension. A lot of his former colleagues couldn't; many had been lost to alcoholism or drug addiction, and some had taken their own lives.

That was why he did not keep a firearm. He knew that many suicides were down to opportunity, the ease of the act when the urge arrived. Had he a weapon at hand, he could not say for certain he would be alive now. And given his line of work, he didn't really need one, and besides, it was a pain in the ass to always have to check a firearm when he flew.

He had seen five young women on his most recent trip. They had been narrowed down from close to thirty face-to-face interviews. There'd been more than two hundred applicants, but a brief telephone conversation weeded out most of them. Of the five successful candidates, two had already declined, two had accepted on the spot, and one was wavering.

Anna Lenihan. Mr. Kovak liked her as a person, but not as a candidate. She seemed tough, like she'd taken more than her share of knocks in life. A friendly exterior, but he got the sense that if he bit into her, he'd find something hard inside. Which made her a difficult prospect, but Dr. Sherman had made himself clear.

Mr. Kovak's job title was Candidate Liaison Executive, which he supposed was accurate enough. He dealt with the women, interviewed them all, mainly because he was a good judge of character. That skill had been acquired as an insurance investigator. When someone tried to claim a payout over a ruined back, Mr. Kovak would study the person from a far-enough distance that the subject would never know. Then he would speak with them face-to-face. It didn't matter how good a show a subject put on for the world, when they sat across a desk from him, sweating, fidgeting, he'd know who was truthful and who was not. Many times, subjects would break down in front of him and confess their sins. He had that effect on people. Something about him made lying to his face seem a terrible idea.

Mr. Kovak enjoyed that part of the job. The initial interviews, the whittling down, the joy it brought to those who succeeded and understood that their ship had just come in. But his work did not end there. He also had to shepherd these young women through the process. If all went well, he would have little further interaction with them. But if it didn't, if the women missed their regular checkups, or didn't care for themselves properly, then he would have to pay them a visit. He didn't like that part, but he was good at it. If a woman began smoking or drinking during the term, then as often as not, a knock on her door and a few sharp-edged words would bring her back into line. And if they didn't? Well, the clinic paid him for results, and he always delivered. In five years, not one woman who had carried a baby to term had failed to appear at the appointed clinic on the appointed date. Mr. Kovak had made sure of it.

At around three in the afternoon, he was at the desk in the corner of his living room, concentrating on his laptop's screen. It displayed a table of names, dates, and events. His employers maintained a network of partner clinics, five in total, in Massachusetts, New Jersey, Pennsylvania, Connecticut, and North Carolina. Each clinic had the facilities to carry out every step from intrauterine insemination, through prenatal monitoring, all the way to delivery and postnatal care. In truth, the headquarters in Brooklyn might have been called a clinic, but he didn't believe there was a single item of medical equipment in the entire place. Rather, it was an office where calls were made, deals struck, payments received. The real work happened far away in other states where such things weren't against the law. Every time a contracted birth mother underwent her regular checkup, the visit was logged through a web interface, ready for Mr. Kovak and his employer to observe. Any anomalies or concerns would be noted, and appropriate action taken.

The same database also contained information on potential birth mothers, those who had been successful in their candidacies, and were awaiting selection by an intended mother. Some were never chosen at all, and simply banked the five thousand dollars for signing the contract and never heard another thing about it. But some fit whatever criteria a client had specified—hair and skin color, build, facial features—and were notified that they should visit their nearest clinic for an initial consultation.

One of the entries in the table bothered Mr. Kovak. A twenty-six-year-old woman from outside Boston had failed to show for her checkup. The notes said that the clinic in Cambridge had tried to contact Mandy Carmichael multiple times, but she had not answered her cell phone. When they finally did reach her, she was uncooperative and would not commit to a time for a rescheduled appointment. This was the second checkup she had missed, and she was becoming troublesome.

Mr. Kovak did not like trouble. He craved peace above all else. Anger came quick and easy to him, always destructive, and years of learning to control his rage had taught him to avoid those things that awoke it in him. He felt his mood dip as he navigated to Mandy's profile and clicked on her phone number, which triggered a Skype window to open. The dial tone grated on his nerves.

"Hello?" she said, her voice sounding boxy through his laptop's built-in speakers.

"Mandy, this is Mr. Kovak."

He counted three seconds of silence before she responded.

"Oh, hey, uh . . . how are you?"

"I'm fair, Mandy, how are you?"

"I'm . . . I'm okay, I just got a little head cold, you know? A case of the sniffles. Nothing serious."

With some effort, he kept his tone measured and friendly. "I guess that's why you didn't go to your checkup yesterday."

"Yeah, yeah, that's right. I didn't want to, you know, pass on my germs to anyone, so I thought I'd leave it a few days."

"Oh, don't worry about that," Mr. Kovak said. "There's no reason why you can't go in tomorrow. I happen to know they have a slot at ten a.m. They would appreciate your attendance, as would I."

He heard her sigh, the sound of distorted air through the speakers.

"Okay, sure, I'll be there."

"And please be aware, Mandy, that they will take blood samples, and they will be checked for alcohol and narcotics. Is that clear?"

Quiet. The thin and distant sound of a dog barking somewhere in Massachusetts.

"Mandy, is that clear?" he asked.

"Yeah," she said, her voice like a child's.

"Good," he said. "I hope this doesn't happen again, Mandy. If I have to fly up there and escort you to the clinic . . . well, I'd rather it didn't come to that."

Silence again. He knew his warning was clear, and that it frightened her. His size intimidated people, no matter how benign he tried to appear. The idea of his being upset would strike fear into anyone. This did not please him at all, but still, it was useful.

"Please don't make me call you like this again," he said. "Goodbye."

She stammered something, and he clicked the red icon to end the call. He closed the Skype app and returned his attention to the tables on the computer's screen. Before he could focus, his cell phone vibrated on the desk. He checked the screen: Anna Lenihan. He picked the phone up and answered.

"Anna, how are you?"

"Yeah, I'm okay."

She didn't inquire after his well-being. He didn't mind.

"Have you come to a decision?" he asked.

"Maybe," she said.

"Is there anything in particular you're unsure about?"

"What happens in the procedure?"

"You mean the insemination?" Mr. Kovak asked. "I think our colleagues at our partner clinic in Pittsburgh might be better placed to go over that with you."

He knew full well what the procedure was; in fact, he'd observed it once through a two-way mirror. But he had no desire to explain the mechanics of it over the phone. He often surprised himself with his queasiness with such matters. The word "speculum," for example, greatly bothered him.

"Will it hurt?" she asked.

"No, it will not," he said. "I can promise you that much."

"What if I change my mind?"

"Before or after insemination?"

"Either."

"Before, well, no one can force you to go through with the procedure, but you will have broken the contract. You'll be obligated to return the on-signature portion of the payment. After . . . well, we've never had that circumstance occur. But, please, if you have any doubts, don't proceed."

"No," she said. "No doubts."

Was that a quiver in her voice?

He ignored it and asked, "So, is it a yes?"

A moment's pause, then, "I guess."

"Good," he said. "Do you still have the contract I gave you in Pittsburgh?"

"Yeah," she said.

"Then sign all three copies and return them to the address on the first page. Can you do that? The sooner you get them back to me, the sooner I can release the five thousand on-signature payment to you. And the sooner we can look for a match."

"Okay," she said.

That quiver again.

"And please understand, for things to proceed, we need an intended parent to pick you out of our portfolio. It's quite possible this will never go further than your signing the contract."

"I understand," she said.

He thought: Do you?

Do you really?

20

ANNA HELD THE PHONE IN HER HAND LONG AFTER THE CALL ended.

She sat on the bed, the comforter wrapped tight around her, trying and failing to keep out the cold. Frost had begun to form on the inside of the windows. She really should have put the heat on, but the propane was so expensive these days. Another blanket might do the trick. She pulled one from the bed and layered it over the comforter.

Yesterday she had spent fifty-three dollars and forty-eight cents on groceries. That left her not quite four hundred and eighty dollars to her name. God knew how long it would take to get the money from the clinic. And she supposed she would have to pay tax on it. Five thousand sounded like a lot when you said it out loud, but when you thought about it, when you thought about rent and gas and propane and electricity and all those tiny things that ate the cash right out of your pocket, it really wasn't much at all.

It would be almost nothing to some rich New York couple who wanted a baby so bad they'd pay, against the law, to get one.

Anna wondered what it would be like to feel a life grow inside of her. To feel it move, kick, toss and turn. To watch her belly swell day after day, week after week, for all those long months. And nothing but an empty space at the end of it all.

Can I really do that?

She had asked the question a hundred times over the last two days.

Yes, I can.

With the answer given, finally and for real, she gathered the comforter and blanket around her, dropped the phone on her bed, and went to find the contract and a working pen. She'd signed nothing more significant than the lease on her home before today. Now she was going to sign away a living, breathing piece of herself.

And she was okay with that. Really.

She found the contracts in the manila envelope and dug in the drawers for a pen. The third one worked, black ink that left ugly blots on the back of the envelope. She sat at the table and signed her name six times, twice for each contract.

I will carry and deliver a baby that I will never know, she thought, that will be raised by someone I will never meet. I can do that.

I know I can.

She wept then for no reason she could understand, her tears pattering on the table and the envelope. Only later, much later, did she realize they were tears of grief. She grieved for a tiny life that could never be hers.

Once the sobbing had passed, she counted the money in her head, left her home, and drove to the post office.

And then, for a while, she put it out of her mind.

21

LIBBY SAT NEXT TO MASON ON THE COUCH, DR. SHERMAN ON the armchair. He had driven from Brooklyn to Albany just to see them, and he seemed excited when they answered their door to him. Libby and Mason shared a modest house in the city's suburbs. They could easily afford a bigger place in a better neighborhood, but there were other things to spend money on.

Like this.

"We've got a candidate that I'm very excited about," Dr. Sherman said, grasping an iPad.

They had signed up with the clinic three months earlier. It was an agency of sorts, an introduction service, no more. Dr. Sherman had been very clear about that, and insisted that they also be clear about it, given the legal issues with paid surrogacy in the state.

Mason had been skeptical from the start. Libby had shown him the clinic's website, the images of their pristine offices, all white surfaces and glass. Mason had wondered if they were stock photos, but Libby had stopped listening to his objections.

Dr. Sherman tapped at his iPad and said, "Take a look."

He handed the tablet over, and Libby had to turn it this way and that to make the photograph orient correctly. When she did, she saw a portrait of . . .

"That's you, isn't it?" Mason said. "An older photo, but it's you, right?"

Libby shook her head slowly, trying to make sense of it. The woman in the photograph did indeed look like her, but a few years younger, and a few pounds lighter. She stood against a door, shoulder-length red hair pushed behind her ears, a nervous expression on her face.

"No, it's not me," she said.

"Jesus," Mason said.

Dr. Sherman grinned and said, "It's a remarkable likeness, isn't it?"

"Who is she?" Libby asked.

"As we discussed, Mrs. Reese, I'm not at liberty to reveal the candidate's identity. You can't know anything about her, other than her appearance and her health. Which is excellent, by the way. No conditions, genetic or otherwise, no issues with alcohol or drugs, she's never smoked, she's a good weight for her height. All in all, you couldn't ask for a better candidate. And when you factor in the resemblance to the intended mother, well, I guess you can see why I'm so excited about this prospect."

Libby looked to her husband. His face remained blank. She nudged him.

"She's perfect," she said. "Isn't she?"

He forced a smile. "Sure."

Libby felt the urge to shake him, to scream at him. Every step of the way, he had acquiesced but never freely given his approval. He had never wanted it, not like she did. Now here was the opportunity she'd been seeking, and she wouldn't let his apathy alter her course. She turned back to Dr. Sherman.

"What's the next step?" she asked.

"The candidate has already signed a contract, so the next step is insemination."

From the corner of her eye, she saw Mason wince, stoking her anger once more. Come on, she thought, it's not like you have to fuck her. You jerked off into a cup. That's as far as your contribution goes. That and the money, of course.

"She'll attend a clinic in her area to have the procedure. It's very simple, completely painless, she'll be in and out in an after-noon. Then in about two weeks, we'll know if she's conceived."

Libby's anger faded away, replaced by a welling joy that made her giggle.

"And you know," Dr. Sherman continued, "with such a close resemblance, there's really no reason for anyone to know you didn't carry the child yourself. Not unless you choose to tell them. All I need is your signatures on the final agreement to execute the contract, the next-stage payment, and we're off to the races."

He drew the papers from his briefcase and said, "I assume a bank transfer will be the easiest option?"

Mason spoke, his voice ringing loud with anxiety. "Can you leave those with us? Just so we can talk it over one more time."

Dr. Sherman looked to Libby, eyebrows raised.

"We don't need to talk it over again," Libby said, the anger back and burning. "We've talked it over a hundred times. The decision has been made. We have the perfect candidate, every-thing's in place, there is no reason not to do this."

He looked back to Dr. Sherman and said, "Forgive me, but I'm still hazy on the legality of what we're discussing here. I know we've been over this, but—"

Dr. Sherman smiled and nodded. "Absolutely no need to apol-ogize for being confused. It's the lack of clearly defined regula-tions that causes the confusion. First of all, please be assured that neither you nor I are proposing anything illegal."

"But it *is* illegal," Mason said. "New York State doesn't allow paid surrogacy."

"That's correct. But the surrogacy will take place in another state, one where paid surrogacy is perfectly legal. The clinic is merely acting as a facilitator."

Mason pointed to the papers in Dr. Sherman's hand. "But here, where we live, those contracts aren't worth the paper they're printed on. Same as whatever agreement you have with the birth mother. If she changes her mind after we have the baby, then what?"

"That's why we keep a barrier between the birth mother and the intended parents. You will never know her identity, and she will never know yours."

"She could take you to court," Mason said. "A judge could order you to hand over that information."

"Well, she'd have a fight on her hands," Dr. Sherman said with a forced chuckle. "And, quite frankly, the clinic can afford better lawyers."

"That's pretty cold," Mason said.

"It's reality, that's all. Please remember, you're paying a premium price for a premium service. You're not dealing with a front for some baby farm in Mexico or India. Your child will be carried to term under the best of care, let me—"

Libby pressed her fingertips against her temples. "Enough. We've been over and over this. Every question has been answered. I want to sign the papers now."

Mason reached for her and she resisted the desire to slap his hand away.

"Libby, honey, it's such a big step, I don't see the harm in giving it one more day to—"

"One more day? One more . . . how about another week? Another year? Jesus, Mason, we've been trying for this since the day we got married. We are not backing out now."

"There's still the adoption route."

"We've been on the waiting list for nearly four years now. How much longer do we give them?"

Mason clenched his hands together, held them in front of his face for a moment, then lowered them. He inhaled once through his nose, exhaled through his mouth.

"Dr. Sherman," he said, "please leave the papers, and I'll mail them to you tomorrow."

Libby got to her feet and hissed, "Goddamn you."

She walked to the stairs, climbed them, and slammed the bedroom door behind her.

LIBBY FELL ASLEEP at some point. It had been light outside when she lay down, but when she opened her eyes, the room was inky dark and cold. A wintery shower pattered against the window, wet drops that weren't quite snow flattening on the glass and sliding down. She listened for a while, wondering if Mason was still in the house, or if he'd gone to the range like he often did when stressed. Shooting relaxed him, he said. He had tried to interest her, even bought her a small pistol of her own, but she didn't like it. Whatever he got from pulling the trigger and hitting a target, it was lost on her. She never told him how pathetic she found it all.

They should talk, clear the air, but in truth she hoped he'd gone. She had no will to fight again. They'd done so much of that over the last few years, since she was finally diagnosed with endometriosis. Tissue from her womb drifting up into her fallopian tubes, the gynecologist had said, relishing the details. That explained the suffering brought on by her periods, which had returned in full force when she stopped taking the contraceptive pills. Even though she now had an explanation, confirmation that it had never been her fault, the guilt still bore down on her.

But as infuriatingly understanding as Mason was, he still remained hesitant about their only real solution. She knew each of his arguments by heart.

Will you love the baby like it's your own?

It *will* be my own, she countered. And it'll be yours.

What if there's a problem with the pregnancy, a miscarriage, an abnormality?

That's the same risk every parent takes. Why should we be any different?

Why not wait a little longer for the adoption agency?

But we've been waiting so long for them already. If we wanted a troubled seven-year-old, we'd be at the front of the line, but we don't.

It's not legal, and the contract can't be enforced. The birth mother can claim the baby anytime she wants, dragging us through the courts to get it back.

Only if she finds us. She won't know who we are, and we won't know who she is. The baby will not be taken from us. She can't find us. There's no way. It could never happen.

Never.

But there was one argument she couldn't push back against, the one that always ended the discussion: the baby won't fix you. In that strange way of his, he drilled down into the soul of her, finding that live nerve. You think this baby will heal you, he'd say, and it won't.

Libby always walked away at that point, closed the door behind her. And he never followed her, knowing to push further would be to risk everything.

She sat up and stretched her arms, working her shoulders and neck loose. The house was quiet, covered with the stillness of being alone. Mason wasn't here, she was sure of it. She had asked Mira, their cleaner, not to come today. They would pay her anyway, but today they had needed privacy.

Libby got out of bed, opened the door, and listened again. Nothing but the wind against the gable wall and the sleet against the windows. Cold drafts swam up the stairs to brush against her skin. She pulled her robe tight around her and went downstairs.

The contracts still lay on the coffee table, three copies, only a name on a line between her and the life she desired so badly. She stared at them for a time before walking to the dresser, where her cell phone rested.

The last call had been from Dr. Sherman, early this morning, to tell them he was on his way. She found his number in the recent-calls list and tapped it with her thumb. The dial tone sounded and she wondered if he'd gotten back to New York yet. When he answered, the sound of his voice resonating inside a car answered her question.

"Dr. Sherman," she said, "can you talk?"

"Yes, certainly. I'm stuck in traffic, but I have you on speaker."

"It's just, I wanted to ask a question."

"Yes?"

"The final agreement," she said. "Does it have to be signed by both the intended parents?"

A pause, the noise of distant traffic, horns blasting.

"Not necessarily," he said.

22

"GOOD NEWS," DR. HOLDSWORTH SAID. "YOU'RE PREGNANT." It was not news to Anna. She had felt the change within days of the procedure. It wasn't something she could define with words, even if she had been good with such things. The best way she could describe it was that it felt as if the world had shifted somehow, changed around her, so that the air smelled and tasted different, that her skin felt new textures, her eyes saw new light.

Her mood had changed too. She had never been quick to anger, which was how she'd stuck with waitressing so long, but over the last two weeks she had found her temper growing shorter and shorter. Just yesterday she had snapped at a cashier in the supermarket, and two days before that, while she had traveled to the clinic for the blood test, she had given another driver the finger for not letting her merge. It was an odd feeling, like standing on one foot, ready to fall at any moment.

Dr. Holdsworth was an older woman who spent more time looking over her spectacles than through them. When Anna had arrived for the procedure at Dalton Gynecology and Obstetrics, she had been relieved to find it would be carried out by a female doctor. There'd been no pain, as promised, but it sure as hell was uncomfortable. That had been two weeks ago.

"So what now?" Anna asked.

Dr. Holdsworth smiled and said, "What now is you go home and relax. Eat well, rest well, use your common sense. Any pain, any bleeding, call me immediately, don't wait. But right now, everything seems good."

A question had been nagging at Anna since she'd arrived at the clinic, and now she felt she could ask it. "When will I get the next payment?"

Dr. Holdsworth dropped her gaze, as if the question shamed her. "I'm afraid I don't deal with that end of things. If you've no other questions, I'll see you in a month."

As Anna returned to her car in the clinic's parking lot, her mind turned to the thing inside her. A cluster of cells, she reminded herself. Nothing more. The drive from Pittsburgh back to Superior took hardly any time at all, the midmorning traffic moving freely. She thought of Betsy and whether she should call her and tell her the news.

The news.

As if this were her baby, and she would breathlessly call friends and loved ones to share in her excitement. But it was not her baby.

Just a cluster of cells. That's all.

23

LIBBY CRIED WHEN DR. SHERMAN CALLED TO TELL HER THE NEWS. She was at her desk in the office she shared with three other members of the department's admin staff. Nadine looked up from her computer terminal, mouthed the words, What's wrong? Libby shook her head, smiled, and waved away her concern.

"How long?" she asked.

"Counting from the candidate's last period, it's four weeks," Dr. Sherman said.

Libby covered her mouth to stifle a giggle. Her eyes brimmed. Nadine watched her, a mix of worry and bemusement on her face.

"Everything looks good at the moment," Dr. Sherman said, "but please remember, it's early days. There's no guarantee we'll make it to twelve weeks. The first trimester can be tricky. A lot of women miscarry in the first few weeks without even realizing they were pregnant."

"A lot of women?" Libby asked, the smile falling from her mouth. "What's the risk? I mean, how likely is it—"

"Libby, Libby, Libby, don't panic. Everything appears fine right now. I just want you to be aware that there's always a possibility. And if it happens, which it probably won't, then we can try again. Now, stop worrying."

"Okay," she said in an expulsion of air. "It's just . . . I've wanted this so much for so long, you know?"

"Of course," he said. "It's an emotional time. In ten weeks, the candidate will come in for the first full scan and we'll have a better idea of how things are progressing. In the meantime, try not to worry, all right? It won't do you any good."

"Okay. I'll try. And Doctor?"

"Yes?"

"Thank you," she said.

Dr. Sherman chuckled, said welcome, and goodbye.

Libby hung up and noticed Nadine still staring at her. Nadine got up from her swivel chair so fast it spun into her desk. She dashed across the room and hunkered down by Libby's side.

"Tell me," she said.

Tears ran down Libby's cheeks. Nadine reached up and wiped them away.

"Tell me," she said again.

A laugh escaped Libby, high and ringing. Nadine smiled now, her expression one of amused confusion.

"Come on, don't do this to me. Tell me what it is."

Libby sniffed back more tears.

"I'm pregnant," she said.

"YOU SAID WHAT?"

Mason stared at her from across the kitchen.

"I told her I was pregnant," Libby said.

He stood there, back against the fridge, mouth open, shaking his head. It was the first moment when she really, honestly asked herself if she still loved him. The question rang inside her like a fire bell, insistent, until she pushed the thought away. No time for that now. They had a family to build.

"Why did you do that?" he asked.

"I don't know," she said, truthfully. "Does it matter? We're going to have a baby in eight months. It has to come from somewhere."

Mason hadn't been as angry as she'd imagined when she told

him she'd gone ahead and signed the agreement without him. He had come home from work that evening, two months ago, and told her he'd noticed the money gone from their savings account, and to whom it had been transferred. He had remained ferociously calm while she explained to him how she'd signed the papers and mailed them to New York and then made the payment.

"I guess I knew you would," he'd said.

She remembered the emotions that crossed his face in those few seconds: anger, fear, regret, and more.

"It's what we wanted," Libby said.

He was about to argue, but she raised a finger.

"Don't you say it isn't. Don't you dare. We talked about it every day for ten years."

"I should leave you," he said through tight, thin lips. "I really should."

"But you won't," she said, knowing this to be true.

And he didn't. Now, two months later, he stood ten feet away, and she could feel the turmoil in him from across the room. He held his hand out in a questioning gesture.

"So, what, you're going to pretend to be pregnant for the rest of the year?"

"If I have to," Libby said.

"How?" he asked, his voice rising in exasperation. "What, are you going to stick a pillow up your sweater? Wear a padded bra? How are you going to do it?"

"I don't know, but I'll figure it out. That's not what's important right now."

"It kind of feels like a big deal to—"

"What's important is we have a baby on the way," she said, cutting him short. "We have to be ready. We need to learn what to do, how to look after it, all the things parents deal with. Because that's what we are now. We're parents."

He shrugged, sneered. "Funny, I don't feel much like a dad."

"But you are," she said, her voice softening, as she took a step toward him. "I might not be this baby's real mother, but you're its real father. It'll be your flesh and blood. This baby is really yours, and you have no idea how much I wish it was mine."

The last words splintered in her throat as the tears came. Timed just right, they filled her eyes. Through the blur, she saw his shoulders drop, then his hands, then his head. She saw him surrender, and silently, she rejoiced.

He crossed the room and she took him in her arms. She buried her nose and mouth between the hardness of his jaw and his shoulder, breathed deep, tried to find the scent of her love for him. Tried to remember the feeling in her belly, back when they were young, when he could make her quiver at his touch.

"I love you," he said, the words hot against her ear. "You know I do. And you know I want to make you happy. But I'm afraid. Can you understand that? I'm afraid this won't be what you need it to be. I'm afraid it'll break you."

"I'm already broken," she said.

He said nothing because he knew she was right.

24

ANNA LEANED OVER THE TOILET AND VOMITED UP HER LUNCH, holding on to the cistern to keep herself upright through the rolling waves of nausea. When the cramps in her stomach had subsided, she spat into the bowl, then flushed it away. She went to the basin and ran cold water from the faucet, scooped handfuls of it up to rinse her mouth.

Almost two thirty in the afternoon.

"Morning sickness, my ass," she said to her reflection in the mirror.

She studied herself there. Her hair had thickened, had never looked so good in fact, but the benefit was offset by blotches and pimples around her chin and nose. She hadn't experienced acne since she was a teenager, and she did not welcome it back. Turning, she examined the reflection of her stomach side-on. No sign of anything there, but she knew it was too early. Her bra felt tight and uncomfortable, and she tugged at the straps, thinking she should arrange a fitting somewhere.

The bathroom opened onto the bedroom of the apartment that had been provided for her. She'd been here almost three months and had enjoyed making it her own. Not that she had much to clutter the place up with, but she'd bought some cushions and throws. Nothing expensive. She had been frugal with her money so far, and most of the forty thousand dollars she'd been paid to date had remained intact. With no rent or utilities to pay, the living allowance more than covered her needs. She'd even managed to put a little extra away for the first time in her life.

The bed, still unmade since the morning, called to her. She had planned to go out for a walk, partly for the exercise, partly to enjoy a little spring air. But the tiredness clung to her constantly, weighing down her limbs, her head, her eyes. She climbed into bed, lay down, and pulled the comforter up around herself, burrowed in beneath it, letting the warmth swallow her.

Sleep came, black and thick, punctuated by garish dreams of old strange houses with winding hallways and undiscovered rooms. When she woke, the world had dimmed, and her bladder ached for release. She sat up, yawning and rubbing her eyes.

Then she saw the figure in the doorway.

Anna froze, staring at the shape. Part of her mind knew full well that it was a man standing watching her. The other part told her that it couldn't be, the doors were locked, and anyway, why would anyone be here? Adrenaline-fueled tremors rippled through her limbs and she wondered if she should run, but where to? And what from?

"Hello, Anna," the man said.

She gasped, felt a sudden chill, from her toes to the top of her head.

He reached for the light switch, flicked it on. She saw his face and found her fear matched with anger.

"I'm sorry, I didn't mean to startle you," Mr. Kovak said.

Anna put a hand on either side of her head, trying to keep the rage inside. "Startle me? You scared the shit out of me. What the fuck do you think you're doing?"

He gave a patient smile and said, "Please don't swear at me, Anna."

"What? Don't swear?" She grabbed a pillow from the bed and hurled it at him. "Fuck you!"

He batted the pillow away with one of his meaty hands and entered the room. "Again, I'm sorry, I didn't mean to frighten you.

I was in town, so I wanted to see how you were getting along. I called your cell, but there was no answer. I was starting to get a little worried, so I came over, and you didn't answer your door."

"How did you get in?"

"I have a key," he said. "I do work for your landlord, remember."

"This is not okay," Anna said, her initial terror ebbing away to leave only anger in its place. "You can't just show up here and let yourself in."

He went to the chair beneath the window, picked up the few items of clothing that rested there, and set them aside.

"Like I said, I did call, and you didn't answer."

"Doesn't matter. There are laws. I've been renting places ever since I left home, and I know my rights."

Mr. Kovak sat down and said, "You're absolutely correct, and I apologize. It won't happen again."

Anna felt her anger cool, but the fear returned, coiling like a snake inside her. Even though she was fully clothed, she pulled the comforter up around herself.

"What do you want?" she asked.

"To see how you're doing." He crossed his legs, an oddly feminine movement for a man of his size. "To make sure you're comfortable and you have everything you need."

"I'm doing okay," Anna said. "I could've told you that over the phone."

"But I like to see my girls in person."

Mr. Kovak smiled, and she wished he wouldn't. It didn't suit his face, showed too many teeth, made him look like a predator.

"Well, now you've seen me. I'm fine, honestly."

"Any sickness, nausea?"

"Some," she said.

She could have told him about earlier, how she threw up her lunch, but she didn't want to tell him any more than was absolutely necessary. His intrusion had rattled her beyond the fear of it; it had left a feeling of vulnerability, the knowledge that he could do this at any time, even if he promised he wouldn't. She felt her anger bubble up and rise again.

"How about headaches?" he asked.

Look at him, she thought. Sitting there all prim like some priest or pastor when he could rip me to pieces without even breaking a sweat.

"Not really," she said.

"Are you eating okay?"

"Yeah."

"Have you been taking your folic acid and vitamin D?"

"Yes, and yes."

She unconsciously rolled her eyes, and he gave a small condescending laugh that angered her more than anything he'd said or done so far.

"You know what's not so good?" she asked.

"Mm-hm?"

She looked him in the eye and said, "I haven't taken a decent shit in, like, four days."

He nodded and said, "Eat plenty of fruit and drink lots of water. That should help."

"And the farting," she said. "My God, I've never farted so much in my life. And they stink so bad."

"The hormonal changes slow down your digestive tract, the gases build up, it's perfectly normal. Almost every woman experiences it when she's pregnant. What about hemorrhoids? Any of those? If you haven't yet, you will in the later months, so you've that to look forward to."

"Fuck you," she said.

"Anna, there's no point trying to gross me out. I've been doing this job for a few years now, I've guided many dozens of women through the process, even attended a few births. You know you'll probably soil yourself during labor, right? Believe me, I've seen everything. All the stuff people don't mention in polite conversation. You don't have anything to scare me off with."

"All right, so you're Mr. Maternity, I get it. I'm fine, the baby's fine as far as I can tell, so I don't know what else you need from me."

Mr. Kovak got to his feet, put his hands in his pockets, and approached the bed. Anna shrank back against the headboard, her courage evaporating. He came to the nightstand on one side, examined the top, then opened the single drawer and peered inside.

"What are you doing?" she asked. "Stop."

He walked around the bed and did the same at the other nightstand, this time pushing a few items in the drawer aside to get a better look.

"I said stop, you can't do that."

"Yes, I can," he said.

He closed the drawer and went to the dressing table against the far wall. His fingers picked through the detritus on top, occasionally turning items over for a better look. Some makeup, a hairbrush, a paperback that she never got around to reading. Then he began to go through the drawers.

"If you don't stop, I'll call the police and tell them you broke in."

"Fine by me," he said.

"Well, Jesus, tell me what you're looking for if you're that—"

"Are you using?" he asked, continuing his search.

"Using what, exactly?"

"Anything."

He closed the last drawer, seemed satisfied.

"No," Anna said. "I've never used drugs. I told you."

"Users lie," he said. "I need to be sure."

Mr. Kovak went to the still-open bathroom door and turned on the light. As he opened the cabinet below the basin, Anna threw back the comforter and got out of bed.

"If that's what you're looking for, then you're wasting your time."

"No, I'm not," he said as he left the bathroom. "I get paid for this, remember?"

He headed for the living room, and she inserted herself between him and the door, her socked feet backpedaling across the carpet.

"Be careful, please," he said, stepping around her. "I wouldn't want you to fall and hurt yourself."

She followed him around the living room, from the couch to the armchairs. He picked up an empty glass from the coffee table, brought it to his nose, sniffed.

"It was a Diet Coke," she said. "Look, I haven't had so much as a sip of beer since before the procedure."

"Diet Coke?" he echoed. "Please watch your caffeine intake. And the sweeteners, they're not good for you. No more than one can a day. Sparkling water is better."

He set the glass back on the coffee table and took a deep breath through his nose.

"You're not smoking cigarettes," he said. "I'd smell it."

He went to the kitchenette, opened cupboards, looked behind mugs and beneath plates, rattled the cutlery in the drawers.

"You can't tell me what to do," Anna said.

He didn't turn from his work, lifting boxes of cereal out of the lower cupboards, looking inside. "Excuse me?"

"I signed the contract, and I'm bound by that, that's fine, but you don't get to come here unannounced and start telling me what to do, what to eat, what to drink."

Mr. Kovak took one of the cereal boxes and dropped it in the trash.

"Too much sugar," he said. "You should be mindful of gestational diabetes. There are plenty of low-sugar alternatives."

"Did you hear what I said?" Anna asked, her anger building by the moment. "You don't tell me what to do in my own home."

He turned to face her. "Yes, I do."

"I'll do what the contract says, but you can't—"

136

He crossed the room with a speed she'd never have imagined a man his size could possess. She stumbled back against the couch, almost fell over, but he reached for her upper arm and kept her from falling. He moved in close, his stomach pressing against her chest.

"I'm here for your safety," he said, his voice gentle as he loomed over her. "That is my primary concern, along with the well-being of the baby. I don't care what you think I can or can't do. This is my job, and I'm good at it. Whether you like it or not is of no concern to me."

He released her arm and stepped away, turned toward the apartment door.

"Please take care of yourself, Anna, and don't hesitate to call me if there's anything you need. And don't be late for your appointment next week. End of the first trimester. It's a big one."

He stopped at the door and turned back to her.

"And please, don't change the locks. That would only cause a headache for both of us."

Mr. Kovak opened the door, stepped through, and closed it behind him.

Anna ran to the kitchen sink and threw up.

25

ANNA LAY BACK ON THE BED AND PULLED UP HER SHIRT. THE lights in the ceiling made her squint, but through the glare, she saw Dr. Holdsworth lift the ultrasound transducer probe from the wheeled terminal. From a tray underneath she took a bottle of gel and squeezed some onto the business end of the transducer. Anna flinched from the cold as Dr. Holdsworth pressed it against her belly and used it to smear the gel across her abdomen. She'd been told to drink plenty of water that morning but avoid going to the bathroom. When the doctor pressed the transducer beneath her navel, it reminded her how badly she needed to go.

"Let's see now," Dr. Holdsworth said. "There's your bladder, nice and full, so baby should be right around . . . here."

Anna turned her head to see the screen and gasped when she saw the image. So clear. She hadn't expected to see much, but there, the head, the arms, the pulsing heart.

"My God," she said.

Dr. Holdsworth manipulated a tracker ball on the terminal, clicked at points on the screen, laying out connected lines across the image.

"Just measuring the length, size of the head," she mumbled, talking to herself more than Anna. "Good. Excellent. Going by the size, we're bang on the money with the delivery date. You doing okay?"

Anna looked up at the ceiling, rested her forearm across her brow to shield her eyes from the light. "Yeah. I mean, I'm tired all the time, and I throw up a lot, but apart from that."

"The sickness should pass soon," the doctor said. "And the tiredness. Make sure you exercise, that'll help. And what about you? Up here, I mean."

Anna couldn't see Dr. Holdsworth, but she heard the sound of finger tapping skull.

"I'm all right," she said. "More or less."

"You're going through a huge life event, about as big a thing as a woman will ever face. And you'll have nothing to show at the end of it. You must feel something about that."

"I'll have money," Anna said. "I'll have a future."

"Is that really all it means to you?"

Anna lifted her forearm from her eyes so she could see the doctor. "What else can it mean? The baby won't be mine, no matter what. The money's all I have to get me through. Do I sound hard?"

Dr. Holdsworth couldn't hold her gaze, set about tearing handfuls of paper towels from a roll and mopping up the gel on Anna's belly.

"No," she said. "You sound like you know what you're doing. But if you ever feel like you need to talk, I can give you a few numbers, help lines, counseling services, that sort of thing."

Anna looked once more to the screen, the tiny life frozen there.

"Can I get a copy?" she asked.

"No," Dr. Holdsworth said, "you can't."

26

IBBY USED A MAGNET TO STICK THE PICTURE ON THE FRIDGE door. She stepped back to admire it. Such a perfect thing. She had giggled when she opened the first email attachment, a video file showing the baby moving its tiny arms and legs, its little heart thrumming like an engine. Even the nose was there. The second file was a still image she immediately printed out on a letter-sized page. Mira had paused her cleaning and joined Libby in gazing at the image.

"*Guapísimo*," Mira had whispered.

"I know," Libby had said with an unabashed grin.

She had barely stopped staring at it since.

Mason would be home any minute and she wanted him to see it. To see his child. He had become distant in recent weeks. Never an outgoing man at the best of times, he had grown more reserved, and she seemed to see less of him every day. He had taken to leaving for work early, always saying he had things to catch up on or wanted to get a few shots off at the gun range before he went in, and evenings had become a grind of silence over dinner followed by his retreating to his den to do yet more work, though she suspected he spent more time playing those shooting games, living out whatever toy-soldier fantasies he harbored.

In truth, she was relieved to see him go most nights. She had stopped drinking, said it was for the baby, and ignored the rolling of his eyes. So, he would open a bottle of wine to have a glass with his meal, then take it to the den to finish. Libby didn't like him when he drank; he became sullen and quiet, and when he did speak, it was to snap and argue. Let him go play his games, she thought.

She hoped the scan would change things. Looking at it again, she traced the shape of the head, the arms, the legs. It was real now. Surely he couldn't turn away from this? Surely when he saw the child—his own baby—he would accept that he was a father along with everything that entailed? He would love this baby.

He. Would. Love. This. Baby.

He had to.

"What's that?"

His voice startled her, and she cried out. She hadn't heard his car in the driveway, or his key in the door. He stood in the kitchen doorway, briefcase still in hand, his shirt collar undone, tie loose. Libby moved the magnet aside and lifted down the printed picture. She brought it to him, held it out. He looked at the image but did not take it from her.

"Isn't it beautiful?" she said.

The muscles in his jaw worked, his Adam's apple bobbed. He let out a long breath of air that skimmed her extended hand.

"It's our baby," she said. "Your baby."

Mason sagged, his shoulder pressed against the doorframe. He finally took the paper from her hand. His eyes brimmed, his breath quivering.

"It's real," Libby said. "This is happening. You have to understand that. Either accept it or go."

He dropped his briefcase on the floor, walked to the table, and sat down, the picture still in his hand. "How long to go?" he asked.

"Twenty-seven weeks," Libby said. "Six months."

He looked from the page to her. "I guess we'd better start planning."

Libby crossed the room to him, wrapped her arms around his shoulders, kissed his cheek. She smelled the burnt, acrid odor of spent gunpowder in his hair, on his clothes, and knew where he had been.

As she lowered herself into his lap, she said, "It's going to be all right."

"Is it?" he asked.

She shushed him with a kiss.

"WHAT IS THAT?" Mason asked.

Libby turned away from the mirror. "It was delivered today. What do you think?"

He didn't answer, just stared. The artificial belly, formed from flesh-colored silicone, had been expensive, but worth it. At least she thought so, anyway. It was formed like an undergarment with Velcro fasteners at the back and transparent shoulder straps to support its weight.

"I don't know," Mason said. "Seems a little . . ."

"A little what?"

He didn't answer, stood there mute, his mouth open but no words coming. Libby supplied one of her own.

"Weird?"

He shook his head and put his hands up. "I didn't say that."

"You didn't have to," she said, running her hands over the silicone, feeling the strange coolness of it. "It's what you were thinking, right? I know it's strange, but it's important for me, okay? I should be showing by now. Look, see? I can pad it to make it grow, then I can order bigger sizes as the pregnancy goes on."

It had been a month since the image of the ultrasound scan had arrived in her email inbox, and things had been better between them. He had opened up a little, they had talked more, and he'd been drinking less. Wine was saved for the weekends, with the odd beer on workdays, and he always asked permission. They had discussed the nursery, the things they needed to buy, how and when they would begin to tell people. Every now and then, he even seemed excited. Like a father.

"How's dinner coming?" she asked, stepping into her new dress.

"Should be ready by the time everyone gets here," he said. "Say, about thirty, forty minutes."

Libby pulled the dress up over her thighs, over the artificial belly, and slipped her arms through the holes. She turned her back to Mason and said, "Zip me?"

He crossed the bedroom and did as she asked, then leaned in and kissed her neck. His breath warmed her ear and made her tingle in a way she hadn't felt in some time. But that happened, didn't it? Women's hormones go crazy when they're pregnant, and they get horny, right?

Libby caught herself in that thought and felt suddenly foolish and ashamed. I'm not pregnant, she reminded herself. Am I?

She turned in front of the full-length mirror, viewed her body side-on. She ran her hands over her breasts, her fingers unable to discern the padding in her bra, and over her rounded stomach.

"Yes, I am," she said.

"What?" Mason asked.

She smiled at him and said, "Oh, nothing."

"YOU'RE NOT DRINKING?" Shannon asked as Libby topped off her glass of Prosecco.

The four women stood at one end of the kitchen while Greg watched Mason at the stove, admiring his work. She'd known Shannon since Greg—then still her fiancé—had been an usher at Libby's wedding. Diane had been their neighbor at their first home together, and tonight she'd brought along her new girlfriend, Meadow, who Mason thought was far too young for her. They huddled around now, all of them glancing at Libby's figure, but none of them ready to come right out and ask.

"Nope," Libby said, raising her glass of cranberry juice. "Not for a few months, anyway."

Shannon's eyes widened while Diane and Meadow shared a glance.

Libby feigned exasperation. "Oh, come on and ask me already!"

"Are you?" Diane asked. "For real?"

Libby grinned and said, "For real."

Shannon squealed and threw her arms around her. "Oh, thank God, I was so worried you'd just gained weight."

"Congratulations," Meadow said with the polite reserve of a new acquaintance.

"Let me in there, dammit," Diane said, squeezing her way into the hug.

The three of them shared the embrace, Meadow on the periphery, until Greg piped up from the other end of the kitchen.

"What's going on over there?"

Libby managed to extricate herself enough to say, "Mason, tell him."

Her husband turned away from the bubbling pots and pans, blushed, and said, "We've got a baby on the way."

"Really?" Greg said, pointing at Libby. "You're pregnant?"

Before she could reply, he took Mason in a back-slapping hug. "Oh, man, I'm so happy for you. I know you guys have been trying for so long."

Mason returned the embrace, thanked him, while his eyes met Libby's. She saw the doubt there for the first time in a month, and it stung like a needle in her heart.

DINNER PASSED TOO quickly for Libby. It had been so long since she'd seen her friends, and their joy for her news made her glow inside. Even when she exchanged glances with Mason and saw that same unease in his eyes, it didn't dilute the happiness she felt. Greg and Shannon shared war stories of their own parenthood; they had two boys and a girl, aged five, seven, and ten. Tales of bodily functions and household chaos reduced everyone to tears of laughter. All except Mason, who politely smiled along.

By the time their guests had left, all of them loose with alcohol, it was past midnight. Libby walked back to the kitchen to find Mason loading up the dishwasher.

"Leave that for the morning," she said. "Let's go to bed."

"It won't take long," he said, keeping his back to her.

She approached, slipped her arms around his middle, feeling his warmth, the soft and firm of him. He smelled of faint cologne and wine. She stood on her tiptoes and kissed his neck, just as he had done hours earlier.

"Leave it," she said. "Come to bed."

He turned inside her arms so their bodies met. She kissed his mouth, at first unyielding, then his lips parted and their tongues met. As their torsos pressed together, she became aware of the prosthesis beneath her dress. She pulled away from him and took his hand.

"Come on," she said.

She led him upstairs to their room, guided him to the bed, and sat him down. Gently pushing him back down onto the bed, she straddled him, felt his hardness against her. She leaned down and they kissed again. As she unbuttoned his shirt, he reached around and unzipped her dress. She slipped it over her head, tossed it to the floor, then reached around her back to undo her bra. As it fell away, he kissed her there, and she sighed, grinding her crotch against his.

He moved his hands around her back, and she felt a tugging, heard the sound of Velcro unfastening. Without thinking, she twisted her body, slapped his hands away.

"Stop," she said.

He stared up at her, confusion on his face. "I was just going to take it off."

"No," she said. "I have to keep it on. It needs to be a part of me."

He shook his head, his brow creasing. "Even just for—"

"No," she said.

Mason reached up, gripped her at the waist, and moved her aside. As she lay down on the bed, he got up, redoing his shirt buttons.

"I'll finish clearing up downstairs," he said. "Get some sleep."

He left her there, alone, and she cursed him.

27

THE FIRST TIME ANNA CONSCIOUSLY FELT THE BABY MOVE, SHE was in a semi-doze on her couch, watching *Friends* reruns on TV, the remains of her breakfast still on the coffee table. She had experienced odd sensations for a week or so before that, like tiny bubbles popping inside her belly, but she'd put them down to gas, her stomach settling as the sickness became less frequent, less severe. But this was different. There could be no mistaking it. Like a butterfly taking flight inside of her.

She put a hand over her mouth as she giggled, then sat quite still, waiting for the feeling to return. And it did. Little butterfly wings beating, ready to ride the breeze. She laughed again and lost the sensation. Thirty minutes passed while she sat motionless, hoping for it to come again. When it didn't, she reached for her cell phone.

When Betsy answered, Anna said, "I felt it move."

She heard her friend's breath against the mouthpiece and wondered if it was a sigh of sadness or joy.

"You better get used to that," Betsy said. "Couple months, the little so-and-so will be kicking the hell out of your bladder."

"You want to come over before your shift?"

A pause, then, "Maybe for a half hour. I'm on lunch duty today. I guess I'd better get ready to go."

"Thanks," Anna said, meaning it. "You're a good friend."

"I know," Betsy said. "See you soon."

Anna set the phone down and began clearing up. Since

Mr. Kovak's surprise visit, she had become fastidious in her housework. Of all the things that bothered and scared her about that intrusion, it was not the implied threat that weighed heaviest: for some reason it was the idea that he might have considered her a slob. Therefore, she washed up after every meal, vacuumed every day, even made her bed each morning. She would not be found lacking again.

Mr. Kovak had visited once more since that day, this time giving her an hour's notice. Anna had rung Betsy immediately after hanging up on him, and begged her to come over. She had arrived at almost the same moment he did, and the two were rigidly polite with each other for the thirty minutes he stayed in the apartment. He asked after Anna's well-being, if she had everything she needed, was she taking care of herself. You don't have to worry, Betsy had said, I'm keeping an eye on her. With a cold smile, Mr. Kovak expressed his appreciation.

When he'd gone, Betsy had said, "I don't like him."

"Me neither," Anna had said.

Neither of them had elaborated on their reservations, only that Betsy insisted she be present the next time Mr. Kovak called to visit. Anna couldn't argue with that.

Betsy arrived at a quarter of eleven, and they embraced on the doorstep.

"How you been sleeping?" she asked.

"Okay," Anna said. "I have to get up to pee more than I'd like, but other than that."

She poured them each a glass of sparkling water and they sat in the living room, talking a lot about not much of anything. Betsy had learned quickly that Anna simply wanted the company, to see a friendly face, to not be alone, even if it were only for a few minutes.

Anna had called her mother after the twelve-week scan, the first time she'd tried to contact her in five years. There had never been a real falling-out, no bitter explosion that had blown their relationship apart. Not like with her sister, who had screamed at her to never talk to her again. Instead, it had been a slow and unstoppable drift. Marie had always been her mother's golden girl, Anna her maternal inconvenience. When Marie expelled Anna from her life, the fissure inevitably extended around their mother. There could be no other outcome.

As Anna dialed her mother's number that morning seven weeks ago, she sensed that same cold betrayal, but she pushed it aside, concentrated on the good news.

"Hello?" her mother had answered, the hint of her Irish accent elongating the *o*. She had come to America with her family in the late '70s and had never quite left the old place behind.

"Mom," Anna had said, "it's me. Anna. How are you?"

A sigh, then, "I'm fair. What do you need?"

"I don't need anything," Anna said. "I have some news."

A pause, then, "Oh?"

"You're going to be a grandma," Anna said.

"I'm already a nannie," she said, using her preferred nomenclature. "Twice over, in fact. Your sister has two now, not that you'd know."

"Oh yeah?" Anna said, feeling the sharp sting of knowing Marie had bested her. "What are they called?"

"Do you care?"

" 'Course I do."

"Patrick's the oldest," her mother said. "He's a good boy. Chelsea's the youngest. After the Clinton girl. I didn't like that, but sure, what can you do?"

"It's a good name," Anna said. "I like it. When was she b—?"

"So you're pregnant," her mother said.

Anna placed a hand on her belly, thought of the ultrasound scan, the image already losing its detail in her mind's eye.

"Yeah," she said.

"Who's the father?"

The words *I don't know* almost slipped from her mouth, but she caught them in time. She scrambled for an answer and blurted out the next clear thought to break through her confusion.

"He's an architect," she said. She liked that idea. So much so that she said it again. "An architect."

"Did he marry you?" her mother asked.

Lies beget lies. Honesty has no regrets. Anna knew these things like she knew the sun would rise in the morning, like she knew her own name. But she had started on this path. She had no choice but to follow it.

"Not yet," she said. "We decided to wait. Nobody should get married just because they got pregnant. We'll see. I mean, we both have our careers, and—"

"Your sister left her job," her mother said. "She took a, what do you call it, a career break. She wanted to be at home with her children. She's a good mother."

"Yeah," Anna said. "I know she is. I think I could be too."

"Maybe. You could try being a good daughter first, and a good sister, see how it suits you."

"That's not fair," Anna said, unable to keep the swell of anger from her voice.

"Fair's got nothing to do with it. It's just the truth."

Foul words threatened to burst from Anna's mouth, but she swallowed them. Instead, she spoke with a chilly, smooth calm.

"You know, I don't think it'd matter if I was the best mother in the world, or if I had the best marriage since they invented wedding rings. It'd still be shit to you, wouldn't it?"

"Goodbye, Anna," her mother said, and the phone died.

Seven weeks ago, and the phone call still had Anna cursing into her pillow in the early hours. Thank God for Betsy. Without her she had nothing but four walls and a bald-headed man who scared the shit out of her.

As she came back to the present, Anna realized she had no idea what Betsy was talking about. Some reality TV show, how someone was being an asshole to someone else, but the someone else didn't even know it, and boy, the someone was going to get their comeuppance. Anna was about to interrupt and ask what the hell she was talking about when she felt those wings again.

She giggled, placed a hand on her belly, and said, "Hey there, Little Butterfly."

Looking up, the grin still stretching her cheeks, she saw Betsy staring back at her.

"What?" Anna said.

Betsy held her gaze for a moment, a look in her eyes that caused Anna to ache, before she said, "I should go."

28

ANNA JUGGLED TWO PAPER BAGS FULL OF GROCERIES, BAL-
ancing them on her swollen belly, as she turned the key in
her apartment door. She almost dropped them as it swung open,
but she recovered, letting only a few loose oranges spill and roll
across the floor. Kicking the door closed behind her, she wrestled
the bags over to the kitchenette and dumped them on the counter. When she went to retrieve the oranges, she saw the man on
the couch.

"Jesus!" she said.

"Hello, Anna," Mr. Kovak said.

He sat with his arms draped across the back of the couch, one
leg crossed over the other. Anna gathered up the spilled oranges
and placed them on the counter alongside the bags.

"I asked you not to let yourself in here," she said, shock turning to anger.

"That you did," he said. "And yet here we are."

"You're a real asshole, you know that?"

He smiled as she set about unpacking the groceries. "Need
any help with those?"

"No, I don't need help, and I sure as shit don't need it from
you."

"You're irritable today, aren't you?"

"Yeah, I'm irritable," she said, opening the fridge. "Somebody
sneaking into my apartment will tend to do that."

"It's not your apartment."

"So you keep telling me. What do you want?"

"Just checking in on you," he said.

She stashed the last of the groceries away, closed the fridge, and said, "You checked. I'm fine. Now you can go."

"I wanted a word first."

She looked him in the eye and said, "Fuck off. There you go, that's two words."

Mr. Kovak remained still for a moment, staring hard at her, before leaning forward and lifting a sheet of stiff, glossy paper from the coffee table in front of him. Anna's heart thumped in her chest, and her mouth dried. He turned the page so the image faced her.

"What's this?" he asked.

A perfect image of a perfect baby. She knew she'd left it in the drawer of the nightstand beside her bed. She had fallen asleep gazing at it last night and put it away this morning.

"It's a scan," she said. "Of the baby."

"Why do you have it?" he asked.

"The clinic, Dr. Holdsworth, she wouldn't let me take a copy of the twenty-week scan away with me, so I had one done someplace else. There's places that do that, you go in, get a scan, and they print it for you. They even put it on a disc, or a memory card or whatever, and they do, like, 3-D scans. They asked if I wanted to know the sex, but I said no. It wasn't that expensive, like a couple hundred for—"

"Anna, there's a very good and specific reason why Dr. Holdsworth won't give you a copy of the scans. Come sit down, I want to talk with you."

"I'm fine here," she said, staying behind the kitchenette counter.

Mr. Kovak pointed at the armchair. "Come," he said, his voice hardening. "Sit."

Anna knew an order when she heard it, and she obeyed, crossing the room to him in slow, fearful steps. She lowered herself into the armchair, easing herself down, managing the weight of the baby as she did.

Mr. Kovak turned a little to face her, clasped his hands together, his forefingers pointing out. "The reason Dr. Holdsworth doesn't give you a copy of the scan is very simple, Anna. We encourage all the women who sign our contracts to keep an emotional distance from what they're doing. Of course you have feelings about what you're doing, about what's happening with your body, that's only human."

"You don't know shit about my feelings," Anna said.

"You're right, I don't," he said, "and that's the problem, isn't it? How do I know you're not invested in this baby beyond its birth? Normally, I'd take you at your word, trust you to be mature about this arrangement, but then I see something like this . . ."

He placed the paper facedown, hiding the image.

"You can imagine how something like this would give me doubts about your ability to honor your contract, can't you? You can see why I'm concerned, yes?"

Anna wiped her fingertips across her lips and said, "You have nothing to be concerned about."

"I wish I could believe you," he said. "You're well into the third trimester now. This is when the doubts most often kick in. You're scheduled for an elective caesarean in, what, ten weeks? It's my job to make sure this all goes smoothly, that you are given the best care, and the intended parents have a healthy baby delivered to them. If I feel like you're going to impede the fulfillment of my company's promise, then we have a serious problem. Now's the time to talk it through. Not on the way to the clinic in ten weeks, not in the delivery room. Now."

She looked him in the eye and said, "I have no doubts. I want this done with, and I want my money. That's all."

He watched her for seconds that spooled out into endless time, a coldness about him that she could feel cross the distance between them. Finally, he spoke.

"Anna, I have been nothing but patient, courteous, and professional with you. Please don't give me a reason to treat you any other way."

"Is that a threat?" she asked.

"I would never threaten anyone, and I resent the suggestion," he said. He got to his feet, placed his hands on the arms of her chair, leaned over so she could feel his breath on her skin. "Threats are for schoolteachers and weary mothers, Anna, and I am neither of those. I only make promises, and I keep them. Every single one." He straightened and said, "Enjoy the rest of your day, and please think about what we've discussed."

Mr. Kovak walked to the door and let himself out without saying goodbye.

Anna remained in the armchair, her hands clasped tight together to suppress the shakes. Fear and anger chased each other through her being, snapping and biting at her. She didn't know whether to cry or scream or hide or smash something or—

Then she felt it. That feeling that had become a friend over recent weeks, always visiting when she was at rest. It calmed her, chased the terror and rage right out of her.

She placed a hand on her belly and said, "Hey there, Little Butterfly."

THE MATERNITY SECTION of the department store rang bright with life, like Christmas mornings had been when she was a kid. Anna walked among the mothers-to-be, doing what they did, lifting dresses from their rails, holding them against her body, checking the width and the hang. She enjoyed the rituals of shopping, now more so than ever because there was no guilt attached. No feeling of wasting what little she had on frivolous things. Not only could she afford these things, she could honestly say she needed them. The maternity clothes she had at home were plain and dowdy, and she had reached the limits of her loosest sweaters and leggings.

155

She was uncomfortable enough at the best of times; the least she could do for herself was buy something that fit, something pretty.

"When are you due?" a woman said, startling her.

Anna turned and saw the saleswoman, an older lady with lines that arced out from her eyes when she smiled.

"Oh . . . about six weeks," Anna said.

"Not too long, then," the woman said. "But oh my, those last weeks can drag."

"Yeah," Anna said, turning back to the rack of dresses, all of them reduced.

The woman reached past her, saying, "With your color, I think this."

She lifted a bottle-green dress and held it against Anna.

"Yes, with your eyes and hair, this is lovely. You can try it on if you'd like."

"Thanks," Anna said, taking it from her. "I will."

"And just so you know, there's twenty percent off everything in baby clothes today. You might want to take a look and stock up. I mean, trust me, you'll go through the little onesies like you wouldn't believe. You can't have too many, take it from the voice of experience."

She smiled and left Anna to her browsing. Anna examined the dress, checked the price. It was more than she'd planned to spend, but not too much. And it was pretty. Not that she had anyplace to wear a dress like this, but still. She could always take it back.

Anna looked around for the checkout, saw a row of registers over on the other side of the floor. She headed in that direction, leaving the maternity wear, and found herself among the baby clothes. Twenty percent off everything, a sign read, just like the saleswoman had said. Anna picked up three multipacks of plain neutral-colored onesies, a pack of three footies, two sets of hats and mittens, and a bundle of muslin cloths because she'd read somewhere they were good for swaddling and cleaning up.

When she got home, she tried the dress on, and was pleased to find it a good fit, showing the swell of her belly without making her appear fat. She took it off and hung it in the closet, above the box where she'd hidden the baby clothes.

Anna didn't want Mr. Kovak to see the onesies and the mittens, or the diapers and wet wipes she'd bought in the drugstore the day before.

She didn't want him to get the wrong idea.

29

LIBBY ARRANGED THE ONESIES AND FOOTIES IN THE TOP DRAWER and smoothed them over with her hand. She'd probably bought too many, but she'd read online that you can never have enough. Mason had believed her when she told him she'd bought them in Target rather than that upmarket place in town. So what if they were three times the price? They could afford it. Mason would only ask why she spent all that money when the baby was going to puke all over them anyway.

She closed the drawer and stood back to admire the dresser. It was from an upcycling place, an old piece given new life by a few coats of white chalk paint. The rest of the furniture matched, including a diaper-changing station, which had been transformed from an old hostess trolley. Mason complained that new furniture would have been cheaper than this gussied-up secondhand junk. But it wouldn't have the character, she had argued. They didn't discuss it further after that.

Libby had spent the last few days painting the nursery a soft mushroom color, keeping it neutral because she didn't want to know the baby's sex. This way a few items in blue or pink could be arranged around the room, once they knew what they had.

She hoped it was a boy.

One hand went to her artificial belly, the other to the small of her back. The pain had been there for three months now, and Mason had pleaded with her to take it off, even for a few hours, but she refused. The only time she separated it from her body was when she showered, and even then it was because the buildup of sweat beneath it had begun to smell.

Last night, she had woken from a dream with a terrible start. She had dreamed the baby was kicking in her belly. The silicone one that was of her but not of her. She could see it move, its feet and hands pressing against the not-flesh, and it was in distress. It needed to come out. But it couldn't because there was no opening in the silicone to let it free, let it into her arms. She unstrapped the prosthesis and laid it on the bed, felt around for a fissure, anything she could get her fingers between to tear it open. And the baby writhed and roiled, and she heard it crying, crying for her to let it out, and she couldn't, she couldn't, she couldn't . . .

She had woken with a gasp, clutching at the silicone mound that remained attached to her. Quiet and still. No baby there. Never had been, never would be. While Mason slept on, she cried in the dark.

Now the dream still lingered despite the daylight. The fear and the desperation of it. The hopelessness. Mason's words kept coming back to her: Having this child won't fix you. She had dismissed the idea then, and a hundred times since, but still it lurked in the shadows of her consciousness. What if he was right?

Libby turned in a circle, looked at all the things she'd bought. What if these were only here to fill the gap in her soul? And what if they didn't? When the baby came, what if it didn't provide the center to her life that she'd been craving all these years?

After dinner yesterday evening, as Libby lay on the bed reading, Mason announced he was going to the range. She had watched as he knelt down at the closet and entered the four-digit code to open the safe. Zero-five-one-nine. The month and date of his birthday. Except this time, he entered something different. He had changed the code without telling her.

Once he'd retrieved his pistol, locked in its case, he closed the safe's door and stood upright. He turned and saw her looking back.

"What?" he asked.

"Nothing," she said.

"I'll be an hour, ninety minutes, tops," he said, and left her there.

He's locked me out of the safe, she thought as she listened to his car drive away. I'm not to be trusted with the code, she thought. For ten minutes, she tried to resume her reading, but it was no good. This was a blister that needed to be burst.

"Goddammit," Libby said, and climbed off the bed.

She went downstairs, straight to Mason's den. His desk stood against one wall, the computer there on top, along with whatever paperwork he'd taken home with him. Next to the telephone, where she knew she'd find it, sat a small hardback notebook. The kind of book people used to keep numbers and addresses in before cell phones and contact lists. She lifted the book and leafed through it, seeing numbers that had been scribbled there maybe twenty years before. Old friends they'd lost touch with, dentists they no longer used, an auto mechanic that Mason swore by until he overcharged him for an oil change.

But Libby knew that not all of the entries were real telephone numbers. Some were PINs for bank cards hidden among the contacts, or passwords for email accounts, or any number of clumsily guarded secrets.

Here, a fresh scribble, bright-blue ink standing out against the older digits. This entry was for the gun club that Mason frequented. Libby couldn't help but laugh aloud at the silliness of it. A phone number had been crossed out, and the middle four digits happened to be zero-five-one-nine, just like the code for the safe upstairs. Beneath that, a new number in fresh blue ink.

"Oh, Mason," she said.

Libby recited the new number a few times, then closed the notebook, and returned it to its resting place. She went back upstairs to the bedroom, opened the closet, and kneeled down by the safe. Sure enough, the four digits opened the door. Even though she had no interest in what lay inside, she felt a pleasing surge of triumph. It kept the smile on her lips as she closed the safe again and returned to the bed and picked up her book once more.

Before long, however, both the triumph and smile faded to leave behind the sour resentment of his attempting to keep a secret from her, no matter how poorly done. The resentment lingered as she pretended to be asleep when he came home, as she kept her back to him when he climbed into bed, smelling of the wine he'd drunk before coming upstairs.

She still felt it now as she surveyed the nursery, and it melded with the bitterness she felt at his warnings about the joining of this new life with hers. Maybe he was right about that. And maybe he was right to hide the code for the safe from her.

"Stop it," she said aloud. "Just fucking stop it."

The quiet of the room engulfed her, and she blushed in irrational embarrassment, as if the whole world had heard her talk to herself. Mira was downstairs, cleaning the kitchen, humming to herself as she worked. She couldn't have heard.

Libby checked her wristwatch. Almost one. Time she had some lunch. She made her way downstairs, smiled at Mira. She fetched some cheese from the fridge, some crackers from the cupboard, and poured a glass of water. As she ate, Mira found work to do elsewhere. She was always discreet like that, and Libby liked her for it.

As Libby sat at the counter, finishing the last cracker, Mira came back, a worried expression on her face.

"Mrs. Reese?"

"Yes, Mira?"

"Are you okay?"

Libby smiled and said, "Yes. Why?"

"It's just, in the toilet." She pointed to the laundry room off the kitchen, and the small bathroom beyond that. "There is blood. On the toilet paper. In the water, there is blood. And upstairs, I change your sheets this morning. There was blood also."

Libby stared at her, thinking. Her period had come on overnight, not long after she'd woken from the dream. The bleeding wasn't as severe these days, having gone back on the pill after being diagnosed with endometriosis, but it was heavy enough that she had to rush to the bathroom for a tampon. She'd forgotten to strip the bed after Mason left for work, and then she'd used the downstairs bathroom at some point. When she'd flushed, some of the paper must have remained.

"It's all right," Libby said. "Nothing to worry about."

Mira took a step closer. "But bleeding there. It's bad when you have a baby. Maybe you should go see the doctor."

"It's fine, Mira, honestly."

"But maybe—"

"Maybe you should mind your own goddamn business," Libby said.

She hadn't realized she'd thrown the glass until it shattered at Mira's feet. Mira stumbled back, almost lost her footing, until she grabbed at the edge of the sink. She stared at Libby, her eyes and mouth wide.

"Oh my God, Mira, I'm so sorry."

Libby got off her stool and came around the island, her hands outstretched.

Mira began gathering up her things. "I'll go now."

Her voice quivered, and Libby knew she was fighting back tears.

Libby approached, reaching for her. "Mira, please, I didn't mean to do that. I don't know what—"

"Please don't touch me," Mira said.

Libby stopped, saw her purse on the counter. She went to it, rummaged through the clutter inside, and found a fifty and two twenties. She held the bills out to Mira.

"Here," she said. "Take this. Please. As an apology."

Mira finished packing her things, looked at the cash, then at Libby. "You think everything is money. You think you can buy everything you want. But you can't. Goodbye, Mrs. Reese."

She let herself out through the back door, leaving Libby there alone, ninety dollars in her fingers and shattered glass at her feet.

30

ANNA SAT IN A SEMICIRCLE WITH TWO OTHER YOUNG WOMEN, all facing Dr. Holdsworth. As the doctor talked, Anna observed the others. She guessed the ages as anything between twenty-five and thirty-five. Both of them white, well-dressed, healthy-looking. Just like her.

A projector beamed an image of a baby in a womb onto the whiteboard behind Dr. Holdsworth. It lay upside down, its head down close to the cervix, its legs curled up to its chest, its arms crossed, hands tucked up to its chin. Boy or girl, she couldn't tell. Lately, she'd been wondering about her own baby. She hoped it was a boy.

Not that it should matter to her.

She'd slept poorly the night before. Little Butterfly had been kicking something fierce, and she'd had to get up to pee three times. She knew the shape of him now. Yes, him, Little Butterfly was a him for now, and would be until she found out otherwise. She had tried to convince herself to stop thinking that way, to stop naming him, to stop assigning him—*him*—a gender. But she couldn't. Not when she could see and feel his feet pressing against the inside of her, not when she could cup his bottom in her hand while it pushed against the other side.

Idle daydreaming had become a dangerous thing. The stories she had been imagining for herself were beginning to take on a solidity, as if they were only a step away from reality. Playing, cuddling, running, swimming, riding, talking. All the things she and Little Butterfly would never, ever do together. At the same time, the certainty of having him taken from her had cracked, shards of it falling away. The unthinkable had become more real, the real more unthinkable. It frightened her, so she tried not to think about it.

But then he would move, turn over, remind her he was there, alive, growing, growing, growing. Last night, her mind had raced through the darkness, settling on images that could never be. First steps, first words, first teeth. And she had buried her face in her pillow, willed the images away, because Mr. Kovak would not approve, no, Mr. Kovak would be displeased, and that idea terrified her more than anything.

"Anna, are you listening?"

Anna blinked at Dr. Holdsworth, her mouth opening and closing before she could find her tongue. "Yes," she said.

"Good," Dr. Holdsworth said. "I'm trying to make this easier for you all. The more you know what to expect, the smoother things will go. Now, let's—"

A knock on the door stopped her. It opened, and a young woman stood there, her arm held in the large hand of Mr. Kovak.

"Sorry to interrupt," he said, guiding the young woman inside. "Sarah forgot to set her alarm for this morning, so I gave her a ride here."

Sarah's face was flushed pink, her eyes red and brimming, her fear obvious to everyone who looked on. The room's temperature seemed to drop. All of the women, including Dr. Holdsworth, shifted in their seats.

Mr. Kovak brought Sarah to a chair, holding on to her arm until she was seated. She did not lift her gaze from the floor. He apologized once more for the interruption and left, closing the door behind him.

Dr. Holdsworth cleared her throat and said, "Okay. Let's continue."

One grinding hour later, they broke for refreshments. A choice of sparkling or still water, fruit, and oatmeal cookies. Anna took a banana and a cookie, along with a cup of water, and retreated to a corner of the room. Sarah, the young woman who had been escorted in by Mr. Kovak, sat in the opposite corner, not looking at anyone. Anna had hoped to be left alone too, but one of the women wouldn't let that happen. Anna thought her name was Jocelyn. Or Joy. Or something. She didn't much care, but still and all, here she was taking the seat next to hers.

"Hey," Jocelyn said.

Yes, it was Jocelyn, Anna was almost sure of it now. She gave a noncommittal smile in return.

"How long?" Jocelyn asked.

"About two and a half weeks," Anna said.

"Ooh, you're close," Jocelyn said. "I'm six weeks. How you bearing up?"

"Okay, I guess."

Anna hoped short answers would lead to a short conversation, but she had a feeling she'd be disappointed.

"This part's the worst," Jocelyn said. "I mean, just waiting around for D-day, and you can't get comfortable, you can't stand up, you can't sit down, and when you do, you need a winch to get up again, right?"

Anna smiled in spite of herself. "Right."

"And I don't know what yours is like, but this one, God, I swear she's trying out for soccer. That or she's break-dancing in there."

"You know it's a girl?" Anna asked.

"Yeah. Last one was a boy. He was much calmer. This one never lets up, so I know it's a girl."

"Last one?"

"This is my second. I mean, I have two kids of my own, but this is the second surrogacy."

Anna sat forward in her seat. "You mean you've done this before?"

"Yeah. It's a good thing to do, you know? All those couples just desperate for a baby, and I can help them out and get paid for it. And, you know what? I like being pregnant."

Anna snorted. "Are you serious? Being pregnant sucks."

"First one's always the worst. I mean, I'm assuming this is your first, right?"

"Yeah. I don't think I could do it again. Not like this. Not for someone else."

Jocelyn touched Anna's forearm and tilted her head toward Sarah in the far corner. "Well, it's not for everyone, that's for sure. And this isn't the usual deal. Last time I did it, it was way different than this. The money wasn't as good, but it wasn't run like a military operation. And that Mr. Kovak, he gives me the creeps."

Anna wanted to say she was scared of him. That she was afraid he might do violence upon her if she displeased him.

Instead, she said, "Me too."

Jocelyn went to stand, but Anna said, "Wait."

She sat back down and asked, "Yeah?"

"When it came time," Anna said, "when you were due, how was . . . could you . . ."

"You're asking me, could I give up the baby?" Jocelyn said, leaning close, her voice little more than a whisper.

"Yeah," Anna said.

"It wasn't a problem because it was never my baby. If you see it any other way, then you shouldn't be here."

Anna said nothing. Jocelyn took her hand.

"Look, you and me, we're walking incubators. If you let yourself think anything different, then you're setting yourself up for nothing but heartache. Don't tell me you're having doubts, are you?"

"No," Anna said too quickly, too forcefully. "I mean, not really."

Jocelyn leaned closer still, touched Anna's belly. "Listen, this

167

is not your baby. You will never be its mother. You have to understand that."

"I do," Anna said. "Honestly."

And that was the truth, wasn't it?

SHE AWOKE AT four the next morning and knew she couldn't do it.

There was no gradient of change, no thinking it through, only a certain and solid clarity that settled in her mind the very moment it rose into consciousness. She lay awake for the next thirty minutes, staring at the wall as Little Butterfly danced within her, singing I am yours and you are mine, together till the end of time.

"Oh no," she said in the dimness.

The certainty of it didn't change its impossibility. She had to keep this child but she could not. Two hard and immovable truths, neither of which could bear the existence of the other. And there was a further contradiction: the parallel terror of choosing this path, and the calm of knowing it had been chosen.

She got out of bed, used the bathroom—Little Butterfly was using her bladder for a trampoline—and burrowed straight back under the covers, still warm and welcoming. Tiredness dried her eyes, but she knew sleep would not come with so many things to think about.

Could she raise a child on her own?

Why not? The country was full of single mothers. Lesser women than she did it all the time. She could be a good mother. Money wouldn't be a problem at first, seeing as she still had most of the initial payments. Except she'd have to give that back, wouldn't she? And there was a contract. Could they take the baby from her? Surely not. If she gave the money back, or what was left of it, wouldn't they have to leave her alone?

Then she thought of Mr. Kovak and felt suddenly cold. She pulled the comforter up to her chin, tried to keep the fear of him out. There was no escaping the reality that she would have to tell him. And she knew as soon as he hung up the phone he would be on the very next flight out here and she would have to face him.

But she didn't have to do it alone.

At ten minutes to five, Anna lifted her cell phone from the nightstand and chose the first number in the recent-calls list.

"Hello?" Betsy said, her voice thick and coarse with sleep.

"It's me," Anna said.

"What's wrong?" Betsy asked, her voice sharpening.

"I'm going to keep my baby," Anna said.

31

M R. KOVAK MAINTAINED HIS COMPOSURE AS HE MADE SLOW
progress along the jetway at La Guardia. Right now, he
should have been up in the air, on his way to Boston Logan. Instead, he was boarding yet another flight to Pittsburgh, the city
he'd flown out of just the evening before. All because a foolish
girl couldn't keep her promises.

His cell had vibrated on the nightstand a few minutes before
eight that morning. He had been dressing in front of his full-
length mirror, admiring the new tailored shirt he'd bought online,
delivered from Italy. A sales rep had queried the order, checking
to make sure the measurements were correct. Mr. Kovak had
confirmed that, yes, his chest was really that deep, his waist that
slender in comparison. Three weeks later, the shirt had arrived,
and he had taken pleasure in opening the stiff box and folding
back the diaphanous paper to reveal the pin-striped silk beneath.
The interruption of the phone call as he fastened the collar button
had irked him. More so when he saw who was calling.

"Yes, Anna, what can I do for you?"

"Mr. Kovak?"

Her voice sounded very small and very far away.

"Yes, it's me, what do you need?"

"Mr. Kovak . . ."

He knew then. The fear in her voice, the hesitation, the un-
willingness to say what needed to be said. He knew she had made
that grave mistake of forgetting her purpose.

"Yes, Anna," he said, not letting his calm slip.

"Mr. Kovak . . . I . . . I need to talk to you about something."

He wetted his lips and said, "Go ahead."

"I wanted to ask you . . . I mean, I need to know, what happens if I change my mind?"

"What do you mean, change your mind, exactly?"

"I'm going to keep my baby," she said, followed by an exhalation, and he knew the effort it had taken her to say it.

"Anna, it is not your baby."

"No, but it is, it really is, it—"

"Anna?"

"—is mine, it's been in me all these months, and I know this baby, and it knows me, and—"

"Anna."

"—I'm his mother, yes it's a he, I know it is, and I can feel his feet with my hand, and—"

"Anna, stop."

"—I can feel him move inside me, I can feel him there, and I can't—"

"Anna, stop talking."

"—just give him away, like he's nothing, because he's a part of me, and I can't give—"

"Shut your fucking mouth!"

The casing of the phone creaked under the pressure of his grasp, his throat burned with the force of his anger. Silence, then. He inhaled through his nose and exhaled through his mouth. Twice.

Rage, be still, he thought.

"Anna, please don't say anything, just listen. You signed a contract. You have no moral or legal right to that baby. There is no question of your keeping it. That simply will not happen. Do you understand me?"

"You can't enforce the contract," she said.

"Excuse me?"

"It's illegal in New York State. I looked it up on the Internet. You can't enforce it."

He began to pace in his bedroom, clenching and unclenching his fist.

"You signed the contract in Pennsylvania."

"Yeah, but you're taking the baby to New York. All I have to do is show up at the door of whoever bought my baby and take him back."

"That's not how it works, Anna, you're being ridiculous. You can't just snatch a baby. You'd have to go to court, and believe me, our clients can afford better lawyers than—"

"No. I'm right, and you know it. You think I'm just some rube, that I know nothing, but you're wrong, Mr. Kovak. I won't give up my baby and you can't make me."

He paused for a few moments, searching for his calm center, being in the moment, just like his counselor had instructed him. Then he spoke.

"Anna, I'm coming out to see you. I'm not sure what time, but I expect you to be there when I arrive. If you're not, if I have to look for you, then . . . just be there."

He ended the call and stood quite still for a time, at the middle of the room, his arms hanging loose by his sides. Find the center, find the center and find balance. This was not the time for rage because rage blinded and deafened the unwary, could make a man do things he shouldn't. Now was the time for reason, for calm, for rational thought. Once he felt the world even out, he went to his laptop and set about finding the next flight to Pittsburgh.

Now he stood in the doorway of the Embraer ERJ-145, waiting for the passenger in front to quit arguing with the flight attendant about where to stow his bag. A businessman with a bad haircut and a cheap suit, he seemed displeased that there was no space in the overhead bin above his own seat.

"There's plenty of room to the rear," the flight attendant said, the polite smile nailed to her face.

"I told you, I don't want to put it back there," he said. "I need to make a connecting flight, that's why I booked near the front, so I could get off quick, and if I put it in the back I have to wait for everyone else to get off before I can go get it."

Her smile widened, showing the lipstick on her teeth. "Sir, I understand that, but all the same, there is no room toward the front of the cabin. Now, if you could just stow your bag in the first available space, then I'll be able to get these other passengers seated."

"But I have a connecting flight, I need to—"

"Sir, the quicker you stow your bag, the quicker we can be on our way."

"Now, listen, I booked a seat up front so—"

"Sir," Mr. Kovak said, taking a firm hold of the man's upper arm. "Stow your damn bag and let this lady get on with her work."

The man looked around at Mr. Kovak's chest, which was at his eye level, then let his gaze crawl upward to his face. What he saw there made him reconsider his position, and he took his bag down to the rear of the cabin without another word.

Mr. Kovak found his own seat halfway down. He'd have preferred one on the other side of the aisle, in the single row, but at least he didn't have to squeeze his frame up against the window. Had he the choice, he wouldn't have booked this flight, because he hated these tiny jets with their narrow seats and nonexistent knee room, but he had no time to be fussy.

Two hours later, he trapped a scream in his throat as the plane's wheels bumped on the runway at Pittsburgh. He had fallen asleep and dreamed of blood and sand, of the sound bullets made as they passed above his head. The smell of dying men, odors of meat and feces thickening the air. The chaos and the raw terror of coming under attack.

As the jet taxied to the terminal, and he brought his breathing under control, the elderly gentleman seated next to him asked, "Scared of flying?"

"Something like that," Mr. Kovak said.

He presented his company Amex to the assistant at the rental-car desk, and thirty minutes after that he approached the town of Superior, a glowing ball of anger contained within him. He parked across the street from Anna's building and saw the other woman's Jetta nose-to-bumper with Anna's Civic.

Of course she was there. He shouldn't have thought otherwise. Not that it mattered. He climbed out of the rental, and it rocked on its suspension at the relief of his weight's lifting. The gate to the communal entrance had a keypad lock, but he had a PIN. He entered it, went to the stairs, and up to Anna's floor. There, without knocking, he inserted his key into the lock and opened the door to the apartment.

It stopped after three inches, held by a security chain that had not been fitted the last time he was here. Through the gap, Betsy stared back at him.

"Undo the chain, please," he said.

"You want to speak with Anna," Betsy said.

"That's none of your concern," he said.

"No, it's very much my concern."

"Regardless, please remove the chain."

"If you want to speak with Anna, it'll be with a lawyer present. You can call to arrange a time and place. Goodbye."

She went to push the door closed, but he blocked it with his foot.

"Ma'am, this apartment belongs to my employer, and I am authorized to enter whenever I—"

"You aren't authorized to do shit," she said. "Now, get out of here before I call the cops."

Mr. Kovak put his shoulder to the wood, and the chain gave

way as if it were made of candy. The door slammed against the wall. He caught it with his left hand as it rebounded. The woman gave a cry and stepped back. He turned to see the damage to the doorframe where the chain had pulled the slide away. A chunk of wood torn out. No big deal. He closed the door and took three steps inside, reminding himself to hold his temper.

Betsy retreated, but kept herself between him and where Anna sat on the couch. He looked around her.

"Anna, please ask your friend to leave."

Betsy stepped between them once more. "I'm not going anywhere."

"I wasn't speaking to you," he said. "Anna, tell her to leave. Now."

"Listen, I don't know who you think you are breaking in here and harassing a pregnant woman, but I bet your company wouldn't want it in the—"

Mr. Kovak seized her throat in his right hand, forced her back toward the window, her toes skittering across the floor. The back of her head slammed against the double-glazed pane, a ringing, hollow boom. Her eyes rolled back in her head before focusing again on him. Somewhere, Anna screamed at him to stop, but he chose not to hear.

"Your name is Elizabeth McKean, born in New Haven, Connecticut. Divorced, your twenty-two-year-old daughter lives with your ex-husband in Philadelphia, your twenty-five-year-old son lives with you on Kalkirk Road. Do you want me to go on?"

Wide-eyed, she mouthed the word, No.

He felt Anna's hands clawing at his shoulder, heard her say something that did not matter.

"Now, I need to speak with Anna, alone. If you won't allow me to do that, then I will happily speak with your son, alone. Do you understand me?"

She mouthed the word, Yes.

"Good," he said, and released her.

Betsy dropped to the floor, coughing, gasping, hands going to her throat. Anna lowered herself down to her side, struggling with the bulk of her belly. She wrapped her arms around her friend, tears dropping from her cheeks to the floor.

Two women cowering and crying at his feet. Mr. Kovak supposed he should have felt something about that, whether a surge of power or regret, but he felt nothing but a mild annoyance.

"Tell her to get out," he said.

"Just go," Anna said to Betsy. "I'll be fine. He can't hurt me. Not when I'm like this."

She was correct in that. He would not cause harm to her while she carried the child.

Betsy got to her feet, wiped the heel of her hand across her eyes. "Goddamn you to hell, you son of a bitch."

As she went to the door, Mr. Kovak said, "I don't need to tell you not to talk to anyone about this. Do I?"

"Goddamn you," she said as she opened the door. She slammed it closed behind her.

Mr. Kovak stood still for a time, once again seeking the center to all things, and the balance to be found there. He ignored Anna's weeping until, finally, there it was. Inhale, exhale, and again. Then he turned to her, reached out his hand. She stared at it as if it were some alien thing.

"Come on," he said. "Let's get you up off that floor. It can't be comfortable."

"Fuck you," she said, the words hot with hate.

"Come on," he said.

She crawled past him, planted her hands on the coffee table, and pushed herself up onto the couch. A grimace creased her face and she circled her arms around her belly.

"Are you feeling all right?" he asked. "Would you like some water?"

She shook her head, would not look at him.

He went to the armchair closest to her and sat down. "Let's talk," he said.

Anna turned her gaze away from him, toward the window.

"You know you can't keep the baby," he said. No point dancing around it.

"I'll give the money back," Anna said. "Betsy said she'd give it to me out of her savings. The advance and the allowance, all of it."

"It's not as simple as that. You made a promise, you have an obligation. There's a couple right now decorating a nursery, buying clothes, planning a life with this child. You can't just take that away from them because you changed your mind."

"What about me? What about my life with this child?"

"You signed that away, Anna. You put your name on that contract and you can't take it back. I won't let you."

Now she turned her face to him, and he saw the hatred there. He felt it, burning hot. The rage that dwelled in him stirred. He inhaled, a deep breath, to cool it.

"You don't own me," she said. "You don't own my baby."

"Yes, I do," he said. "And you won't be free of me until you hand the child over. You must understand that, Anna. There's nothing you can do to change that now."

"I could go to the cops."

"And what do you think they can do? If it comes to it, this is a matter for lawyers and courtrooms, not the police. Either way, I'd strongly advise against it. I've no desire for things to get any more . . . difficult than they are."

He let the threat hang in the air between them. She wept again, harder than before, hiding her face in her hands. Hiding from him. Mr. Kovak got to his feet and straightened his jacket.

"I'll leave now," he said, "but I'll check in with you tonight. You have a final checkup at the clinic next week. Don't miss it. And you're booked in for the C-section two weeks from Friday. You will be there, Anna. I will bring you myself. If you aren't here when I call that morning, if you run, if I have to look for you . . . your mother's name is Philomena, right? And your sister has, what, two kids now?"

"Fuck you," she said.

"I'll see you in a little over two weeks," Mr. Kovak said.

He let himself out.

Back in his car, he clasped his hands together and closed his eyes. The rage writhed and snapped inside him. He commanded it to be still, and thank God, it obeyed.

32

ANNA FELT THE FIRST CONTRACTION AN HOUR AFTER MR. Kovak left.

She had sat on the couch, crying with both rage and sorrow, torn between her fear of him and her desire to visit harm on him. But beneath it all lay the utter helplessness. She had never experienced such a feeling in her life, a complete inability to choose a path. The knowledge that she would keep her baby remained as certain and solid as before he came, yet his threats still hung in the air like poisoned fruit. So, she had lingered there, unable to move, to do anything but weep and worry.

Then that cramp, almost but not quite like a period pain, low down in her stomach, hitherto unknown muscles flexing through no will of her own. She froze, one hand hovering an inch over her navel.

Was it?

No, couldn't be.

First-time mothers were almost always late, weren't they? It couldn't be now. Just couldn't.

Anna felt the sudden and engulfing urge to be up, to be busy, to be active. Things to do, things to do, things to do. Cleaning, tidying, vacuuming. All these things had to be done right now, this second, this very moment.

She set about gathering up the few mugs and glasses that sat around the place, brought them to the sink, turned the hot faucet, squirted some dish soap into the tumbling water, and began washing with furious intent. This morning's breakfast things too. A pot off the stove she'd forgotten to do last night.

As she drained the sink and began to dry, a sense of calm returned. It had been just a twinge, a spasm of muscles, a cramp. That was all. Nothing to worry about. Besides, she had bigger things to concern her right—

It came again, like a belt tightening painfully around her middle. She dropped a mug and it shattered on the tiled kitchenette floor as she bent forward, using the countertop for support as her knees weakened.

"Oh shit," she said. "Not now. Oh God, please not now."

Anna ignored the scattered shards on the floor and made her way toward the bedroom, using items of furniture as waypoints. She reached the bed and lowered herself down, lay back, used her heels to push herself up so her head rested on the pillows.

"Just you stay where you are, Little Butterfly," she said. "It's not safe out here."

She circled the mound of her belly with her hand, a soothing motion she often found herself making without knowing it.

"Stay put," she said. "It's not your time yet."

And again it came, gripping her tight, squeezing her like a fist.

She screamed at the ceiling in pain and fear and anger and prayed to God, not now, not now, not now . . .

ANNA ENDURED IT until the sun had sunk low in the sky, darkening the apartment. The pains had subsided for a while, maybe an hour or more, and she wondered if it had been nothing after all. Maybe those Braxton-Hicks contractions she'd read about, the ones that get your body ready weeks in advance. Lying on the bed, she had sunk into an uneasy slumber, strange dreams that seemed to carry portents and omens she could not understand. Then another pain woke her, stronger than before, and it didn't let up for a good thirty seconds. When it passed, she lay on her back, breathing hard.

She gently eased herself over onto her side, and she felt something inside, a sensation of breaking, a release of pressure. Then warmth spreading around her groin, soaking through her underwear and leggings, and into the bedclothes.

"No," she said. "No, no, no."

Anna heaved herself upright and dropped her feet to the floor. She used the nightstand to haul herself up, and she heard liquid patter on the floor as she staggered to the bathroom.

"Oh God," she said, stripping the leggings and panties off. "What'll I do? What'll I do?"

Her first thought was to call Betsy. But then she remembered Mr. Kovak's threat. Could she put her friend in that position? The less Betsy knew, the better.

"What do I do?"

Anna thought of the community hospital in Superior. It was small, but they had an emergency room for minor injuries. Dr. Holdsworth had told her to go straight there if anything happened. The baby's safety came first, always. Well, something was definitely happening now. Didn't mean she had to call the clinic or Mr. Kovak.

For an insane moment, she considered getting the mop and bucket from the closet in the living room and cleaning up the mess. No time, no time.

That decided, she cleaned herself up, changed into a loose maternity dress, the bottle-green one she'd bought just a few weeks ago, and began gathering what she needed. The bag from the bottom of the closet, a nightgown, a change of clothes, a few sets of underwear, a thousand dollars in cash, pausing only when another contraction hit. Then, following some instinct that she could not identify, she packed a handful of diapers and onesies.

After yet another contraction, Anna left the apartment and locked the door behind her. She paused at the balcony, looked down at what she could see of the street from here, watching for a large well-dressed man. As satisfied as she could be, she made her way downstairs and out to the street. She stopped outside the gate, looked up and down the street. No sign of him. She opened the driver's door of her Civic, tossed the bag over to the passenger seat, then groaned as the next contraction hit.

She leaned her forearm against the roof, her head on her forearm, and counted the seconds until it passed. When it had receded, she looked up and saw an elderly man with a small dog on a leash.

"Miss, are you okay?" he asked. "Do you need any help?"

She smiled at him and said, "No, thank you, I'm fine."

"You sure? You don't look so good, if you don't mind me saying."

"I'm fine," she said again. "Thank you."

Slowly, she lowered herself down into the driver's seat and pulled the door closed. As the man watched, she started the engine and pulled away from the curb without checking her mirrors. A car horn blared somewhere behind her, but she ignored it, concentrating on the road ahead.

The hospital was maybe ten minutes away. She figured the contractions were not quite five minutes apart. If she timed it right, she could pull over and wait the next one out, then set off again.

Three and a half minutes later, while she waited at a set of lights, the contraction came, a full minute before she expected it. She gripped the steering wheel tight, clenched her jaw, and breathed hard. Counted the seconds, fifteen, twenty, thirty, forty, and more. Horns sounded and cars pulled around her, drivers glaring at her.

"Fuck," she said as the pain ebbed away.

Anna put the car in drive and pulled away from the lights as they changed back to red, accelerating through the intersection. She checked the time on the dash and told herself to pull over in three minutes.

A deep ache had settled into the small of her back, and the muscles around her midsection and thighs tingled with fatigue. She ignored the signals of pain that came in from all over her body and focused on driving, on closing the distance between her and the hospital. When the third minute ticked by, she pulled to the side of the road, didn't care that she blocked someone's driveway, and waited. It came right on time, the giant fist squeezing her hard around the middle. She let loose a string of curses and rode the pain to the end. When it had subsided, she pulled away once more.

At last, the hospital came into view. A squat building, taking up one corner of the block. She followed the signs into the small parking lot and didn't care that she left her car across two spaces. The walk to the building seemed to take an age, the bag slapping against her thigh as she trudged down the sloping driveway. No one around to help. Full dark now, the windows glowing like beacons.

The next contraction came, overwhelmed her so the pain and the pressure were the entirety of the universe. If not for the car she used for support, she would have collapsed to the ground. Once it had passed, she stood upright and resumed walking.

She saw the word "Emergency" above a set of doors, glowing green. She fixed her gaze on the sign, refused to stop until she reached it. The doors hissed open as she approached, and she shuffled through, her legs losing strength with every step. Ahead, she saw a reception desk. A woman behind it, talking to a security guard. She noticed Anna, and her eyes widened. She pointed, and the guard turned to see.

Another contraction hit, and she dropped her things to the vinyl-tiled floor. She saw the security guard running toward her, then the world spun away, the floor rushing up, strong arms circling her, catching her, bright light everywhere, sparks and fireworks, then a choir singing the most beautiful melodies she had ever heard.

33

LIBBY AWOKE WITH A START, NO IDEA WHAT HAD ROUSED HER, only a sense that something was very wrong. Then the fragments of the dream reassembled into a blur of images. The baby writhing, trying to find a way out. The pain of the contractions, even though the belly was no more than a mass of silicone. Waters breaking. The panicky rush of fear, thinking, It's now, it's now, it's now.

She lay trembling on the bed for a time. Alone, Mason hadn't come upstairs. He had developed a habit of falling asleep on the couch and staying there for the night. In the mornings, he would rouse, still wearing yesterday's clothes, then shave and shower before going to work. Then they would see each other at dinner, inquire about their days, before he would go to the living room or his den while she went to the small upstairs study she'd made for herself to write in. Short stories, mostly, but she had the beginnings of an idea for a novel. She indulged in fantasies of her child playing on the floor while she composed flowing sentences and beguiling plots.

All of that seemed so far away now. All she had at this moment was a hollow dread for which she could find no source. She shifted onto her side, the weight of the prosthetic belly following her, and wrapped her leg over the body pillow that had been recommended on a pregnancy forum. Sleep would be slow to return; it had been hard enough to come by at all in recent weeks. She closed her eyes, tried to focus on her breathing, in, out, in, out, to wash away the sense of fear and—

A giant invisible fist gripped her around the middle, a tightening band of pain low down in her back, circling around to her stomach. She opened her mouth, wanted to cry out, but could only find a low groan from deep in her throat. The pain kept coming and coming until she thought she might pass out. Then, as quickly as it had arrived, it faded again, leaving behind flutters and tingles in the muscles it had seized.

Libby remained still for perhaps a minute, breathing hard, gathering the courage to move. When she felt she could manage it, she pushed herself up into a sitting position, shoved the body pillow out of the way, then swung her legs out of the bed, feet to the floor. It seemed an unholy effort for such a simple maneuver, and she rode a wave of dizziness as the room found its balance.

What the hell was that? She went to put a hand to her stomach but found the prosthesis in the way. Maybe she should have taken it off, but she dismissed the idea. It hadn't left her body in weeks, except for when she showered, and she would not remove it now.

A bright craving appeared in her mind and her throat: cold water, from the filter built into the fridge. At that moment, there seemed no better thing in the universe. She hauled herself to her feet and went to the bedroom door, opened it, and stepped through, out onto the landing. From the stairs she could hear the television, a man's voice giving a monologue, punctuated by the laughter of an audience, one of the late-night talk—

The fist gripped her once more as she descended the stairs, draining the strength from her legs. She gasped, then cried out, reached for the handrail, but it had somehow become slick and slippery and she could not grasp it. The steps shifted under her feet, and then up was down and up again, and something slammed into her shoulder, jerked her neck, kicked her thigh, punched the side of her head, and then there was darkness, and finally floating somewhere she could look up at the ceiling above the stairs, many miles away, and here was Mason, so handsome, looking down at her, worry on his good face, and then it was dark again.

SHE CAME TO in an ambulance full of dazzling lights and shrieking noise. Her eyes could not focus, there was too much to see, but she was aware of a man to her right. She reached out, touched a shirtsleeve, an arm too thick and heavy to be Mason's.

"Libby, everything's all right," the man said.

She tried to turn her head to see him, but it would not move. Oh God, no, she thought, please no, not that. The thought of crushed vertebrae and severed spinal cords flashed in her mind, horrifying in their possibility. She heard a rising wail, a woman's voice, taking flight in terror, up and up and up, only vaguely aware that it was her own.

"Libby," the man said. "Libby, listen to me."

A big hand on her arm, squeezing.

"Libby, it's all right. You have a concussion, and maybe a few pulled muscles in your back and neck. There's a brace on your neck to keep your head still. You're going to be fine. Libby, can you hear me?"

He appeared in her vision now, leaning in. A moon-shaped face, black hair, brown eyes. He clicked his fingers once, twice, three times, snapping her focus to his hand.

"Libby, can you hear me?"

She opened her mouth to say yes, but it came out as a dry croak.

"Do you remember what happened?"

"I fell," she said.

"That's right," he said. "You fell down some stairs. Can you remember how you fell? What made you fall?"

"The pain," she said.

"What pain?"

Her hands went to the mound of silicone beneath her nightgown, circled it, and she felt a moment of relief in realizing that she could move them at all.

"Here," she said.

"In your stomach?"

She spread her fingers across the prosthesis. "Here," she said.

"Libby, I know that isn't real. Your husband explained it to me. Was the pain in your stomach? Your real stomach?"

"Don't know," she said truthfully.

"We'll make sure the emergency-room staff checks it out, okay? They'll have to remove the prosthetic belly to—"

"No, they can't," she said.

"They'll have to. Your husband asked us not to remove it at your home, but in the ER, there won't be any choice. It'll have to come off."

She did not answer. She couldn't. The unseen fist had taken hold of her again, stealing the words from her mouth, the voice from her throat.

IN A BAY in the ER, as a nurse and an orderly helped her onto the gurney, Libby asked, "Where's Mason?"

"I'm sure he'll be right along," the nurse said.

"But I need him," Libby said. "He should be here."

"I think he was following the ambulance," the nurse said. "I'm sure he won't be long."

"No, you don't understand, he should be here."

"All right," the nurse said. "I'm going to need you to calm down. Todd, will you see if you can find him?"

The orderly nodded and drew the curtain as he left the bay.

"Now, let's see if you can lie back for me."

The nurse eased Libby from a sitting position onto her back, making soothing noises as she did so. Libby gasped as the muscles in her upper back and neck protested. The brace still held her head locked in place, but it didn't stop the spasms that shot up from between her shoulder blades to the base of her skull.

The curtain whisked aside and a doctor stepped through, clipboard in hand. He closed the curtain behind him and approached the gurney.

"Hi, Libby, I'm Dr. Garner. How are you feeling?"

"Sore," she said. "Scared."

"You took quite a spill," he said. "We'll get you down to radiology for some X-rays, but I don't think you've done anything too serious to yourself. Right now, I'm more concerned by the abdominal pains. If you don't mind, I'd like to give you a quick examination. I believe you're wearing a prosthetic pregnancy vest, correct?"

Libby didn't answer. She closed her eyes.

The doctor's voice softened. "Listen, no one's judging you here. Many women wear prosthetic bellies for all sorts of reasons. That's none of my concern. But I have to check you out and see what's causing this pain. So I'll need you to remove the vest for me."

She opened her eyes and said, "No."

"Libby, I need to examine you. Whatever this pain is, it was bad enough to take you off your feet. We can't just ignore it."

"No, I—"

The fist again, tighter than before, crushing the air out of her. She drew her knees up, opened her mouth wide, let out a high whine.

"Libby?"

Through the pain, she heard Mason's voice, and she reached blindly for wherever he was. Strong hands took hers.

"Don't let them," she said.

He came close, said, "Don't let them what?"

"Don't let them take the baby," she said. "Please don't let them."

His fingertips brushed her cheek. "Honey, there is no baby."

She grabbed his shirt in her fist. "Don't say that. Don't you dare say that."

"Libby, you're not making sense. They want to take the vest off so they can examine you, that's all."

"Don't let them. You keep them away from me."

"They have to, honey."

"No."

Then he reached around her back, pulled her upright, and held her as the nurse undid the button at the back of her collar.

Libby screamed. She tried to shake them off, but Mason's arms circled her, pinned hers to her sides. She screamed again, shouted for someone to help her, to make them stop.

But they didn't.

34

ER CAR WAS GONE. THIS TROUBLED MR. KOVAK. ALTHOUGH there was no real reason why Anna Lenihan shouldn't leave home in the evening, it still bothered him. He had planned to catch the late flight back to La Guardia, checking in on her before he left for the airport. That had been at a little after nine, and he had found her usual space empty.

He had been waiting here in the rental for her to return for three hours now, and there was no hope of catching that flight. He checked his wristwatch once more: three minutes past midnight. Something was most definitely wrong. He took a long deep breath, opened the car door, and climbed out.

Deathly quiet on the street, he crossed, entered his PIN to open the gate, and made his way up to the apartment. No point in knocking, he let himself in, and switched on the light. Perfectly clean and tidy inside. Except for the shattered mug on the kitchenette floor. The unease grew in Mr. Kovak's gut. A brief tour of the living area revealed nothing, so he entered the bedroom.

The closet door stood open. He reached inside and pulled the light cord. On the floor were scattered loose diapers, a baby's onesie hanging over the side of an open suitcase.

"Goddammit," he said.

So she had run. It wasn't the first time one of his girls had taken off. He would find her and convince her to honor her agreement, just like the others. But still, it was a giant pain in the ass.

Maybe she'd gone to her friend's home. Although it seemed the most likely choice, he believed Anna to be smarter than that. She would know it to be the first place he'd look—and she'd be right—but he would try it anyway. There was her mother, but as far as he knew, they weren't on speaking terms. Still, a new baby has a way of bringing sundered families back together. That would be the next place to look.

He turned the light off and went to the bathroom door. The light was on already and he saw the mess inside, the clothes on the floor, the tumbler in the basin that had held a toothbrush. He went to turn away, but something snagged his eye.

What was it?

He turned his attention to the clothing on the floor. A pair of leggings, panties, a T-shirt. He nudged the pile with the toe of his shoe and realized by their weight that they were soaked through. Turning back to the bedroom, he saw the trail of liquid across the floor that he hadn't noticed until now. He went to the light switch by the door, turned it on. A large wet patch stained the comforter on the bed.

"Goddammit, she's in labor," he said.

He took the cell phone from his jacket pocket and went to the contacts list, found the number for the clinic, and hit Call. A man's voice answered within seconds.

"Dalton Gynecology and Obstetrics, how may I help?"

"This is Mr. Kovak from the Schaeffer-Holdt Clinic. Was a young woman admitted this evening? Name of Lenihan, Anna—"

"No one this evening," the man said. "Both delivery suites are empty, no one admitted since—"

Mr. Kovak ended the call.

"Goddammit," he said.

He closed his eyes and thought for a few seconds. Superior had a small hospital, but he didn't think it had a maternity unit. It did have an emergency room, however. Ten, fifteen minutes away. She could have driven herself there.

Mr. Kovak closed the apartment door behind him and went to the rental car.

35

AFTER IT WAS DONE, ANNA REMEMBERED LITTLE ABOUT THE
birth. She remembered the lone doctor on duty telling her
they didn't have a maternity unit or midwives there, they'd have
to transport her to a hospital in Pittsburgh. They kept asking her
name, and she must have given them half a dozen, none of them
her own. Who was her insurance provider? Did she have any
credit cards with her? Any identification?

They had brought her to a private room without a bed, and
she lay on her back on the gurney, her knees up and spread wide.

"My God," one of the two nurses had said, "she's ten
centimeters."

Anna was dimly aware of them crowding at the foot of the
gurney, panicked and confused.

"What do we do?" the nurse asked.

"Where's that ambulance?" the doctor asked.

"Has anyone delivered before?"

"I have," the older nurse said. She came close, took Anna's
hand. "I'm Nurse Tiernan. Don't worry, honey, we're going to
take care of you."

The contractions had become near constant, as had the urge
to push. The pain all-consuming, the beginning and end of
everything.

Nurse Tiernan leaned in close, wiped sweat from Anna's forehead. "I know you want to push, honey, but don't. Okay? Don't
push yet."

"But . . . but I have to, I have to . . ."

The nurse squeezed her hand hard. "Not yet, sweetheart. Just hold on."

Someone entered the room, asked the others about insurance, identification, who was going to cover the cost of this? Nurse Tiernan shouted at him to get the hell out, couldn't he see what was happening here?

"I . . . I have to . . ."

"What, honey? You have to what?"

Through gritted teeth, Anna said, "Have to move."

"Wait, wait—"

Anna ignored her because her body commanded her to get on all fours, the urge, the need so strong she could not disobey it. She rolled to her side, almost tipped over the edge of the gurney, but the nurse caught her.

"What are you doing, sweetheart?"

"I have . . . I have to."

Anna got onto her hands and knees, and the contraction hit hard, and she had to push, there was no stopping it, she had to, she had to, she had to . . .

"Jesus Christ, she's crowning." The doctor's voice, panicked. "Nurse Tiernan, you'd better come down here."

The nurse disappeared from Anna's view.

"Let me in there, you get up that end and hold her hand. This baby's coming and that's all there is to it."

Time turned to a bloody smear. Anna's conscious mind seemed to dissolve, leaving behind a body running on pain and instinct. Voices sounded around her issuing instructions and re-assurances, but she heard little of them. Nothing mattered but the need to push, to breathe, to push, to breathe, to push, over and over again.

"There's the head," Nurse Tiernan called, her voice the only one to cut through the turmoil. "Keep going, honey, you're doing good. When you feel the need again, you give it one more big push."

I can't, Anna wanted to say, I can't, it's too much, I can't do it, but still the urge came thick and hard and she had to push and push and push.

Then she heard the piercing, beautiful cry.

"It's here," Nurse Tiernan said, her voice bubbling with joy. "It's here. It's a boy. You have a little boy."

Anna collapsed onto the gurney, tried to roll onto her back, couldn't, she didn't have the strength left to heave herself over. The doctor slipped an arm beneath her, eased her onto her side, then her back. Nurse Tiernan carried a bloodstained bundle to her.

"Unbutton her dress down the front there," she said to the doctor. The doctor looked from the nurse to the buttons and back again. "Come on, now's not the time to be shy, baby needs to meet his mama. Skin-to-skin."

The doctor did as he was told, and Nurse Tiernan brought the bundle closer, pulled aside the blanket, and Anna gasped at the sight of him. Pink and wrinkled and bloody and perfect. The nurse slipped him down inside Anna's dress, and he nuzzled into her breast, mewling, eyes open and unseeing.

Anna sniffed back tears and said, "Hey, Little Butterfly."

36

MR. KOVAK TOURED THE TOWN UNTIL HE FOUND A PAY PHONE on a corner. He used a paper tissue to grip the handset and wrapped the forefinger of his other hand in another to dial the community hospital's nonemergency number. He was not concerned about fingerprints, but rather the hygiene of the telephone.

"Superior Community, how can I help you?"

A woman's voice, somewhat breathless, harried and tired, as if she had recently come through an ordeal.

"Good evening," Mr. Kovak said. "I believe a young woman in labor came to you tonight. I wondered how she was doing."

A pause, then, "She's doing fine. May I ask who's calling?"

"A friend. Is labor still ongoing?"

"Labor is done," the woman said. "She had a healthy baby boy."

Mr. Kovak silently cursed, then said, "That was fast."

"It was. And that's all I'm able to tell you without the patient's consent. If you let me know who's calling, I'll pass on your concern."

"Just give her my best wishes, thank you."

He hung up and cursed aloud.

Mr. Kovak had spent an hour driving the few blocks around the small community hospital. A squat two-story building with a small parking lot beside it. The kind of place that might stitch up a cut or give eye tests to seniors. Not a suitable facility for a birth or its aftercare. They would have to move her to a hospital with an obstetrics department before too long, and that would make things all the more difficult. If he was going to do anything, now was the time.

Checking his watch, he saw it was after one. Late, but he thought Dr. Sherman would want to know. He took his cell phone from his pocket and found the number in his contacts list. A voice thick with sleep answered.

"Mr. Kovak? Do you know what the time is?"

"It's late, I'm aware of that, and I apologize, but I thought you'd want to know straightaway."

A pause, then, "Know what?"

"Anna Lenihan, the candidate in Superior, outside of Pittsburgh."

Mr. Kovak walked back to where he'd parked the rental car, in a litter-strewn alley between a convenience store and a Realtor's office.

"Ah, yes, I spoke with the intended mother a few days ago, she's very excited."

"We have a problem. Anna told me this morning she wanted to break the agreement, keep the baby."

Dr. Sherman sighed. "I assume you pointed out that Miss Lenihan had signed a contract and—"

"She went into labor this evening and took herself to the emergency room at the local community hospital. She had the baby within the last few hours."

Dr. Sherman went quiet. Mr. Kovak felt more certain than ever that he wasn't a real doctor, at least not a medical one. He always seemed fuzzy on the details of childbearing for a man whose business depended on it.

Eventually, Dr. Sherman asked, "Have you seen the child?"

"No, but I gather it's a healthy boy. I doubt they'll let me in to see it."

"Well, now, that *is* a problem, isn't it? What's the likelihood she'll abscond with the baby, do you think?"

"I'd say it's a certainty that she'll at least try."

"But you won't allow that to happen, will you, Mr. Kovak?"

"Not if I can help it. Should I call Biggs?"

Howard Biggs was a local lawyer, a cheap ambulance chaser who made his living from compensation claims. The clinic kept him on a small retainer in case of emergencies. But nothing like this. Mr. Kovak knew the answer before Dr. Sherman gave it.

"Think about how that would look. You showing up with a lawyer and a contract demanding the baby be handed over. Even with a better lawyer, we could do without drawing that kind of attention. No, you're going to have to be more creative."

"I'll try," Mr. Kovak said.

"'Try' is the wrong choice of word. I expect you to call me in the morning, at a more civilized hour, and I expect you to tell me that you have Miss Lenihan and the child. My client has paid a lot of money for this baby and I won't disappoint her. Your future at the clinic depends on it. Is that clear, Mr. Kovak?"

"Yes, Dr. Sherman, it is."

"Good. We'll speak in the morning."

The call ended and Mr. Kovak kept walking as he returned the phone to his pocket. The consequences of messing this up didn't bear thinking about. It was clear that he would lose this job, and it was perhaps the best job he'd ever had. After the military, he'd done security work all over New York, which involved too many late nights, too many evenings standing out in the cold. Then he'd done some debt collecting, but he'd found that soul-crushing. Then his time as an insurance investigator, which he had enjoyed. But this job had been the best, nothing else was even close.

Truth was, he enjoyed working with the women, shepherding them along their journeys. And most of them fully understood what they were doing, that they were helping out some unfortunate couple, and earning good money in the process. Maybe they would need reminding of their responsibilities from time to time, but not often, and it usually only took a little nudge to get them back on track.

But not this one.

He'd had doubts from the beginning, and he should have nipped it in the bud as soon as she started talking back. Or even better, nixed her from the candidate list. No use in ruminating on it now, though. If he wanted to keep his job, he had to deal with the current situation. Tonight.

Mr. Kovak reached the alley and the car parked in the darkness. He went to the trunk and hit the button on the key to open it. Inside was the small leather overnight bag that he always traveled with. And inside that were the few items of clothing that he kept for occasions when he desired to be less conspicuous.

In the darkness of the alley he changed out of his suit, folding it carefully on the floor of the trunk, and into a cheap hooded top and sweatpants that he'd bought at the Target on Queens Boulevard, along with a pair of knock-off sneakers that he'd got from a street stall in Chinatown. He grimaced when he had to stand on the damp ground, nothing but the thin layer of cotton between his feet and the dirt, as he slipped them on. Finally, he forced his hands into a doubled-up pair of surgical gloves. They had to be ordered online; no brick-and-mortar store carried gloves big enough for him.

He placed his cell phone on top of the folded suit and closed the trunk. Once he'd locked the car, he found a spot behind a dumpster to hide the key. He pictured the route to the hospital, visualized the turns. Maybe a fifteen-minute walk.

Mr. Kovak raised his hood, buried his hands in his pockets, and set off.

37

AS LITTLE BUTTERFLY SLEPT AGAINST HER SKIN, HIS TINY BODY between her breasts, Anna drifted in and out of a fitful doze. She straddled the hinterland of half dreams and blurred reality, exhaustion keeping her weighted down, her baby keeping her afloat. Things had become terribly quiet since the rush of activity only a short while ago. Despite the pain, she had been in a state of dizzy euphoria, a high like nothing she'd ever felt before. But now the fatigue had gotten the better of her, and a crash would surely follow.

Little Butterfly stirred, snapping Anna awake, frightening her.

"What?" she whispered, breathless. "What is it, L'il B?"

He mewled, his face creasing, his mouth working.

"You hungry?" she said.

As if in answer, the mewl swelled to a small cry. He pressed his mouth to her skin, seeking her.

"Okay," she said. "Just wait, L'il B. Gimme a second."

Holding him in place with one hand—he was so small, a little over six pounds, that one hand was all it took—she used the other, along with her feet, to push herself up the bed. The movement aggravated the pain between her legs, that deep itching sting. She had a shadowy memory of the doctor stitching her down there, but she had no idea how many. By that time, once the afterbirth had come, she was focused on only two things: her child and her exhaustion.

"Aaahhhh," she said, then hissed through her teeth.

One more push and she got herself into an upright position, but at the cost of more pain, and what felt like more bleeding. She sat still for a time, let the pain ease and her breathing steady. Then she looked down at her boy and realized she didn't know how to feed him. Feeding had not been discussed in the class she went to, nor diaper changing, or bathing the baby, or any of the day-to-day tasks she'd have to perform. Of course not, she thought. I was never supposed to have him.

Can't be that hard, Anna thought.

She undid a few more buttons on the nightgown they'd given her, exposing Little Butterfly's back. He shivered and cried louder, a higher, longer wail.

"I'm sorry, baby, I'm sorry."

She took his body in one hand, his head in the other, and turned him, maneuvered him into place so that his lips rested against her nipple. His mouth opened and closed on her skin, searching.

"Here," she said, trying to move herself within his reach, but he couldn't seem to get hold, even as his lips moved, making sucking sounds. "Here, baby, it's right here."

But still he couldn't manage, and she felt something crumble inside of her, like her soul cracking and splintering.

"I don't know what to do," she said, her voice trembling as tears came. "Nobody showed me, L'il B, and I don't know what to do."

She wept then, feeling the crushing reality of what lay ahead. All the things she didn't know, and no one to help her. For the first time since the conscious thought of keeping the child she'd carried appeared in her mind, she did not believe that she was equipped to care for him.

"What do I do?" she asked the baby. "Show me what to do."

"Oh, sweetheart," a voice said from the doorway. "Not as easy as it looks, is it?"

Anna gasped and turned her head, saw Nurse Tiernan looking back, a soft smile on her face.

"It's a pity they don't come with instructions, isn't it?" She entered the room, closing the door behind her. "Here, let me help."

She approached the bed, leaned over so she could see, pulled back Anna's nightgown.

"Now," she said, "lift baby away for a second. Don't push it into his mouth, let him take it. Bring him in close, put your nipple against his top lip, and he'll tilt his head back and open his mouth. There, see? And just let him . . . there you go. That's it."

Little Butterfly latched on, and Anna giggled as he filled his mouth and swallowed.

"He's getting the good stuff now," Nurse Tiernan said. "Your first milk is different, colostrum, it has all the antibodies and the nutrients and everything he needs for his first few days. Attaboy. Look at him go. The little ones always feed like crazy, just so they can catch up."

"Thank you," Anna said, resting her head back against the pillow.

"You're welcome, honey." Nurse Tiernan stroked Anna's hair, swept it away from her eyes. "You got a tough time ahead of you. But I promise, it'll be worth it. You thought up a name for him yet?"

Anna smiled. "I've been calling him Little Butterfly, L'il B for short, but I guess that won't do, will it?"

"Not when he gets bigger, it won't," Nurse Tiernan said, returning the smile. "This guy's going to be a bruiser, just look at those hands. And there's a rapper called Lil B. My daughter listens to him."

"There's room for more than one L'il B, isn't there?" Anna asked. "But I'll think of something else. L'il B works just fine for now."

"I wish I knew *your* name," Nurse Tiernan said, her voice gentle. She fixed Anna with her eyes.

Anna couldn't hold her gaze.

"A man called, asking for you."

Anna tried to keep her voice even, casual. "Who?"

"He didn't give his name, just like you didn't. He wanted to know if he could visit you."

Anna closed her eyes and pictured him out there somewhere, waiting for her. No. Not waiting for her. Waiting for L'il B.

"Sweetheart, tell me what's going on. What kind of trouble are you in?"

"Nothing," she said. "There's no trouble. Honestly."

"Look at me," Nurse Tiernan said.

Anna did as she was told.

"You've been lying since you walked into this hospital. Now it's time to tell the truth. I can't help you if you don't. You tell me what's going on, and I promise, we can fix it."

"You can't," Anna said, her eyes welling. "No one can."

"You don't know that."

"Yes, I do."

Nurse Tiernan became silent, looking down at the baby feeding, a distant expression on her face. Eventually, she spoke.

"I'll make sure no one is allowed in," she said. "But you can't stay here. The manager wants you moved over to Magee Womens Hospital in the city. They can take proper care of you and your baby. An ambulance is booked for six a.m. That gives you three hours to think it over. They'll want to know how you're going to pay for your care, for one thing. You need to start talking. Then we can figure out how to help you and this little one."

She placed a hand on the baby's head, then on Anna's cheek.

"I promise, I will do everything I can to help you," she said. "But I can't if you won't let me. Three hours. Think of your baby."

She turned and left the room.

Alone, as Little Butterfly fed, Anna gave in to the tears.

38

M R. KOVAK PRIDED HIMSELF ON HIS ABILITY TO MOVE IN
silence, particularly for a man of his size. The aging security guard knew nothing of his approach until it was too late.
The guard wasted the few seconds of consciousness he had left by
grabbing at the thick arms wrapped around his neck instead of
reaching for the pepper spray or the pistol on his belt. The cigar-
ette he'd been enjoying only moments before dropped from his
lips, its embers sparking on the concrete outside one of the hospital's emergency exits. Mr. Kovak lowered him to the ground,
maintaining the choke hold, knowing he had only eight or nine
seconds before the guard awoke and tried to fight back.

He flipped the old man onto his front and pulled the cable ties
from the pocket of his hoodie. The guard groaned as Mr. Kovak
bound his wrists behind his back, and his body had begun to
buck and writhe as the ankles were secured. Mr. Kovak placed
a knee at the small of his back, his hand at the back of his head,
forcing him down.

"Be still," he said.

"What . . . what . . ."

"You've been unconscious for a few seconds," Mr. Kovak said.
"You're not in any danger so long as you remain still and quiet.
Do you understand me?"

"I . . . I don't . . ."

"Just be quiet. Don't move, and you'll be fine."

"Please, don't . . . don't . . . I . . ."

"It's okay. Everything's all right. You're confused, that's all. Breathe deep and stay calm. All you have to do is lie here until help comes. Do you understand?"

"I think . . . I think so."

"Good. Because if I have to come back and deal with you, I will hurt you very badly. Do you understand?"

"Yes. Yes, I understand."

"All right," Mr. Kovak said, and stood upright.

The guard breathed hard, in and out, and Mr. Kovak noted the puddle that spread from his groin. He looked to the emergency exit. The door had been propped open with a fire extinguisher. He slipped into the darkness inside.

As his eyes adjusted, he saw a row of lockers to one side, a mop and bucket to the other, along with stacked boxes. Some sort of staff changing room that doubled up as storage. Light cut through the cracks around a door directly opposite. He crossed the room to it, held his breath, and listened.

A woman's voice, speaking softly. Perhaps the same woman who had answered the telephone earlier. There had been three cars in the lot when he had arrived a few minutes ago. One he recognized as Anna's. He guessed the other two belonged to the security guard and the woman. A place like this, there was no need for overnight staff. He was glad of that.

Mr. Kovak pressed the metal finger plate and the door opened outward without a sound. He leaned through, head and shoulder first. On the other side, a dimmed ward made up of three curtained bays faced by three doorways. A nurse stood in the farthest, speaking to someone. And Mr. Kovak knew to whom she spoke.

He slipped through the door, careful it made no noise as it closed behind him. Still and watchful, he waited while the nurse stepped away and walked to a pair of doors at the other end of the ward. He moved toward her, feet whispering on the vinyl tiled floor, closing the distance between them in seconds. As he reached for her, the nurse sensed his presence, spun on her heels. But it was too late for her.

She emitted a high squeak as his right hand closed on her throat, his left on the back of her neck. Her eyes bulged, her mouth opened wide. The tips of her toes skittered along the floor as he carried her toward the double doors, then through, using her as a battering ram to open them onto a narrow corridor. There, he pinned her against the wall.

His nose close to hers, he said, "Listen to me very carefully. I'm going back into the ward and I'm going to talk to the young woman in that room. If you try to stop me, if you interrupt me, if you call anyone, I will break your neck. Do you believe me?"

He loosened his grip long enough for her to say yes, then he tightened it again, and her heels kicked at the wall. As her eyes began to roll back in her head, he let go, and she crumpled to the floor like a sack full of rags. She coughed and writhed, spat on the floor. He went back to the doors, threw them open, and hurried to the room he'd seen the nurse leave a few moments before. He shouldered the door open, let it slam against the wall.

Empty.

He entered, turned in a circle, stared into the darkened corners, under the bed, into the open closet. The bathroom door was closed. He went to it, kicked it open, found it as empty as the room.

"Goddammit," he said. "Where is she?" he demanded, turning back to the ward, and the doors beyond.

Except his path was blocked by the nurse. Too late, he saw the glint of metal in her raised right hand, heard her scream. He raised his left arm to block the scissors, but they pierced the flesh of his neck, just inside the hood. Stinging pain followed. He balled his right fist, swung it up, caught her beneath the chin, felt her jaw shatter as her head snapped back, compressing the nerve cluster at the base of her skull. She dropped, out cold, the scissors falling at her side.

"Fucking goddammit!"

He reached for his neck, pressed his palm against the cut, his left eyelid involuntarily fluttering. It wasn't that bad, little more than a scratch. But it could have been much worse, and he had been too slow in blocking the attack.

Mr. Kovak stepped over the nurse's still form and out into the ward.

Where could Anna have gone? She must have slipped out when he was dealing with the nurse in the corridor. He was about to curse, but a faint draft froze the hateful words in his mouth. He looked toward the door, the one that led to the locker room and the emergency exit. It moved back and forth, barely perceptible.

"Shit," Mr. Kovak said.

He bolted for the door, shouldered his way through, and ran for the emergency exit. His gaze was fixed on the young woman staggering across the small parking lot, so he did not see the security guard kick out. He felt his feet taken from under him and reached out to break his fall. The concrete grazed his hands, tearing the surgical gloves as he sprawled there. He cried out in fury and kicked at the guard before he gathered his senses and clambered to his feet.

He heard a car's ignition cough and wheeze as he stood upright. Anna Lenihan's Civic. As he launched himself toward it, the headlights came on, dazzling him. Still, he kept going, his legs pushing him across the asphalt as his arms churned. He heard the engine sputter, then catch, followed by spinning tires. The car lurched forward, then veered away, heading for the exit. Mr. Kovak adjusted his course, calculating that he could intersect its path. He summoned all the speed he could muster as the car accelerated. The passenger door handle would be within his reach if he could just keep—

The car jerked toward him, the tires shrieking, and he saw her then, staring at him with more hate in her eyes than he'd ever seen before. Her teeth bared, twisting the steering wheel in his direction. He tried to halt, but his momentum was too much, carrying him forward and into the car's front wing.

His legs were whipped from under him, his shoulder hit the hood, then all he could see was the starry sky above, then the asphalt coming up at him so fast he couldn't save his skull from connecting hard with the ground.

Then all was silence and the world full of sparks and constellations.

39

IBBY BECAME CONSCIOUS IN A QUIET HOSPITAL ROOM. SHE supposed, in the dimness of her mind, that she was awake. And that she had been awake before. She had a sense, if not a memory, of having come and gone, losing and finding herself in the dark. But this time was different. This time she could see and know. She knew it was a hospital by the sounds all around, and the ceiling above, and the high sides to the bed.

"Hello?" she tried to say, but the sound barely left her mouth. She swallowed, and it felt like her throat was lined with sand.

Something was biting on the forefinger of her left hand. She lifted it into her vision, saw the plastic clip, and recognized it was one of those devices that keeps track of a patient's pulse. The persistent beeping she heard was her own heartbeat. She gathered whatever saliva she could find in her mouth, swallowed again, and tried to speak once more.

"Hello?"

Movement somewhere across the room, then she saw Mason, leaning in. A day's worth of stubble lined his jaw, his eyes underlined with dark circles. He stroked her hair and her cheek.

"Hey," he said.

"What happened?" she asked.

He gave a weary smile. "This'll be, what, the fourth time I've told you?"

"I don't remember. Please, I need some water."

He reached across her and brought a paper cup to her lips,

helped lift her head so she could take a sip. It was tepid and stale, but wonderful nonetheless.

"Tell me," she said.

"You've had an appendectomy," he said. "It was bad. You could've died if they hadn't operated in time. But you're okay now."

Her hand went to her stomach. "The baby," she said.

He reached down to her hand, brought it back to her chest.

"There is no baby," he said.

"No," she said, "what did they do? What did you let them do?"

Mason bowed his head, the exhaustion written clear on him.

"They removed your appendix," he said. "It had burst. You had poison inside of you. They saved your life."

She began to cry, trying to make sense of it.

"You're confused," he said. "The anesthetic. You don't know what you're saying."

"Where's my baby? They cut it out of me. Did they? Is that what they did?"

Tears came to his eyes. He shook his head and said, "I can't. I can't."

He disappeared from her vision, and she heard a door open and close, and she called after him, called after her baby until her voice had gone and then she fell once more into the black.

A DAY PASSED, and Libby became fully aware. When Mason returned, she apologized.

"I didn't know what I was talking about," she explained, "everything was a blur."

As she had come to her senses, she had grown embarrassed at her own raving. She knew she had never been pregnant, that the silicone belly was merely a prosthetic, that she would never give birth. And yet she grieved. She couldn't help but reach for her stomach and feel the deep sorrow of finding it as flat as it had ever been. It was sore and tender over to the side, but even so, she ran her fingertips up and down and across, missing the rise of not-flesh that had been a part of her for months. And even if none of it was real, there was nothing fake about the grief that opened beneath her like a hungry mouth, ready to swallow her.

But there was the baby to come. Not the make-believe one she had carried all this time until it was taken from her, but the real one, the child who would be here in just a matter of days. She held that thought up and examined it often because it gave her comfort.

"Did they say how long it'll take to heal?" she asked Mason.

"They said you'll be up and about by tomorrow. They want to keep you in just in case there are any complications from the poison, but you'll be home by the weekend. You just have to take it easy for a while."

She thought about it for a few moments.

"I guess that'll be all right," she said. "I mean, you'll have to help out more, but that's fine. We can manage."

"Help out?"

"With the baby. It'll be here in a couple of weeks. But we'll be fine. Right?"

Mason cast his gaze down to the floor.

"What?" she asked.

He shook his head, did not lift his eyes.

"Mason, what?"

He glanced up at her but couldn't hold her stare. He lifted a hand as if to explain something, but all he could do was let out a long exhalation.

"Tell me, goddammit."

"She absconded," Mason said.

Libby had a sense of falling, of tumbling through space. She gripped the rails at the sides of the bed, tried to sit upright, but the pain was too great.

"What do you mean, absconded?"

"That's how Dr. Sherman put it. She's run away with the baby, they don't know where she is."

Dizzy now, the air rippling, the room turning.

"With . . . with the baby? The baby? How . . . ?"

"It came early. She gave birth in the emergency room of a little community hospital. Then she ran. She's gone."

"She took my baby?"

"It wasn't our—"

"She fucking stole my baby?"

Her voice boomed between the walls, and Mason flinched as if she'd struck him with her palm.

He buried his face in his hands and said, "That's all I know."

Libby stared at the ceiling, the suspended tiles, the support struts, the fluorescent light panels. Still falling, falling, falling.

"Was it a boy or a girl?"

"Does it matter?"

"Tell me," she said, her voice steely.

"Dr. Sherman said it was a boy."

She closed her eyes. Imagined the perfect little baby boy.

"Listen," Mason said, "maybe it's for the best. Maybe we should—"

"Get out," she said.

"Libby, just think about—"

"Get out!"

Her shout tore at her throat. She heard Mason stand and shuffle toward the door.

"Try to rest," he said. "We'll talk more later."

She said nothing as he left the room, kept her eyes fixed on the ceiling as hellish rage burned within her. Then she screamed and cursed until a nurse came running in asking what was wrong and Libby could not answer because the anger blotted out everything and became the only thing in the whole wide world.

40

M R. KOVAK STARED AT HIMSELF IN THE MIRROR AS HE CHANGED the dressing on his head. He had used butterfly strips to seal the wound above his left eye, but it still seeped red, soaking the gauze pads so they had needed to be changed several times a day. The spasms in his neck had eased in severity and frequency, but he still had to be careful in his movements. He'd had such an injury before, a strain on the tendon that joins the neck muscle to the clavicle bone. Not a serious injury, but painful nonetheless. Then there was the bruising to his shoulder and thigh, as well as the aching in his hip.

All in all, however, he knew he'd been lucky. A few inches to his right and he'd have been caught by the front of the car instead of the wing, and his head would likely have connected with the windshield. And the raised hood of the top he was wearing had saved him from a more serious cut to the head. So, his wounds weren't as bad as they could have been, but everything else? Everything else was shit.

He had regained consciousness lying on his back on the asphalt. The sky had been inky black and the stars faint, he remembered that. He didn't know how long he'd lain there, but he believed he'd only lost consciousness for a matter of seconds, otherwise someone would surely have found him there. It was the sound of sirens approaching that convinced him to finally move. The simple motion of rolling over onto his side had triggered a blinding cluster of spasms in his neck. He placed a hand there and it came away wet; then he remembered the nurse and the scissors.

The sirens became louder, closer. Couldn't be far away now. He had to get out of here. To hell with the pain. He pushed himself up onto his hands and knees, groaned as every part of his body protested, then hauled himself onto his feet. The world tilted, and he staggered side to side, almost fell. He turned in a circle, trying to find his bearings, picturing the streets in his mind, making a map of them. West. He needed to go west. Still fighting nausea, he set off, heading for an alley on the other side of the street. As he slipped into its blackness, he looked back and saw blue and red reflected on the buildings all around.

It had been a fifteen-minute walk here but it took thirty to get back to the alley where he'd left the car. He didn't know how many wrong turns he took, but he was relieved to have finally found his way. As he stumbled into the side of the car, he felt his stomach lurch, and he vomited into the grime and litter that covered the ground. The retching caused his neck to spasm once more and he emitted a high whine.

For an alarming few seconds, he couldn't find the rental's key in his pants pocket where he was certain it had been. Had it been thrown from him when he collided with the car? Then he remembered he had hidden it behind a dumpster. Regret came with the pain when he had to bend down to retrieve it. He hit the button and heard the click and clunk of the car unlocking. Fresh pain flared all over as he lowered himself into the driver's seat, the spasms of his neck almost unbearable as he reached for the door and pulled it closed. He started the engine, put the car into drive, and accelerated out onto the street.

Mr. Kovak pushed the car as hard as he dared, ignored the traffic signals and road signs, just kept going until the town of Superior was left behind. Then he drove aimlessly, mindlessly, for perhaps an hour until he saw the sign for a cheap motel in the distance.

He slipped the young man at reception a hundred-dollar bill and asked if the motel had a first-aid kit. The young man produced one from behind the desk. Mr. Kovak showed him another fifty and asked how his memory was.

"Kinda shitty," the young man said.

Mr. Kovak took the first-aid kit and the key and went to find his room. It smelled of damp and excrement, but it would suffice. He did the best he could with the wound on his head, cleaned and dressed it, and the cut on his neck, then tried to get some sleep.

Late the following afternoon, while in a fitful doze, he heard a knock on the door. It couldn't be housekeeping; he'd told the maid to skip his room earlier in the morning. Still wearing the hoodie and sweatpants, he dragged himself out of bed, ignoring the clamoring pain, went to the door, and peered through the peephole. It was the young man from reception, standing with his hands in his jacket pockets.

"Yes?" Mr. Kovak called.

"Uh, mister? I need to talk with you."

"Go on."

"Inside, maybe?"

Mr. Kovak bowed his head and sighed. Then he unlocked the door, opened it, and stepped back. The young man slipped through, and Mr. Kovak closed the door behind him.

"Well?"

The young man looked around the room, his eyes and head making jerking movements, betraying his nerves. It had taken him some courage to knock on the door, and even more to enter. Finally, he turned back to Mr. Kovak, but could not hold his gaze.

"I guess I'll get right to it," he said, his voice wavering in pitch like an adolescent boy's.

"I wish you would," Mr. Kovak said.

"You were on the news."

"Oh?"

"I mean, I'm pretty sure it was you. The hospital over in Superior. They said you beat up on a nurse. They showed a video of the guy, and he was wearing a hoodie just like that. I figured right away it was you."

"Even with your poor memory?"

"Yeah, thing is, I knew you were in some sort of trouble when you showed up, but I thought it was none of my business. If I'd known it was something as heavy as this, I don't think I would've given you a key. I mean, they said there was, like, a little baby involved in whatever was going on."

"Get to the point," Mr. Kovak said.

"Well, when you gave me the hundred and fifty bucks, I saw you had a lot more in your wallet. I figured, if you want me to keep quiet, then maybe you should think about—"

"You want more money," Mr. Kovak said.

"Well . . . yeah."

Mr. Kovak went to the nightstand by the bed and lifted his wallet. He counted out five twenties and brought them back to the young man. "That's another hundred. Now get out of here."

The kid looked at the outstretched left hand and the money it held, and slowly shook his head.

"I don't think that's gonna be enough," he said, stretching the words out like they were made of glue.

Mr. Kovak's right hand formed a fist and lashed out, a smooth, quick movement, and struck the young man below the solar plexus. Not hard, but enough to make his knees buckle and drop him to the floor. There, sprawling, the young man retched and gasped and coughed while Mr. Kovak waited patiently.

"How about now? Do you think it's enough?"

The young man eventually got his knees under him as he regained control of his breath.

"Here," Mr. Kovak said, dropping the five bills to the floor. "Take it and get out. You've already taken money from me. That makes you complicit, no matter what you say, no matter who you say it to. And remember what that punch felt like. Imagine what it'll feel like if I don't hold back. Now, pick up the money and get the fuck out."

Without looking at Mr. Kovak, the young man gathered up the bills, struggled to his feet, and stumbled toward the door. Once he was gone, Mr. Kovak went to the dresser and used the remote control to switch on the small flat-screen television set. He scrolled through the channels until he found a local news station. A story about a factory closure played, but the ticker along the bottom was concerned with the events of the previous night. He sat on the end of the bed and read.

POLICE RELEASE VIDEO OF SUSPECT IN SUPERIOR COMMUNITY HOSPITAL ASSAULT. A WOMAN WHO GAVE BIRTH AT THE HOSPITAL A FEW HOURS BEFORE IS ALSO SOUGHT FOR QUESTIONING.

"Goddammit," he said.

It looked like the story was local for now, but he suspected it would go national before too long. A pretty young woman fleeing a hospital with a baby. The news networks wouldn't be able to resist.

"I fucked up," he said aloud.

And it was the truth. Had he thought harder, been smarter, he might have found a dozen ways to resolve the problem. But he had blundered in, let the baby be taken away, and drawn attention to himself. The only saving grace was that no one knew his or the mother's name. His only option now was to remain out of sight. He felt it safe to assume that the clinic would not volunteer any information unless someone made a connection back to them; Dr. Sherman would not expose himself in that way if he could help it.

Mr. Kovak decided he would stay here, in this god-awful

motel, for as long as it took for this to blow over, for the news vultures to seek their carrion elsewhere. He would not shave, would let the hair on his head grow in and a beard come. Four or five days should be enough to make him hard to recognize from what little CCTV footage they had.

Clothing could be a problem. He would have to destroy what he wore now and find something else. And the car; however unlikely, someone from the rental place could make the connection, and they'd have a record of his identity, including his driver's license.

"Shit," he said.

This was a potential problem. He thought back to when he'd arrived in Pittsburgh. There had been only one middle-aged woman on the desk. She had barely looked at him as he signed the agreement and took the key. Would she see him on the television and remember the large man who had been in such a hurry? Unlikely, he thought. His face was not clearly visible in the footage shown on the news. But his size. He was a big man, the kind of big that gets noticed and remarked upon. He would keep an eye on the television over the next few days, and if they seemed close to discovering his identity, he would rethink.

There was, however, one question that occupied his mind more than any other: Where had Anna Lenihan gone?

He had no idea what he would do with that information should he discover the answer. What could he possibly gain from going after her? His job with the clinic was gone, the chances of the child ever going to the intended parents were infinitesimal. So why should it concern him?

Pride.

She had made a fool of him. Some say money is the root of all evil. Mr. Kovak knew that wasn't true. Pride drove all men to their most terrible acts, the immensely powerful fear of shame.

Men are vain creatures and they dread ridicule more than any-thing else.

So, pride was the only reason to hunt her down.

But he was smarter than that.

Wasn't he?

41

WITH LITTLE BUTTERFLY STRAPPED INTO THE PLASTIC BABY seat of a shopping cart, Anna walked the aisles of the first Walmart she found. She loaded the cart with onesies, pacifiers, diapers, powder, cream, wet wipes, sanitizer, everything she could think of. The handful of clothes she'd managed to pack had got her this far, but she needed more of those too. She chose plain tops and jeans, a pair of cheap sneakers, a couple of hoodies, and several sets of underwear.

A few other customers had given her curious glances, their stares going to her feet. Anna looked down to see what they were staring at and saw the red trickle of blood that had traveled down to her left ankle. She headed straight back to the baby aisle, chose a box of maternity pads, and went to find the baby-changing room. She double-checked that the door was locked before strapping Little Butterfly onto the fold-down table. Then she stripped off her clothes and washed at the basin, wiping away two days of grime and sweat. She disposed of the saturated maternity pad she wore and applied a new one before dressing in the clean clothes she'd yet to pay for. Finally, she took the pair of scissors from its packaging and set about chopping off her shoulder-length hair. It took only a few minutes, and she looked a mess. But it would have to do. She swept up the cuttings as best she could and disposed of them in the trash.

Right on cue, L'il B began to mewl and snuffle. It had been a little over two hours since his last feed, and the idea of his draining her again made Anna groan. She had managed to snatch only a few minutes' sleep here and there over the last two days, and fatigue had placed a shimmery veil over the world.

"Okay, L'il B, okay. It's coming."

She unstrapped him from the table and brought him to the chair in the corner. It seemed to swallow her as she sat, and she let her head roll back as she closed her eyes. How sweet it would be to doze awhile, to drift uncaring in the black. Then the baby's grumbling turned to a high cry and Anna pulled up the new top and let him feed. The crying and grumbling turned to suckling and sighing, and she couldn't help but smile even though it hurt like hell.

The idea of food presented itself, and her stomach rumbled in response. She had eaten as little as she had slept over the last forty-eight hours. A sandwich yesterday, a bag of potato chips the day before. She knew if she hoped to keep feeding her baby, she needed real food, and she needed it soon.

But everything had been such a blur, a long, smeared stretch of endless roads interrupted only by stops to feed and the few minutes of slumber here and there. She had stopped at the first thrift store she saw, carried L'il B inside as the doors were unlocked, and found the baby section. The baby cradled in one arm and the other holding a handful of onesies and footies, she went to the register. On the floor, beside the counter, she saw an infant's car seat, grubby and stained. A middle-aged lady approached the register and Anna pointed to the seat.

"How much?" she asked.

"Oh, sorry, honey, I can't sell that to you. Someone donated it with a bunch of other stuff, but we can't put old car seats out for sale."

The lady rummaged through the clothes Anna had set on the counter, looking for price tags.

"Can't you make an exception?" Anna asked.

The lady looked up from the bundle of clothes, studied Anna for a moment, then L'il B.

"No, I'm sorry, I can't. I have to throw that car seat in the trash. In fact, maybe you could do me a favor and throw it away for me?"

Anna smiled and said, "Maybe I could."

After she'd figured out how to fix it to the latching points in her car, and strapped in L'il B, she had called Betsy.

"You were on the news," Betsy said.

"Did they name me?"

"No, it was just a picture, not a very clear one. I was going to call the police, say it was you."

"Please don't," Anna said. "They'll come after me."

"Who will?"

"The clinic. They'll take my baby."

"But you don't know that," Betsy said. "After what happened, that man attacking the nurse, there's no way they could take him."

"They're bad people," Anna said. "I don't know what they'll do if they find me."

"But sweetheart, you need medical attention. So does your baby. You can't do this on your own. Please, go to a hospital, go to the police, whatever, just get help."

"I can't," Anna said. "I just can't."

"All right," Betsy said. "I won't say anything. But tell me one thing."

"What?"

"Is he beautiful?"

Anna choked back a sob. "God, yes," she said.

"Then for Christ's sake, love him all you can."

It seemed like a lifetime ago now. She thought about the journey here, the miles and miles of road between here and there. As her mind drifted, as L'il B found his rhythm, she let her head fall back, closed her eyes. The world became a string of fragmented images, and then grew warm and dark, like burrowing down beneath a blanket, like when she was a kid and pretended her bed was a cave and she an explorer, and there she floated like a leaf on a pond until—

A knock on the door startled her awake. L'il B lost purchase, and his face creased as he readied himself to cry. She quickly moved him across to the other breast before he could get started. He sounded like a damn chainsaw when he really got going.

"Occupied," she called.

"Ma'am, it's store security, is everything all right?"

A man's voice, stiff and polite.

"Yes, fine."

"It's just you've been in there awhile."

"I'm feeding my baby," Anna said.

"That's okay," the voice said. "Sorry to disturb you."

L'il B fed for another five minutes or so before turning his mouth away, his face slack from gorging. She balanced him on her knee, his chin propped in her hand, and she rubbed his warm, smooth back until he let out a long belch. That done, she changed his diaper and dressed him in one of the new onesies and footies she'd chosen.

Anna took a last look in the mirror over the sink. The haircut was rough; she'd aimed for '60s Mia Farrow and wound up with a crazy lady instead. But it would have to do. She returned L'il B to the plastic seat, strapped him in, and opened the door.

The security guard, an overweight man in his thirties, stood waiting for her.

Anna stared at him for a moment before she said, "Yes?"

He gave her a polite smile and said, "I just wanted to check everything was okay, ma'am."

"I'm fine," she said. "Everything's fine."

"Those aren't the clothes you were wearing when you went in," he said. He looked her up and down and up again. "Did you cut your hair?"

"I changed my clothes," Anna said. "That's all right, isn't it? I mean, I have the tags right here, they can still scan them at the checkout, right?"

"That's not normally how we do things, but I guess it'll be all right. Why don't I take you to the registers now, make sure you got everything taken care of."

"No, I can manage," she said.

That polite smile again. "I'd prefer it if I went with you. Just to make sure everything scans okay."

Anna agreed, and he followed her to the checkout, where he hovered while the assistant ran all the items through. She paid cash, and pushed the cart toward the exit, the guard still following. L'il B began to fuss, so she fished a pack of pacifiers from the bottom of the cart. She pulled the packaging apart and went to insert one into his mouth.

"No, no, no, stop!"

The security guard came to her side, took hold of her wrist.

"You need to sterilize that before you give it to him. It's a boy, right? Anything you put in his mouth needs to be sterile."

"I know," Anna said, even though she didn't. "I just forgot, that's all."

"He's your first?" the guard asked.

"Yeah," Anna said, and she pushed the cart away, the exit doors sliding open.

"I got three, youngest one's six months. They're hard work, I tell you."

She ignored him and kept pushing.

"I think maybe I saw you on the news," the guard said, walking alongside her.

Anna felt a chill, and a crackle of adrenaline. Her heart knocked hard inside her chest, her limbs thrumming with a sudden energy.

"No, I don't think so," she said, not slowing as she wheeled the cart out into the evening.

He stepped in front of her, stopped the cart with his pudgy hands.

"Please," she said, "I need to go."

"Just tell me the truth," he said. "Will you and your baby be safer if I call the cops now or if I give it an hour or two?"

She stood silent for a time before saying, "A couple hours, maybe."

He nodded and said, "That's kinda what I thought. And I guess I didn't catch your license plate. But you take care of that baby, you hear me?"

Anna got moving again, heading toward the parking lot. Then she stopped and turned back to him.

"Thank you," she said.

He nodded and walked back to the store.

42

LIBBY SAT ALONE IN THE NURSERY, IN THE WHITE ROCKING CHAIR in which she would have fed him. It creaked as she moved back and forth, a steady rhythm that did not soothe her. A week since she left the hospital and the fury had not abated. She had come in here every day, sat in this chair, and rocked while she stared at the wall and counted the things that woman had stolen from her.

This room got the sun in the afternoon. Glowed with it. Right about now she should have been putting the baby down for a nap. She would have put the bottle on the table, burped him, changed him, and laid him down in the crib. Her days had become running lists of would-haves and should-haves, things that she had imagined for herself for the last nine months, things that were now happening somewhere else to someone else.

Her rage was incalculable. She somehow maintained a calm exterior, somehow managed not to scream and smash anything within reach, but the anger burned hard nonetheless. Mason had wisely kept his distance, letting her be when she came to this room, not arguing when she refused the meals he cooked, not questioning why she dragged a mattress from the spare room in here so she could sleep on the floor.

She supposed it was a kind of mourning. They said there were five stages of grief. Denial, anger, bargaining, depression, and finally, acceptance. There had been denial, certainly. In the twenty-four hours following the discovery of the mother's desertion, Libby had talked around it every way she could think of. Surely, she could be tracked down? She can't just disappear into thin air. She had to show up somewhere.

Mason had listened and nodded and patronized her until she screamed at him to get out. The denial had died before the end of the next day, and anger had taken its place. It had stayed with her ever since and she would cling to it forever if she had to.

A knock on the door.

She turned her head toward it, surprised by the sound. And displeased at the disturbance.

"What?" she said.

The door opened a few inches and she saw Mason's pale and worried face.

"Can I come in?" he asked.

She nodded and looked toward the window, the voile curtains glowing in the sunlight. From the corner of her eye, she saw him enter and close the door behind him. He stood beside the crib, one hand on the rail.

"Can we talk?" he asked.

She did not look at him. "What about?"

"About what happened. About us. About where we go from here."

"I'm listening," she said.

He exhaled, steeled himself. "I know you don't want to hear this, but—"

"Then maybe you should keep it to yourself."

"Libby, please, this is difficult enough."

She closed her eyes and said, "All right. Talk."

"Thank you. I know it isn't going to feel like it right now, but we have to consider that this might have been the best outcome for everyone."

She wanted to scream at him to shut his fucking mouth, but

she kept her own mouth shut, the words behind her teeth. He waited, expecting her to explode. She would not give him the satisfaction. Eventually, he spoke again.

"Why don't we try to make this a fresh start? Try to work on our marriage, see if we can just be happy together. Maybe talk to a counselor, get ourselves right. Then look at whatever options are left to us."

"You keep saying 'us,' but it's really me you're talking about, isn't it? It's me who needs counseling, right? It's me who needs a shrink. Just go ahead and say it. I'm the crazy one, aren't I?"

He crossed the room to her, got down on his knees, took her hands in his. At last, she turned her head to face him. She saw the brimming of his eyes, the darkness beneath them. He thinks he's suffering, she thought. He knows nothing.

"Libby, honey, we both know you have problems. You thought this baby was going to fix everything, but it wouldn't have."

"Not it," she said. "He."

"All right, sorry, *he* wouldn't have solved your problems. You wanted to use a child to plaster over the cracks in you, and it would never have worked. You'd have wound up hating him for it, just like you hate me. Don't deny it. You hate me right now. But I think, I hope, you still love me. One doesn't wipe out the other. But if we'd brought this baby home, and he didn't fill the hole in you, you'd hate him for it. And what kind of life would he have?"

"Better than she can give him," Libby said.

"You don't know that."

"Yes, I do. Think about it. What kind of woman sells her womb?"

Mason shook his head. "That's not fair. All kinds of women do it for all kinds of reasons."

"She's the kind of woman who would steal my child."

"Libby, he was never yours."

228

She looked him hard in the eye. "Don't you dare say that to me."

"Why not? It's true. You know it is."

Her anger flared, bright and hot in her heart and mind. She raised her open right hand to strike him. He did not flinch, hunkered there, waiting for the blow. She held her hand suspended over him, then let it drop to her lap.

"I'm going to get him back," she said. "You can either help me or stay out of my way."

"How?" he asked. "He's gone. There's no way."

"There's always a way," she said.

43

NINE DAYS AFTER HE'D LEFT IT, MR. KOVAK LET HIMSELF BACK into his own apartment. The place still smelled fresh; his cleaner had let herself in while he was away. A note was stuck to the fridge asking him to buy more floor polish and bleach.

His first order of business was to get out of the clothes he wore, the jeans and sweater he'd bought from a Goodwill, and have a shower. Then he planned to sleep through the evening and into the next day.

He had stayed in the motel for seven days, keeping the television constantly on the local news channel, and venturing out only to buy clothes, wash things, and get food. The young man on reception hadn't bothered him again. Early on the eighth day, Mr. Kovak began the long drive across Pennsylvania toward New York. He'd already taken the risk of calling to extend the car rental; if the police hadn't yet found his identity through that route, he could only assume they never would.

After hours of driving, he arrived in the outskirts of Philadelphia and found a twenty-four-hour branch of the rental company where he could drop off the car. They graciously called him a cab to take him into the city, to the 30th Street Station, where he bought an Amtrak ticket to Penn Station in New York. Arriving after midnight, he walked until he found a hotel with a vacant room where he could grab a few hours' rest before the next stage of returning home: watching his apartment.

Although Mr. Kovak had seen no indication that he was being

sought by the authorities, he could not be certain of his safety. It was not impossible that if he went straight home he would feel a pistol's muzzle against his temple as soon as he turned the key in his door. Therefore, he would exercise caution for one more day.

At ten o'clock on the morning after arriving in New York, he rode the subway out to Jamaica. By eleven, he was walking a steady circuit around the block on which his building stood. Only one, though, so as not to draw attention to himself. He went and bought a coffee, took his time drinking it, then did another circuit an hour later. Six hours passed that way, and each time he took note of the cars parked at the sidewalk, the pedestrians on the street, any tradespeople going about their work. He saw nothing suspicious, but still he was not satisfied.

Not long after seven that evening, he entered the lobby of his building. He rode the elevator up to the fifth floor, one below his, and walked to the fire door that led to the stairs. His presence triggered a light that flickered on, and he stood quite still on the landing for a few seconds, listening. He heard nothing untoward, so he ascended the two flights of steps that brought him to his floor. Exiting the stairwell, he strode along the hallway, showing no signs of caution, then stopped at his door. He made a show of fishing in his pocket for his keys with no intention of finding or using them for the time being.

Instead, he listened. A rustle of fabric, a shoe sole on carpet, anything to announce the presence of another.

A door opened, and Mr. Kovak spun on his heels to face the sound. He put his weight on both feet, his hands out and ready, his body tensed. Then he saw it was the skinny, pale millennial boy from two doors down. He wore earbuds and running gear, his phone strapped to his upper arm.

"Hey," the young man said.

Mr. Kovak allowed his body to relax, and returned the greeting.

231

The young man pointed to the cut on Mr. Kovak's forehead. "Were you in an accident?"

"Just a fender bender," Mr. Kovak said. "Nothing serious."

The young man nodded and jogged past him to the elevator, ran on the spot while he waited. Once the elevator had taken him away, Mr. Kovak leaned into his door, pressed his ear against the wood. Heard nothing. Then he knocked on it, two quick raps, before ducking out of view of the peephole.

Nothing. No cops hiding behind the door, waiting for him to enter. He inserted his key into the lock, turned it, and let the door swing open. Empty, as he hoped and expected it to be. As tempting as it was to simply shamble inside and collapse onto his good bed, he made himself pull the door closed, lock it once more, and head back to the stairs leading down to the lobby. A further two hours were lost as he traveled back to Manhattan, collected his things from the concierge at the hotel, and rode the subway out to Jamaica again.

Thus, it was with great relief that he stepped naked into his own shower, cleansed himself, before getting dry and falling onto his bed. As sleep swept in, he promised himself that tomorrow, as soon as he awoke, he would begin forgetting about Anna Lenihan.

That hard nub of pride still shouted at him to track her down and make her pay. He searched for his rage, seeking that burn that always seemed to be just beneath his skin, but it was gone. A strange calm had taken its place.

His right mind told him to forget about it.

Let her have her baby. Let her be happy.

44

ANNA PULLED UP OUTSIDE THE HOUSE AND APPLIED THE PARK-
ing brake. She kept the engine running, unsure whether or
not she would get out of the car. L'il B slept in the good car seat
she'd bought a week ago to replace the one she'd taken from the
thrift store. It was fixed into the backseat, where she could glance
over her shoulder to see him. It had been expensive; there were
plenty of no-name brand models in the store, but she had decided
she could spare it for him. Nothing was more important than
his safety. Nothing was more important than him. She had been
through too much to get him this far.

The house was much as she remembered. A recent coat of
paint had brightened it somewhat, and the wire fence had been
replaced by wood, but the yard was as unkempt as the last time
she'd seen it. A newer Hyundai had replaced the old one in the
driveway, but the same color. Two flags hung above the porch,
one the Stars and Stripes, the other an Irish Tricolor.

Anna counted to ten, instructing herself to either get out of
the car or drive away on the final number, but she did neither.
Her hands still clutched the steering wheel, as if bound there,
shaking. Through the open car window, she heard someone playing scales on a piano, do-re-mi, over and over, shifting up a half
step with each repeat. She remembered taking lessons herself.
Was old Mrs. McEvoy still teaching down the street? Or maybe
her daughter had taken over. She had a daughter, didn't she?
Anna thought so.

Memories clamored for her attention. Playing on the street, hanging out in the park, sneaking out at night to smoke cigarettes and drink the Buds and Coors that the older boys shared. Kissing and fumbling in the hidden places around the neighborhood. One recollection made her smile: her mother sewing up the buttons on her blouses. To keep wandering hands out, her mother had said, I know what those boys are like. As if that would ever have stopped them, Anna thought.

The sweetness of those memories turned bitter when she remembered that it had all gone wrong. That she had left and not been missed. All because of him.

They never believed her. She was eighteen when Stephen, her elder sister's fiancé, had found her alone in her room. It was true that she had not asked him to leave, that she did not object when he sat on her bed, but she did not ask him to try to kiss her, to force his hands where she didn't want them. When Marie walked in and found her husband-to-be entangled with Anna, it was his explanation she took as truth. That Anna had thrown herself at him, that he had been trying to get away from her. Marie reasoned that Anna had always been jealous of her, and sure, it was no surprise that she'd try to take her man from her.

As Anna wept and tried to explain what had happened, Marie and their mother turned their stony faces away and would not listen. Stephen and Marie had a long talk with Father Turlington, and Anna packed a bag and left. She had never returned.

Until now.

With no conscious decision to act, Anna shut off the engine, took the key from the ignition, and unfastened her seat belt. She opened the door, climbed out, and walked around to the rear passenger side where she removed L'il B's seat. He grumbled a little at the disturbance as she carried him toward the house. Anna opened the gate and walked along the path to the porch. She hesitated there, one foot on the bottom step, her heart beating hard, her breath short, a buzzing between her ears.

"It's all right," she said aloud. "I never did anything wrong. You hear that, L'il B? No matter what they say, I never did anything wrong."

Anna mounted the first step, then the next, then onto the porch, the boards creaking beneath her feet. She closed her eyes, swallowed, told herself she had nothing to fear, then opened them again. As she reached for the knocker, the door opened inward, and an elderly lady stood there, staring.

For a wild moment, Anna didn't recognize her mother. Thinner, grayer, smaller. But yes, it was her.

"Hi, Mom," she said.

Philomena Lenihan reached for the spectacles on a chain around her neck, brought them to her eyes. Her lips trembled as she struggled to form words. Then she looked down at the seat that hung from Anna's arm, and the tiny life it held. She slumped against the doorframe and let out a quivering wheeze before her hand went to her mouth, sealing in a sob.

She stepped back and allowed Anna to enter.

IT WAS THE same old kitchen, the same old cupboards and doors, but with a lick of paint that made it brighter than Anna's memories of it. The sunshine touched everything in a way that was strange to her. The walls were still decorated with images of Christ and her mother's favored saints, along with a portrait of JFK and a copy of the Irish Proclamation of Independence. Philomena had read it aloud to the family every Easter Sunday, though Anna had no idea why that day in particular. All except the year her father had died. That had been on Good Friday, when Anna was twelve. Heart failure while he drank at some bar with his cronies. Marie and their mother had been devastated, but Anna could not muster the grief for him, a fact that still bothered her all these years later.

"So where's this architect?" Philomena asked.

Anna remembered the lie she'd told all those months ago, the fiction that had formed in her mind as she spoke it.

"It didn't work out," Anna said, feeling heat on her cheeks and neck.

Her mother's hard eyes told Anna she knew her daughter was lying.

"Run off, did he?"

"Something like that," Anna said. "I'd rather not talk about it."

Philomena reached out to the car seat perched on her table, and touched the tiny hands that lay over the blanket.

"So he left you alone with this one," she said. "Good thing he looks like you."

Her mother had made them each a cup of tea, Barry's, imported by a local store to sell to the Irish population. There were still a good number of first-generation immigrants in the area, still plenty of accents from Dublin and Cork and the Black North, as her mother called it. She recalled the strange men who would sometimes arrive in the night at houses in the neighborhood, running from trouble back in Ireland, to stay for a few days before moving on. You weren't to mention these men in school or in church. They came and went like snow in the spring.

"He's a wee one," Philomena said. "What weight was he?"

"Six pounds two ounces," Anna said. "He's gaining, though. He feeds like a madman."

Philomena sat back in her chair. "What, are you giving him the tit?"

Anna let out a guffaw that resonated in the old kitchen, which felt good and warm deep down. "I never heard it put that way before, but yeah, I'm breastfeeding."

"Well, I suppose people do that these days. My generation were told the bottle was the best thing for them, but things change."

They each said nothing for a while, sipping hot tea, listening to L'il B's soft breathing, letting the sunlight crawl across the wall and the pictures of saints.

Eventually, Philomena asked, "Why did you come here?"

"I wanted you to meet your grandson," Anna said.

"And I thank you for that," Philomena said. "But that's not all, is it?"

Anna tried to hold back the tears, but she couldn't. She sniffed and wiped at her cheeks.

"I've got no one else," she said. "I knew it'd be hard, but I thought I could cope. But I can't. I'm so tired I can hardly think. I need help. Mom, whatever happened before, we can get over it, somehow, but right now, I need my family."

Philomena took her hand, squeezed, and said nothing. She let Anna cry it out until she had nothing left. Before either of them could speak, L'il B began to grumble, his mouth smacking and sucking.

"Someone's hungry," Philomena said, smiling.

They embraced, an awkward union, displays of affection being strange to Anna's mother. But it felt good. It felt like a beginning.

Anna unstrapped L'il B from the seat and cradled him in her left arm, then hoisted up her top. As she worked the fasteners of the maternity bra, Philomena held up her hands.

"Oh no," she said, standing, "wait till I leave the room."

Anna laughed. "Relax, Mom, it's just a boob. You've got them too."

"Maybe so, but I don't get mine out in people's kitchens, not even my own."

As Philomena left them alone, L'il B latched and began to feed. Anna leaned back in the chair and closed her eyes, focusing on the sensation, which she had grown to love even though it often hurt and left her feeling drained.

As the sun warmed her where it touched her skin, she let her mind drift, and she wondered if maybe, just maybe, everything might turn out all right.

A MOVEMENT ON the bed, a shift of weight, pulled Anna up from a deep slumber. After L'il B had taken his fill, Philomena had insisted she be allowed to burp and change him while Anna had a nap. Anna had argued halfheartedly, but it took little convincing to hand the baby over and climb the stairs. She found her old room, all traces of her long removed, and collapsed onto the bed. Sleep had taken her almost instantly.

Now the room shifted and lurched around her as she struggled to bring herself fully to the waking world. She was aware someone was here, sitting on the edge of the bed, but her eyes could not seem to make sense of the shape.

"Hey," a familiar voice said. Deeper than she remembered it, rougher, but still well known to her.

Anna rubbed her eyes until she could see her sister looking back at her. Marie gave a small sad smile.

"What time is it?" Anna asked.

"Almost five," Marie said. "You've been under more than two hours. Mom called me as soon as you went upstairs, told me I should come over and meet someone. He's beautiful."

Anna pulled herself up into a sitting position. "I know," she said. "How are you?"

"I'm okay, considering."

Anna studied her. Marie had gained a little weight, and her red hair, tied back, was now threaded with a few grays.

"Considering what?"

"Stephen and I split," Marie said.

"How long?" Anna asked.

"Not quite a year. He got fired from his job. Sexual harassment, can you believe that? I mean, I knew he'd played around before, but I always took him back on account of the kids. But this time they were talking about assault. This girl he touched up, they paid her off to stop her from going to the cops, but when she complained about him, there was another and another and another, so they let him go. And then he came home to me asking forgiveness, and I didn't have any left in me. So that was that."

"I'm sorry," Anna said, meaning it.

"You shouldn't be," Marie said, her eyes brimming. "You knew what he was before I did. I should have believed you. I'm sorry."

Anna reached out, touched her sister's shoulder. "Does Mom know?"

"Not all of it, but enough. She knows you told the truth about Stephen, but you know how proud she is. She can never be wrong, even if it means cutting her daughter out of her life. But hey, babies fix everything."

Anna returned her smile. She started to speak, but Marie raised a hand.

"Listen, a year ago, when all this happened, I should have gotten in touch. I didn't know where you were, I didn't have a number, but I could've tracked you down, or at least tried. I'm glad you're here now. Really."

"Thank you," Anna said.

"You want to help me make dinner? Chelsea and Patrick are downstairs."

"Sure," Anna said, feeling a quiet thrill at the idea of meeting her niece and nephew for the first time. "Just let me freshen up."

They embraced, then Marie headed downstairs while Anna went to the bathroom and washed her face and under her arms. She returned to the bedroom to fetch the hoodie she'd left there. As she went back to the doorway, she glanced over her shoulder, and something caught her eye. She stopped, turned to face the window and the street below.

From this angle, by the door, she could see all the way down to the intersection with the cross-street. She let her gaze wander over everything, the tired houses and lawns, the scrawny trees, the second- and thirdhand Toyotas and Volkswagens that were parked along the curb. But that one car, the BMW down near the intersection, shinier, newer than the others, better kept, stood out from the rest.

And the man behind the steering wheel.

Anna felt the room grow cold. Even though she didn't want to, she moved closer to the window, keeping the car in sight. She reached the glass and put her nose against it, peering out. Yes, there was definitely a man there, she could clearly make out his silhouette. A large man, one big hand laid across the wheel.

She felt an urge, then, so strong that she could not resist.

Anna raised her right hand and waved.

45

GOD HELP HIM, HE ALMOST WAVED BACK.
Mr. Kovak's right hand lifted perhaps an inch before it dropped and gripped the BMW's steering wheel tight. He cursed himself for letting her spot him so easily. He'd been here less than an hour, and he thought he'd parked far enough away to go unnoticed.

"Goddammit," he said.

He turned the key in the ignition, put the car in drive, and pulled a U-turn, heading away from the house. The town of New Prestwick lay an hour west of Boston, a muddle of Irish and Italian families with a smattering of other nationalities and races. The kind of town a girl like Anna Lenihan would grow up in, aching to get out and away, only to discover that everywhere else was just as shitty if you were poor and uneducated.

His contact had gotten back to him the day before, sending an email with a spreadsheet attached. The spreadsheet had been exported from Anna's checking account, which his contact had been able to access online with a minimum of effort given Anna's personal details. Mr. Kovak deposited two hundred dollars into his contact's PayPal account for his troubles.

The transactions listed in the spreadsheet were frequent and for small amounts. Twenty dollars withdrawn here, fifty there. A McDonald's drive-through outside Philadelphia, thirty bucks and change in a Target in upstate New York. A string of motels, cheap ones at that. Then a few hundred dollars blown in a Buy

Buy Baby in Henrietta. That still left a healthy balance in the account. Anna had been frugal with the money she'd taken from the clinic and had enough left to live on for a year, maybe two if she was careful.

The most recent transactions were what interested Mr. Kovak. She had stopped moving about three days ago, and there were a cluster of ATM withdrawals, all in New Prestwick, which he recognized as being her birthplace, where her family still lived. She had gone home.

There was one large cash withdrawal, five hundred dollars, and Mr. Kovak guessed that she'd paid a deposit on a place to live. He had no way to find where that might be, but he knew that if she'd driven across three states to the town she grew up in, it was a certainty that she would visit with her mother. So, an hour ago, he had pulled up to the curb, a little down the street from the house, and smiled when he saw Anna's Civic in front of it.

And then, goddammit, she'd seen him.

He spotted a diner as he steered onto the main street, and in response, his stomach growled to remind him he hadn't eaten since that morning. Stopping to eat would give him time to think and figure out his next steps. He pulled into the parking lot, climbed out of the car, and entered the diner.

Taking a seat in the rearmost booth, he exchanged greetings with the waitress. He refused a menu and told her he wanted steak and eggs, medium rare, over easy, and a side of fries. She poured him a coffee and told him she'd have his food right out.

While he waited, he felt his cell phone vibrate in his jacket pocket. He fished it out and checked the display, didn't recognize the number.

"Yes, who is this?" he asked.

"Anna," she said. "I wasn't sure if you'd have kept that number or not, or if you'd ditched it like I did."

"I had no reason to," he said. "What can I do for you?"

"You can tell me what you were doing outside my mother's house."

For the briefest of moments, he considered lying, denying it, saying he didn't know what she was talking about. But there was no point.

"Looking for you," he said.

He heard the sound of children laughing and squealing in the background, women's voices, a house full of family. The image caused an ache in him that took him by surprise. He realized then, with a disquieting jolt, that he envied Anna.

"I figured that," she said. "But why?"

"You won't believe me," he said.

"Probably not. Why would I?"

"I guess there's no reason you should," he said, "so I might as well keep it to myself."

A pause, then, "Go on, tell me."

"I wanted to see how you were doing," he said. "I wanted to see if the baby was okay."

"You're right, I don't believe you."

"Well, it's the truth, but there's not much I can do to convince you. You know I got fired, right?"

"That's too bad," she said, her sneer clearly audible.

"It is," he said. "I liked that job. I know you don't believe it, but I cared about the women under my supervision. I cared about the children they carried. I cared about you."

"You had a strange way of showing it. You threatened me, you hurt my friend."

"And I'm sorry about that," he said. "I really am."

"And if you cared about me and my baby, you'd know we belong together. You would never have tried to separate us."

"You're right. I was wrong. And I'm truly sorry."

"You're so full of shit, you know that?"

He might have argued, but instead, he asked, "What did you call the baby?"

"I call him Little Butterfly," she said, her voice softening. "L'il B for short."

He smiled in spite of himself. "That's not a real name."

"So people keep telling me. I'll come up with something else. I just haven't found anything that sticks yet."

"How about Sean?"

"Not bad," she said. "It's an Irish name. My mom would like it. Where'd you come up with that?"

"It's my name," he said. "My mother was half Irish."

"And yet she made you. Listen, I have to go. I want you to stay away from me and stay away from my family."

"All right," he said.

"I mean it. If I see you again, I'll call the police."

"You have my word. This is the last you'll ever hear of me."

"Okay," she said. "I guess it's goodbye, then."

"I guess so," he said. "Take care of yourself, Anna. And your baby."

"Fuck you," she said, and hung up.

As Mr. Kovak stared at the phone in his hand, the waitress returned with his food. His stomach growled at the smell and the sight of it. He was ravenous, but he had something to do before he ate. Opening the phone's Skype app, he logged into the account he'd created two days ago and opened the lone name in the contacts list.

He thumbed out a message: *I've found her.*

46

THREE DAYS AGO, LIBBY HAD TAKEN THE AMTRAK FROM ALBANY to New York, spending the two and a half hours gazing out the window as Poughkeepsie and Yonkers drifted by. At one point, a man with a good suit and a fake tan sat opposite her and tried to make small talk until she asked him to go away and leave her alone.

"Bitch," he'd said as he vacated the seat and walked away.

At Penn Station, she made her way down to the subway and found the 2-line Brooklyn-bound platform. There, she watched rats scurry along the black ground beneath and between the tracks until the next train arrived. She stood for the twenty-minute journey to Clark Street Station. She rode the elevator up to the concourse and exited through Hotel St. George onto Henry Street. From there, she made her way northeast until she found the building she sought on the corner of Middagh Street.

She had expected more. Not this indistinct mass of bricks and windows and fire escapes. The brochure and the website had shown floor-to-ceiling windows, glass and steel and white tile. She approached the door and found a row of buttons with handwritten names of businesses, lawyers, accountants, a literary agent, and there on the sixth row, the Schaeffer-Holdt Clinic. Libby pressed the button and waited.

"Yes?" a male voice answered.

"Dr. Sherman, this is Libby Reese. I need to speak with you."

A pause, then, "Do you have an appointment?"

"No."

"I'm sorry, you'll have to call and make an appointment with Dr. Sherman. We can't accept walk-in visitors."

"Dr. Sherman, I know it's you. You know I could make things very difficult for you, so I suggest you let me in right now."

Seconds passed, then the buzzer sounded and the door loosened in its frame. She entered, let the door swing closed behind her, and went to the small elevator at the rear of the hall. It smelled of urine and bleach, and it rattled as it ascended to the sixth floor. Libby walked along the hallway, turned a corner, and found the sign for the Schaeffer-Holdt Clinic at the very end. A plain door, painted battleship gray. She knocked on it and listened as a lock was undone.

The door opened a few inches and Dr. Sherman's pale face appeared in the gap. "Mrs. Reese, I explained everything to Mr. Reese. Your contract clearly states, among other things, that no surrogacy agreement can be enforced in the state of New York, and the Schaeffer-Holdt Clinic cannot be held liable for the actions of any third party, including, but not limited to—"

"Shut up and let me in," Libby said, letting a sliver of her rage into her voice.

Her tone convinced him of her seriousness, and he immediately stopped talking and moved aside. She entered the office, a single room with a desk and a computer, and a row of filing cabinets. An iPad with a finger-marked screen lay on the desk, just like the one this supposed doctor had brought to her home, showing the image of the young woman who looked almost exactly like her.

"This is it?" she asked. "This is the Schaeffer-Holdt Clinic? Where's the receptionist who always answered the phone?"

"I use a service," he said. "Please take a seat."

She sat down on the cheap swivel chair in front of the desk. It wheezed beneath her weight and sank at least two inches. Dr. Sherman took his seat on the other side, a black faux-leather affair that probably came from some discount office-supply warehouse.

"Mrs. Reese, before you say anything more, I have to tell you there can be no question of a refund. The contract is quite clear on this, so if you want to pursue that line, I suggest you talk to my lawyer. I can give you his—"

"I don't want a refund," she said.

He tilted his head and studied her. "Then what *do* you want?"

"I want my baby," she said.

A nervous smile flickered on his mouth. "The birth mother absconded with the baby, you know that. She broke the agreement. There's really nothing more I can do."

"You can tell me where she is."

"Mrs. Reese, I don't know where she is. Believe me, I wish I did."

"I saw a local news report from a Pittsburgh station," Libby said. "They showed CCTV footage of a man assaulting a nurse. A young woman had given birth there a few hours before, and she disappeared from the emergency room. So did the man. Now, I believe he works for you, and I want you to tell me who he is."

Dr. Sherman smiled and shook his head. "I'm quite sure I don't know what you're talking about."

She looked him hard in the eye. "Maybe I should call the Superior Police Department in Pennsylvania and tell them about your operation here, and that the man in that video works for you. When they come asking, will you know what *they're* talking about? Your operation is completely illegal. Do you think maybe the NYPD would take an interest?"

His smile dropped away. "I don't like threats, Mrs. Reese."

"Neither do I," she said. "I'm just telling you how it's going to play out. Maybe you should take a look on your computer there, see if you have any employees you've forgotten about. I can promise you, Dr. Sherman, if you don't tell me who that man was, I will not be the last person to come up here and ask."

He exhaled, withered in front of her, and reached for his keyboard.

THE NEXT MORNING, Libby left the hotel on Thirty-Ninth Street to attend her breakfast meeting. The hotel was one of those modern places, cheap for Manhattan, aimed at hipsters with its pod-like rooms and its rooftop bar. She had felt old as she entered the lobby, seeing all these young tourists from around the world, the reception staff with their tattoos and piercings. They made her feel vanilla, white-bread, and horribly out of place. She had eaten at an Irish bar around the corner instead of the hotel's own taco place, just so she could feel less like a Midwest soccer mom who'd gotten separated from her tour group.

As morning people rushed about their morning business, she walked the short distance north to Bloom's Deli. Passing the windows, she noticed one man watching her. She held his gaze, and he nodded his recognition; she returned the gesture. At the front desk, she told the waitress she was meeting someone, then weaved her way through the tables until she reached him.

"Mr. Kovak?" she asked.

"Mrs. Reese," he said, standing.

He extended his enormous right hand, and she stared at it for a moment before shaking it. He was an extraordinary specimen: broad at the shoulders, slender at the waist, his body carrying a strength that was visible from the other side of the room. He wore his hair short, which suited his thinning pate, with a beard that looked less like a style choice and more like the result of simply not shaving. A fresh-looking scar marked out an inch-long line above his left eye, mirroring the older scar beneath it. Libby was both frightened and impressed by him, which she supposed was a good thing. He indicated that she sit, and she did so. The waitress offered coffee, which Libby accepted.

He stared at her as if she were a walking wonder.

"You're so alike," he said. "I mean, if I didn't know, I would swear . . ."

"Swear what?"

He shook his head and said, "Nothing. How are you?"

She had not expected such a question, and for some reason it left her without an answer. Out of my fucking mind, she wanted to say. A danger to myself and others, might also have been a reasonable reply. Instead, she asked, "What do you mean?"

His face remained impassive, softening only a fraction. "I mean, it must have been a very difficult couple of weeks for you. After all the waiting and expectation, all these months, to be let down like this. It must have been tough."

"You have no idea," she said.

"I might have some," he said. "I've been a part of this process for the last year, same as you have. Granted, I don't have the same kind of emotional investment as you, but—"

"That's right," she said. "You don't. So please don't patronize me, Mr. Kovak. I don't need your sympathy. I need your help. Given that this mess is largely your responsibility, I think you owe me that."

He sat back in his chair, his features hardening once more. "Ma'am, I lost a good job over this. What do you think the opportunities are for veterans with piss-poor education and bad knees? If I'm lucky, I get to put on a uniform and walk around a department store smiling at the customers for the rest of my days. You don't need my sympathy, fair enough, but I don't need your anger. This wasn't my doing."

The waitress appeared with a notepad. "So, we ready to order?"

"Sure," Mr. Kovak said. "I'll have the smoked salmon and onion omelet, please."

"And ma'am?"

"No," Libby said. "Nothing."

"You should eat," Mr. Kovak said.

She ignored him and said, "You say it wasn't your doing, but you were there. You let it happen."

He smiled at the waitress. "Maybe some orange juice for me too, and that'll be all, thank you."

The waitress gave them each a glance, then said, "That'll be right out for you."

Once she'd gone, Mr. Kovak said, "Yeah, I was there. I've got the scars to prove it." He touched the angry pink line above his eye. "That still doesn't change things."

Libby leaned forward. "But we *can* change things. We can fix them."

"I don't see how."

"You can go and get my baby back. Take him from her and bring him to me. To his mother. Where he belongs."

He stared at her for a time before speaking. "You're serious?"

"You know I am."

Mr. Kovak sat forward, lowered his voice. "Mrs. Reese, Libby, you have to listen to me now. That baby is gone. He is with his mother, his real mother—"

"*I* am his mother," she said, the words forced hard between her teeth.

"No, you're not, goddammit, you're not. This child is lost to you, and you need to accept that and move on. For better or worse, he's with a mother who loves him enough to go through what she did. For Christ's sake, just let them be. Let her have him."

"Never," Libby said. "Will you help me?"

"No," Mr. Kovak said. "I won't."

Libby reached inside her purse and pulled out the manila envelope. She emptied the contents onto the table, loose bills spilling over the place settings.

"How about now?" she asked.

Mr. Kovak became very still. "How much is it?"

"Five thousand," she said. "Ten thousand more when you bring my baby to me."

He began gathering up the bills, his enormous hands moving with a shocking grace.

"I'll see what I can do," he said.

LIBBY LOGGED OUT of the Skype app and returned the cell phone to the dresser in her own bedroom. Her overnight bag lay on the bed, the contents unpacked.

So, her baby was in New Prestwick, Massachusetts. A drivable distance from Albany. She could be there and back in half a day. Back with her son.

Time to pack what she needed, which wasn't much. Some basics for the baby, that was all. And one other thing, which rested in the safe that was bolted to the floor of the closet.

A very small thing that fit her hand perfectly.

47

ANNA AND MARIE SAT ON THE PORCH OF THEIR MOTHER'S house, sharing the swing seat. Marie's eldest lay curled in her lap, sucking his thumb. L'il B slept in Anna's arms, having gorged himself into a stupor.

"I swear, I'm like a milk cow," Anna said. "I mean, it's constant. It's exhausting."

"I sometimes wish I'd done it," Marie said.

"They seem to have turned out fine anyhow."

Marie toyed with her little boy's hair. "Yeah, I guess. That's the thing with being a mother. You spend your time comparing yourself to everyone else, wondering if you're doing things right, worrying you're going to ruin them somehow. Truth is, everyone's just muddling through and doing their best. You can't beat yourself up about it. You just do what you can."

They sat quiet for a while as the evening chill began to bite. L'il B was well wrapped up, but Anna had begun to shiver. But it seemed a perfect moment, and she didn't want to break it.

"So, what's next?" Marie asked after a while.

"I don't know," Anna said. "I need to register the birth, I guess."

"You haven't done that already? Why not?"

"Let's just say it's complicated," Anna said, and Marie seemed to understand she didn't want to talk about it.

"Where are you going to live?" Marie asked. "You can't stay

out in that trailer park. When the weather gets colder, you're going to feel it."

It was the first place Anna had found when she returned to New Prestwick a week ago. The park was half-empty, the trailers falling apart. The single-wide Anna had rented was barely habitable, but the landlord had accepted cash and asked no questions. She would trade comfort for anonymity, at least for the time being.

"I don't know," Anna said. "I'll figure something out. I always do."

"Why don't you move in here with Mom?"

Anna looked at her sister. "Are you kidding? My God, we'd kill each other within a week."

"You don't know that. I mean, yes, our mother is a dragon, but she's so good with my two, and she always loves having them. You know what she's like, if she isn't fussing over someone, she doesn't know what to do with herself. I think you and the baby being here would be good for her. And you too. Just imagine being able to hand him over and go take a nap."

Anna laid her head back on the seat. "Oh God, yes, or even a bath."

"You see?" Marie said. "This shit sells itself, right?"

Anna laughed and pictured it. A good life in a warm home. Food on the table. Help when she needed it. Yes, she and her mother had a knack for bringing out the worst in each other, but perhaps Li'l B would provide the cement between them. She couldn't deny it: the idea had legs.

"I'll think about it," she said. "I might need you to soften Mom up for me, though."

"She doesn't need any softening up," Marie said, giving Anna a sideways glance and a playful nudge. "It was her who suggested it."

Anna smiled. "Ah, sneaky. Well, tell her maybe, and thank

you. And really . . ." She reached across and took Marie's hand in hers. "Thank you for . . ."

"For what?"

"For everything. For not judging. For not asking a hundred questions."

"Oh, I got more than a hundred. But yeah, I'll keep them to myself. You tell me about it when you're ready."

"Thanks," Anna said.

"I maybe ought to get my guys home to bed or else I'm going to have two little monsters on my hands by the morning. Speaking of which, what are you doing tomorrow?"

Anna thought about it for a few moments before a quite wonderful idea appeared in her mind.

"Maybe I'll take L'il B for a walk in the park, go down by the pond, let him see the ducks."

Marie's face brightened. "Maybe I could tag along?"

Anna felt a bright glee that seemed almost like panic. The idea of arranging to see her sister, like a normal family. What a thing, she thought. What a beautiful thing.

"Yeah, let's do that," she said.

"And I could take you to lunch after. How does that sound?"

"Perfect," Anna said.

They carefully embraced around their children, said their good-nights, and Anna didn't feel like too much of a liar.

L'IL B WOKE her at six, and for a moment she imagined she was back in the single-wide in Lafayette, and she was late for the breakfast shift. The nauseous panic dissipated after a few seconds, and she sat herself upright as a hint of dawn crept through the blinds; then she reached into the straw bassinet that lay beside her and lifted L'il B out.

"Oh, such a hungry boy," she said, her voice morning-hoarse.

She lifted her pajama top, and he latched immediately. As

he fed, she leaned her head back, closed her eyes, and allowed herself to drift. Images rolled through her mind, places and people, strange and familiar. She thought of old friends she'd had at school, wondered how many of them were still around. Not many, she thought. New Prestwick was not the kind of town that held on to its young. It bled them out to the cities far and wide until only the old and aging remained.

Her mother's offer entered her mind. A place to live, a *real* place, not this dump. The trailer had been barely adequate in the cooling weather and would be uninhabitable come winter. She could picture the frost on the insides of the windows, and she would not subject her child to that. Besides, although she'd contribute in whatever way she could, it would make more economic sense to live with her mother. She still had a decent amount of money left, but it wouldn't take long to burn it up.

Anna decided then that she would accept the offer. The security of a real roof over her and her baby's heads made too much sense. She would tell Marie over lunch.

Once L'il B had eaten enough, she burped him, then laid him on her chest, where he burrowed into the warmest place between her breasts, his face beneath her chin, his feet lying across her stomach. She listened to his breathing, the contented snuffling, and ran her fingertips over his cheek, his nose, his lips, his chin. His face was not visible to her, but she imagined his reactions to the sensation, the widening of his eyes and his mouth.

"You're a perfect little man, L'il B, did you know that? Just perfect in every way. And we're going to be so happy together, just you and me, because you're my Little Butterfly and I will never let you go."

She allowed her head to fall back, her eyes closing, and decided she would doze a little more, with L'il B nestled between her breasts. You weren't supposed to do that, she'd read, in case she rolled in her sleep. But it was only for a few minutes, and he felt so cozy there.

Anna floated in a thick and warm haze, chasing fragments of memories, glimpsing dreams. Then, for no reason she could understand, she snapped fully, utterly awake, her heart racing.

She blinked at the dim interior of the trailer, suddenly aware of all its shadows, the grays and blacks, the deep pools of darkness. Her eyes strained to focus on the farthest places that seemed full of unknown things. And with a cold certainty, she knew she was not alone.

"Who's there?" she said, her voice feeling very small inside her throat.

The shadows shifted, dark becoming light, light becoming dark.

He stepped into the center of the trailer, the breadth and the height of him filling up her vision. Her bladder ached for release.

His voice, when he spoke, shocked her in its quivering.

"Hello, Anna," Mr. Kovak said.

48

M R. KOVAK HAD BEEN WATCHING HER FOR SOME TIME. HE HAD
stayed in the shadows and observed as she first awoke and
fed the baby. The door to the trailer had not been hard to open,
and he'd been able to do it without waking her or the infant.
Perhaps he should have grabbed the bassinet from the bed while
they slept. He might have been able to take the baby without dis-
turbing Anna. But something had stopped him. The idea of her
waking to find the baby gone. He had been surprised to discover
that he could not be so cruel.

But still, somehow, it had to be done.

Just this one last sin. Like a drunk who swears this is his last
whiskey, like a smoker who promises to quit tomorrow. He had
this final terrible thing to do and then he would be gone, find a
straight job, try to make a decent life for himself.

And really, it'd be doing the child a favor, wouldn't it? Look
at this place, he thought. The trailer park was a dump, half of
the homes derelict and empty, abandoned to rot. The single-wide
she'd been living in was in terrible condition. Even in the fall, a
deep damp chill permeated everything. How could anyone hope
to raise a child in a place like this?

But then he watched as she fed the baby. He saw her wake as
the child cried, reach into the bassinet, lift him out, and bring
him to her breast. And even from here, even in the dimness of
early dawn, he could see how small, how beautiful he was.

He's so small, he thought, and I'm so big. If I snatch him from her, I'll crush him, my hands are too big and clumsy. So precious and beautiful and I am so ugly and my hands are so hard. The idea paralyzed him, held him in the shadows, silent and still like he'd been carved from stone.

When she'd finished feeding the baby, she laid him on her chest and closed her eyes. Soon she drifted into sleep, a gentle, breathy snore coming from her, the child nestling into her bosom.

So perfect, he thought.

So perfect, and I can't take him from her.

The realization hit him hard, a mix of anger at his own weakness, and a relief at not having to do this awful thing. He would turn around and leave, let himself out the way he had come in. She would never know he'd been here.

To his shock, tears sprang from his eyes. He hadn't cried since he was a child. Not since his mother's funeral. He brought his fingers to his cheek, felt the warm wetness there. Against his will, he made a gasping, fluttering inhalation, and the noise of it filled the trailer.

Anna woke, lifted her head, suddenly alert and staring into the darkness where he stood. She can see me, he thought. Or can she? He remained still, holding his breath, until she spoke.

"Who's there?"

Barely a whisper, he could hear the terror in her voice.

Mr. Kovak realized then that he too was scared. In fact, he'd never been so frightened in his life. Afraid of himself, afraid of what he might do. He stepped out of the darkness, into a dim gray pool of light cast by the window.

"Hello, Anna."

She stared up at him, eyes wide, breathing hard, her shoulders rising and falling. The baby stirred on her chest, mewling and huffing. So tiny, his legs kicking.

"What do you want?" Anna asked, her voice firmer now.

For want of a lie, Mr. Kovak said, "I came to take the baby."

"You'll have to kill me," she said.

He couldn't hold her gaze, looked away. "I know," he said.

Her breathing was audible from across the room, hard and ragged. He imagined the adrenaline charging through her, the fight-or-flight instinct raging for release.

"Look at him," she said.

Mr. Kovak kept his eyes on the floor.

"Look at him."

He raised his head. She lifted the baby from her chest, turned him so Mr. Kovak could see his face in the early light. How beautiful and perfect he was.

"You know he belongs to me," Anna said. "No matter what you do, no matter what happens, you can't change that. I am his mother, he is my son. He belongs here, with me."

"I'm sorry," Mr. Kovak said. He took a step closer.

Anna retreated across the bed, pushing with her feet.

Mr. Kovak raised his hands. "Please, no."

"Don't come any closer," she said.

"I shouldn't have come here," he said. "I'm sorry."

"Then go," Anna said.

He opened his mouth to speak, but he felt a cold draft touch the back of his neck. Anna leaned to the side and stared past him. The draft vanished as the door closed. He didn't turn his head to look.

"Who is that?" Anna asked. "What did you do?"

"I'm sorry," Mr. Kovak said.

49

IBBY HAD FELT A MIX OF FEAR AND EXCITEMENT AS SHE LOOKED at herself in the mirror that morning. Mason still slept downstairs on the couch while she dressed and prepared. As she left the house, quiet as a cat, as she started her car and backed out of the driveway, she had the sense of an end of things. Today was not like other days. This day was a threshold, and when it was done, there would forever be a before and after. One life split in two.

That feeling remained as she drove east, following her phone's directions until she found the achingly dull town of New Prestwick, and felt a gladness that her child would not be raised here. She took two wrong turns before she found the Rest-EZ Mobile Home Community on the outskirts of the town. Following the final directions Mr. Kovak had given her, she parked her car on a dirt road behind the trailer park. She had to work her way through a small wood, navigating in the darkness between the trees as night creatures rustled in the fallen leaves all around, until she came upon the rear of a row of trailers.

From what she could make out, many of them appeared deserted. Several had begun to shift on the cinder blocks that held them off the ground, their structures giving way, deteriorating. And this was the place to which Anna Lenihan had taken the baby she had stolen? Did she really plan to raise a child in such squalor? Part of her mind recalled that she had been raised in a place not much better than this, and that realization stung her deep in her heart.

No, she thought. That cannot be allowed. She felt more convinced than ever of the correctness of her actions. This was a just thing that she was doing.

Before she could give it more thought, a shape moved on the other side of the trailers, not quite directly ahead of her. She tensed at the sight of Mr. Kovak as he moved like air toward the nearest trailer, climbed the wooden steps to the door. He took something from his jacket pocket, slipped it between the door and its frame, and within a few seconds, the door opened. Her skin tingled when he paused and looked straight at her before slipping inside. All without a sound.

That had been thirty minutes ago, maybe more. The sky had turned from oily black to milky gray. Birds stirred in the trees, called to one another, and she felt they scolded her, told her to get out of here.

What was he doing? He should have been in and out in seconds. She had heard nothing, no struggle, no screaming. What was happening in there?

"Just take him," she said aloud.

The sound of her own voice frightened and shamed her, and she no longer wanted to stand here among the trees, powerless. Mr. Kovak had told her to keep her distance, stay back, and he would bring the baby to her. But how could she wait any longer? How could she stay hidden in the trees while her baby was right there waiting for her?

She felt something cold in her right hand, though she had no knowledge of lifting it from her jacket pocket. The Walther P22 Mason had insisted on buying for her three years ago when he suddenly got into guns. He had gotten himself a Glock something-or-other, explaining they were for home protection, and certainly not toys for him to play with. She had humored her husband by accompanying him to the range a handful of times, but she did not derive the pleasure from shooting that he did. The tiny pistol had lain untouched in the safe for two and a half years, until this morning, when she had slipped it into her jacket pocket before she left the house. It had lain against her side all the way here, a heavy, dark presence that she could not ignore. Now it filled her right hand and told her to move.

Libby walked fast, not caring about the rustling of leaves beneath her feet or the cracking of twigs. The time for quiet had been and gone. She crossed the distance to the steps and the trailer door in seconds, pushed the door open, stepped inside, raised the pistol with her right hand, supported it with her left.

Anna Lenihan sat on the bed, Mr. Kovak standing over her. Libby heard her speak, ask who she was, but she was transfixed. It was like watching a movie of her younger self, something tucked away on her phone or on a Facebook post, unseen for years. Just like me, she thought. Just like me.

"Who is that?" Anna Lenihan asked again.

Mr. Kovak did not move, did not turn his head.

Libby aimed the pistol somewhere above Anna's head. "Take him," she said.

Mr. Kovak did not react.

"You bastard," Anna said. "What did you do?"

"Just take him," Libby said.

Mr. Kovak glanced over his shoulder at her, and she saw the wetness on his cheek, like he'd been crying. What had happened in here?

"For Christ's sake, just reach out and take him," Libby said. "That's all. Just take him. Take him."

Anna shook her head, held the child close.

"Libby, go home," Mr. Kovak said.

"What?"

He turned to her now.

"I said, go home. There's nothing here for you."

She felt the fury that had been balled up inside her for weeks begin to unfurl, to untether itself from her restraint.

"You son of a bitch," she said. "You're going to say that to me now? After all I've gone through, you're going to tell me to go home?"

Anna laid the baby in the bassinet on the bed, made soothing sounds, like she was his mother, like everything was going to be all right.

"I'll give you back the money," Mr. Kovak said. "But you need to turn around right now and go, Libby. It's over. This child will never be yours. The sooner you accept that, the sooner you can—"

She turned the pistol's aim on him, her forefinger curling inside the trigger guard. She aligned the front and rear sights on his broad chest.

"Jesus, Libby, what are you doing?" Mr. Kovak asked, bemusement in his voice.

"Give me my baby," Libby said, her voice firm.

Anna kept her eyes on Libby as she moved the bassinet, trying to ease away from the bed.

"What is that, a .22?" Mr. Kovak asked, taking a step toward her. His voice rose until it boomed between the walls. "It's a goddamn peashooter. What do you think you can do with that? You think you can intimidate me? Give it to me right now, or I will take it from you."

"Shut your mouth," Libby said. "Just take the baby and give him to me."

She saw his weight shift, his arms moving out from his sides, his hands open. Ready to move, ready to snatch the pistol from her.

"Stay there," Libby said as she pulled back the hammer.

But he did not. He stepped closer, his big hands reaching for her, cursing between his teeth.

Reach out and knock 'im down, the instructor on the range had said. When faced with a threat, don't think too hard about it. All you have to do is reach out with the pistol and knock 'im down.

So, she did.

The Walther gave one jarring POP! and jumped in her hand, and Mr. Kovak staggered back, reaching for the new hole in his chest, so small, hardly anything at all, an inch or two below his clavicle. His legs met the bed and he flopped down to sit on its edge. The mattress rocked under his weight. Anna screamed.

"Jesus, Libby," Mr. Kovak said. "Look what you did."

He coughed, then tried to stand again, so once more she reached out and knocked him down, once more the Walther popped and jumped.

Another hole appeared, this one in the center of his chest, and now he slumped, his forearms on his knees, keeping him upright. He gave a bubbling exhalation, his wide eyes staring at her, then past her, and he tried to say something, but his mouth moved silently.

Anna slipped off the bed, past Mr. Kovak, one hand closing the straw handles of the bassinet. What did she think she could do? Get past Libby?

"Stop," Libby said, but if Anna heard, she paid no heed.

Anna's body looked like a spring, ready to launch her toward the door.

"Stop!"

Anna lifted the bassinet, her body between it and Libby. Time slowed, almost froze.

"Stop, please, stop!"

No good. Libby's finger found the trigger once more.

The first shot missed.

And the second.

The third did not.

50

SOMETHING PUNCHED ANNA HARD IN THE RIGHT SHOULDER and left behind a deep burning heat. The air beside her left ear split and cracked, then another punch, lower down in her body, in the ribs, and now it was hard to breathe. Something zipped past her head again, and her legs became ever so tired and heavy. She kept hold of the bassinet, tried to lift it, but it was so heavy. She turned, used her other hand to try to hoist it up.

Then a hot punch low down in her back, and this one hurt, this one burned so bad, and her legs were no use to her anymore, just liquid things that could not support her, because now there was pain and the pain was everything. Another strike to the back of her neck, and it felt like a hammer blow that bit through the muscle and into her jaw and her mouth filled with blood and hard things that she thought might have been teeth and it didn't matter anymore because she had lost hold of the bassinet and she was falling.

Lift it, she commanded herself, lift it and run.

But she couldn't because she was on her knees and the floor was sucking her down and her arms were so heavy, and she couldn't hold her head up anymore, it felt like a balloon on a stick, and she coughed and she sprayed a fine red mist from her nose and mouth and the floor rushed up to meet her. She found herself lying at Mr. Kovak's feet, and that struck her as funny, and she wanted to laugh, but it hurt too much.

Anna heard quick footsteps approach, but she couldn't turn

her head to see. No matter, the woman appeared above her, towering, and once more Anna thought how much she looked like her. Like she had a twin her mother had never told her about.

The woman, Mr. Kovak had called her something, what was it? Sounded like L'il B, but it couldn't be, that was her baby's name.

"L'il B," she said aloud, but it came out as a gurgle and a sputter and red dots spattered Mr. Kovak's shoes. She spat, and she saw glinting white among the red.

"L'il B," she called again, louder this time.

The woman stopped, stared down at her.

"L'il B."

The woman looked back to the bassinet on the bed, reached for it, but stopped, frozen like a rock.

He's beautiful, Anna thought, I know he is, thank you for saying.

Then the woman screamed, and Anna didn't know why.

She screamed again and again, doubling over with the force of it, shouted, No, no, no, no, no, no, and screamed again.

Just lift him, Anna thought, see how beautiful he is. Why don't you lift him?

The woman screamed some more, her voice shrieking between the walls, and then she raised the pistol so the muzzle pressed beneath her chin, and she tried to pull the trigger, but nothing happened, so she screamed again.

"Why don't you lift him?" Anna asked through a mouthful of warm, wet grit.

She closed her eyes, rested her head on her arms, and listened to the woman scream as she drifted away into the cold black.

51

L IBBY PULLED INTO THE DRIVEWAY AT SEVEN IN THE EVENING, rain pelting down, bouncing off the car and the asphalt. She had driven all day, unseeing, like a machine, pulling over now and then to scream into the windshield or to open the door and vomit onto the verge. Turning the ignition off, she listened to the hammering of the raindrops on the roof, the ceaseless clamor of it, and she savored the way it seemed to blot out everything else. A blanket of white noise, and she wanted to hide within its folds.

She could not recall how long she had remained in the trailer. It had felt like hours, though she imagined now it was more like seconds or minutes. She wished she'd had a bullet left in the magazine, that she hadn't used all ten of them. Just one, and everything could have been wiped clean.

But no. She had endured hours of living beyond seeing what she'd done, but there would be only a few minutes more. All she had to do was get into the house and find the box of ammunition. She knew there were several boxes in the safe, mostly the larger ones for Mason's gun, but there were smaller ones for hers. Once inside, she would load the pistol, go into the bathroom, lock the door behind her, and end it.

There was no other way now.

As the rain fell, she wept. She grieved. For herself as well as him.

"What did I do?"

She had asked that question a thousand times in the hours

since she ran from the trailer park. And the answer was always the same.

Her stomach lurched and flexed, and she retched into her lap. The car already stank of it, drying on her clothes, on the upholstery.

Didn't matter. Nothing mattered.

Just get out, she told herself. Just get in there and get it done.

She pulled the handle, pushed the car door open. Then she climbed out, letting the rain soak her through, ignoring the cold. The hateful weight of the pistol, still in her jacket pocket, thumped against her hip. She walked around the car, her feet splashing through the water that coursed down the driveway. Lights on inside. Mason was home. She hoped she would not have to face him before she could put the bullet in her mouth.

The front door was unlocked, and she stepped through, treading softly. Music played in the kitchen, and Mason sang along, unaware of her listening. She heard the oven hum, pots and pans rattling. A bitter ache throbbed in her heart and part of her wanted to go to him, tell him she loved him, tell him goodbye. Instead, she stood in the hallway, dripping water onto the floor, one hand over her mouth to silence the hacking sobs.

Move, she thought, before he finds you out here.

She went to the stairs and climbed, reached the landing, and slipped into their bedroom. No need for the light, she went to the closet, opened it, and dropped to her knees. She entered the code for the safe and waited for it to finish whirring before she pulled the metal door open and reached inside. Feeling around, she found the smaller box and lifted it out, felt the weight shift inside as the contents rattled in their plastic.

Libby got back to her feet and crossed to the bathroom. She entered, pulled the light cord, and closed the door, locked it. The light seemed so bright in here, so painful and hard. Her reflection moved in the mirrors, but she could not see that, could not bear to look at herself. She sat down on the closed toilet lid and opened the box. The bullets spilled across the tiled floor, dozens of them rolling with their dull sheen of brass and lead.

She pulled the Walther P22 from her jacket pocket and found the lever beneath the trigger guard. The magazine popped free, and she set the pistol aside. She leaned down and gathered exactly ten rounds from the floor, then fed them into the magazine one by one until it was full. The fact that she needed only one flitted across her mind before she dismissed it. She reinserted the magazine into the pistol, slapped it home with her palm, then pulled back the slide assembly to chamber the first round.

Libby remembered the numbers: eleven pounds of pressure if the hammer wasn't cocked, only four if it was. She pulled the hammer back with her thumb, opened her mouth, and placed the muzzle between her teeth. Angled it up toward the roof of her mouth. Tasted oil and metal. The trigger moved beneath her finger.

"Libby?" A knock on the door. "Libby, you okay in there?"

She withdrew the muzzle from her mouth, removed her finger from the trigger.

"I'm fine," she said, suddenly aware of how hollow and hoarse she sounded.

"You sure? You sick or something?"

"A little," she said. "Go on down, I'll be there in a bit."

"Where've you been all day? I tried to call you, but you left your phone in the kitchen."

"I went out for a drive, that's all. I'll be down in a minute, all right?"

"And the two days before that. You know, if you need time to yourself, that's fine, I get it, but I've been worried."

"I'm fine," she said. "Everything's fine. Just let me be for a minute."

"I made us dinner. Penne arrabiata with chorizo. There's wine,

I picked up a couple bottles of a nice Tempranillo in town, I might maybe have had a glass or two already. You want I should pour you some?"

She closed her eyes and pressed her hands against her temples, the hard metal of the pistol digging into her scalp. "No, Mason, please just go."

"Thing is, there's news," he said, his voice sounding close to the door.

"Please, Mason," she said, unable to keep the sobs from her words.

"Mrs. Sinclair called. You remember, from the adoption agency? She's been trying to reach you for a couple of days, but you didn't answer, so she tried me instead. Thing is, she thinks she might have a match for us."

Libby opened her eyes. "What?"

"She says it's a really good prospect, a newborn, a little boy. She wants to come and talk to us about it tomorrow. I told her to come at noon. I can call in sick to work or take a personal day or whatever."

"A boy?"

"Yeah. Just what we always wanted, Libby. I told you, didn't I? I said it was for the best, right?"

"Yeah," Libby said. "You did."

52

"SHE TOOK HIM."

Anna told them a hundred times over. She couldn't fathom why they wouldn't listen to her. Why they kept lying, saying he was dead. Her sister, her mother, the police officers, the doctors, the nurses. All of them were in on it. It was a conspiracy.

They told her nothing at first, only that she had been asleep for a long time. Weeks, they said, held under by sedation. She hadn't been able to speak at first. A kindly doctor explained that the bullets had been low caliber, but high velocity, and at least two of them had passed right through her body, damaging her lung and liver. One had only just missed her spine, could have left her paralyzed from the waist down. Another had torn through the muscle of her neck and hit the back of her jaw on the left side, shattering bone and teeth. They had wired what they could back together. There would be more surgery to come.

Those first few days of waking were a long smear of bright pain and dark nothing, which she drifted through in a state of only partial awareness. She began her return to the world by noting the routines of the day, the opening and closing of blinds, the presence and absence of light, the renewals of painkillers, the changes in shifts as faces came and went.

She had been trying to speak for some time before anyone noticed. In the end, it was a young male nurse who first acknowledged her. He leaned in over the bed and waited patiently while she grunted up at him.

"Anna, you're in St. Bartholomew's Hospital in Boston. You were brought here from New Prestwick. Do you know what happened to you?"

Shot, she tried to say, but she choked on her own saliva, coughed, setting off a chain reaction of pain around her body.

"Okay, okay," he said, his voice low and soothing. "Just relax. Anna, you were in a shooting incident. You were struck several times, and you were seriously hurt, but you're going to be fine, all right? We have a very experienced trauma team here, they're well used to dealing with gunshot wounds, and they've been taking very good care of you. You're having difficulty speaking because your jaw is wired shut. Now, I want you to take it easy and one of the doctors will be in to talk with you in a while."

She tried to shout after him, Where's my baby, where's L'il B? But the words remained trapped in her throat and he left her there alone.

The first doctor did indeed explain everything, as did the second, and the third. But none would answer when she forced one word out between her teeth.

"Baby," she said to all three.

All three shrugged the question away, said her family would be around in the morning.

It was Marie who first told her the lie.

She sat at the side of the bed, no one else in the room, clutching her rosary in her hand, pressing the beads to her lips. Face flushed red, eyes brimming.

"Where is he?" Anna asked, her voice a low hum behind her teeth.

Marie's head dropped so it rested on the blanket. "Oh, Anna."

"Tell me."

"Anna, he's dead."

"No," Anna said. "Not."

It was not a screaming denial, but a statement of fact. The way one wearily tells a child there is no monster under the bed.

"He is, Anna, oh God, he is." She lifted her head. "The police doctor, what is he, the, the medical examiner, said the bullet passed through you and hit him. He died in the hospital. They couldn't do anything for him."

"No," Anna said. She would have shaken her head if she could, but the pain was too great. "Took him."

"We buried him in St. Patrick's, in Grandpa Henry's plot, under the cherry trees. It was a beautiful service, hundreds of people came even though they didn't know him, I mean, Christ, I didn't know him, only for a day, and now he's—"

"No, listen," Anna said, growling. "She took him."

Marie stared back at her, shaking her head. "No, Anna, he died. I'm so sorry, but you have to—"

Anna's hand lashed out, the palm striking Marie's cheek and ear, rocking her head.

"Bitch," she said, and struck her again. "Lying bitch."

Then she grabbed a handful of her sister's hair, pulled so hard some came away between her fingers, then slapped her again, and once more.

Marie got to her feet and backed away. Tears soaked her cheeks, leaving black trails of mascara across the red. She moved to the door, saying sorry, I'm sorry, so sorry, and Anna didn't see anyone for hours.

The next day, the police came. Two detectives, a man and a woman, plus a young man in uniform who carried a sketchpad and pencil. The male detective was called Mearns and he looked more like an accountant than a cop. A big man, tall, the room's fluorescent lights glinting on his bare scalp. The female, called Veste, looked like she could tear the head off of anyone who displeased her.

Anna told them everything from start to finish, from Betsy telling her about the ad in the free paper to watching that woman tower over her. Much of it they knew already.

"Sean Kovak," Mearns said, "he died at the scene. No one's

spoken up for the body yet. Until very recently, he worked on a contract basis for a company called the Schaeffer-Holdt Clinic. That turns out to be a one-man operation run out of an office in Brooklyn, New York, by a Donald Sherman who claimed to be a doctor, though he was nothing of the sort. Same day the incident in New Prestwick hit the news, he burned it all down. Wiped every damn record of every transaction he was a part of, got the storage facility he used to flush all the sperm samples they were keeping for his clients, pulled every penny out of every bank account he had. Last trace of him was crossing the border at El Paso. After that, he's up in smoke.

"We know there were a series of calls to and from Mr. Kovak's phone in the couple days leading up to the incident, all from a cheap prepaid cell, all placed from the midtown area of Manhattan. We suspect these calls were made by the shooter.

"We have one witness. A man who lives four down from the trailer you were staying in. He heard the shots and went to investigate. He saw a woman run from the trailer and into the trees. We asked for a description, and he swore on his mother's grave that it was you, the same woman who'd been living in that trailer for the last week. He never entered the trailer, just went back to his own and called the police. As far as he's concerned, it was you who pulled the trigger.

"Anyway, the upshot of all this is that the woman you've described is only a couple of links in the chain away from being found, but we're struggling to find those links right now. But we'll keep looking, Anna, I promise. We'll find the woman who killed your son."

Anna tried to shake her head but couldn't. "She took him," she said. "Not dead. She has him."

The cops looked nervously at Marie, who stood in the corner. Marie said nothing, looked down at her feet.

"Libby," Anna said. "Her name was Libby."

"How do you know?" the woman cop, Veste, asked.

274

Marie spoke for her. "She's confused. She called her boy L'il B, short for Little Butterfly."

"No," Anna said. "Listen. Mr. Kovak called the woman Libby. That was her name."

"Anna, I think you're confused," Marie said. "Maybe you need to rest awhile."

The anger burned in Anna's breast, impotent and useless. She wanted to scream at them to get out, to look for her boy, but she knew they would not listen. Instead, she stared at the ceiling and disconnected, switched herself off, disengaged from their reality until she could get out of here.

TWO WEEKS AFTER she left the hospital, the detectives arranged a visit with Anna at her mother's house. She held off applying a fentanyl patch and endured the pain because she wanted a clear head for the discussion. Marie helped Philomena clean the place, and they laid out coffee and tea and store-bought cookies on the kitchen table. Heavy snowflakes pattered against the window.

This time, it was Veste who did the talking, Anna sitting across the table from her.

"Before we begin," she said, "I want you to know that we're still working on this. We haven't given up on finding your son's killer."

Anna had decided that morning that she would not argue with them again. She would let them lie to her face and say nothing. Veste waited for a response from Anna, but as had become her habit, Marie gave it in her place.

"That sounds a lot like there's a 'but' coming," she said from the corner, where she leaned against the wall.

Veste shifted in her seat, unable to hold Marie's gaze.

"We've explored every avenue we possibly can. We have partial fingerprints from the shooter that we found on the trailer's door handle and the spent cartridges on the floor. We have footprints from the wooded area behind the trailer. But that's it for physical evidence. Even if we had usable DNA, we'd still need to find the person it matches, same as the fingerprints. Unless there's a record from a previous crime, we've got nothing to match it to. Boston PD gave us a forensics team to go over the scene, and that's the best they could come up with."

"What about the money?" Marie asked. "Last time, you said there might be a way to make the connection through the bank records."

Veste shook her head. "This Sherman guy, the fake doctor, he's a clever bastard. And careful. Not only to keep a separation between the surrogates and the people who bought the children, but to avoid the IRS seeing how much money he was taking in. As far as we can tell, he kept a chain of shell companies to funnel the payments through. We think the people paying for this service transferred money to one of these shell companies, which then moved the funds into an offshore account. Sherman then bounced just enough back into the clinic's account to pay the rent on his office and whatever he gave to the young women. Even the clinics and lawyers he used in the various states got paid from that account, and we can't trace the money back any further."

Marie spoke again. "How about his clients? There must be some out there who saw what happened."

"A few," Veste said. "We asked all the local New York news stations to run an appeal with the story to find other clients of the clinic. Only six came forward. My guess is that of the others who saw the appeal, most didn't want to run the risk of their children being taken from them. Of the six who did come forward, only three of them volunteered their own bank records to show the payment going out. In each case, it looks like Sherman created a new shell company and bank account to accept the payment. As soon as the money went in, it was moved offshore and that's as far as we can trace it. To get the other three records, we'd have to get an order from a judge, which the clients could appeal and we'd be tied up in court for God knows how long, and in all probability, we'd wind up with the same dead end."

"What about contracts? Anna signed one. The people buying the babies must have signed one too. Where are they?"

"Gone," Veste said. "We don't know where, whether they've been destroyed or stored somewhere. All electronic records have been wiped."

"There must be a way to get them back," Marie said. "Don't you have people who can do that sort of thing? Computer experts?"

"No, ma'am, we don't," Veste said. "We're a very small department with limited resources. Boston and New York PDs have given us a lot of help, but their indulgence only goes so far. I've personally spoken with contacts at the FBI, and although there are some aspects to this case that fall under their jurisdiction— mostly the financial irregularities—they don't see it as a priority."

"Not a priority," Marie echoed. "My nephew's murder is not a priority."

"Our best hope now is that the IRS goes after Sherman and turns up something we couldn't. They have resources we simply—"

"Murder," Marie said. "You want some government accountants to somehow solve a—"

"No," Anna said, even though she had promised herself she wouldn't. The restriction of her jaw and the missing teeth made it difficult for her to speak, but she could not remain quiet while everyone around her avoided the truth. "Kidnap. Abduction. Not murder."

Veste looked to Marie, who shook her head and lowered her gaze.

"Anna," Veste said, "we've been over and over this. You have to—"

"I looked it up," Anna said, her tongue struggling to form the words. "Child abduction is federal. Should be FBI."

"Anna, please, we can't—"

277

She would not listen to this. Not again. Anna stood, using the table for balance as everyone remained silent, grunted and hissed at the pain. She made her way to the kitchen door and the stairs beyond.

Veste called after, anger now unhidden. "Frankly, Anna, your lack of cooperation isn't helping. It's hard to investigate a crime when the only witness refuses to acknowledge it took place at all."

"Stop," Marie said. "Just stop, please."

Their voices receded as Anna climbed the stairs, each step taking painful effort. Up in her room, she applied a fentanyl patch and let it spirit her away.

IT WAS SPRING, and Anna sat on the top step, listening.

Marie paced the living-room floor. Anna saw her shadow move along the wall, back and forth, back and forth. She pictured the phone pressed to her ear.

"No, not for weeks . . . We're trying, believe me, but you know what she's like . . . Yeah, always, just like our father . . . She won't go . . . No, not at all, we tried and tried . . . I mean, I offered to drive her, just to look, I thought if she saw the headstone, maybe she . . . She just refuses to discuss it . . . I know . . . I know . . . But short of dragging her by the hair, how can I make her go anywhere? . . . I know, but it's almost six months now, and she hasn't even . . . I know . . . I'll keep trying . . . But the reason I called is . . . yeah . . . I called to see if we could get some more fentanyl patches . . . Yes, already . . . I know . . . I know . . . She says she needs them . . . The pain . . . I don't know, that's what she tells me . . . Okay . . . I understand . . . Really, don't mention it . . . I completely understand . . . Thank you, Doctor . . . I'll try . . . You too . . . Goodbye."

Anna waited, listening as Marie continued to pace. Angry steps, the shadow quickening.

"Goddammit," Marie said, then the sound of the phone being tossed onto a table.

She appeared in the doorway down below, crossed the hall, and mounted the bottom step. Looking up, she saw Anna, watching. Anna was struck by how pretty her big sister was. How tall she was, how good her skin, the intelligence in her face. And how much she looked like that woman, Libby, because Marie looked like Anna and Anna looked like that woman. For a burning, blinding moment, Anna hated her sister for it.

"Well?" she said.

"He said no," Marie said, one foot on the bottom step. "He says you shouldn't need the fentanyl by now and he's concerned you're crossing into dependency."

"But it hurts," Anna said, the lisp riding the sibilants, the audible remnants of the injury to her jaw still strange to her ears.

"Dr. Cooper said you should be able to manage your pain with over-the-counter meds. Tylenol, Advil, whatever. Dr. Myers said the same thing yesterday."

Anna swallowed the bubble of anger and said, "I know my own body, Marie, I know my own pain. If they won't prescribe what I need, then we go to a doctor who will."

Speaking was easier now, but the left side of her jaw still felt stiff, the movement lopsided. It blunted her words and she always kept a tissue at hand to mop at the corner of her mouth.

Marie climbed the stairs and sat on a step three below Anna's, took her sister's hands.

"Can't you see what you're doing to yourself?"

"Please don't lecture me," Anna said.

"But I'm worried sick, so is Mom. We can't go on like this. It's going to tear us all apart. Please, Anna, you have to get help."

"I have to get my boy back," Anna said.

Marie's head dropped, and she hid her eyes with her hand. "Oh Christ, Anna, oh my fucking God, I can't keep doing this. I can't keep telling you over and over and over. I'm going out of my mind here. I can't do it. I can't."

"Then stop," Anna said.

Marie became silent, her face hidden. Her other hand kept hold of Anna's, tight, as if she might be carried away on the wind. Minutes passed before she spoke again.

"All right," she said. "I'll make you a deal. Come with me to St. Patrick's and—"

"No," Anna said.

"Come with me to St. Patrick's and see the grave and I will get you more fentanyl."

"No," Anna said.

"Then you can do without. How's that? You can take some Advil or aspirin or whatever the hell you like, but you don't get any more fentanyl unless you do this one thing that I've asked you."

Now Anna became quiet.

"Well? What's it going to be?"

"All right," Anna said, her voice dry like fallen leaves. "I'll do it."

53

LIBBY SAT ON THE STAIRS, BALANCING ETHAN ON HER KNEE. HE pulled at her necklace, turning the pendant over in his fat little hands. She took it from his mouth, ignored the spit.

"I guess that's it, then," Mason said.

He stood by the door, two bags at his feet. His eyes were red; he'd been crying as he packed. She'd heard him from downstairs.

"I guess," Libby said.

She had no more tears left to give.

"Call me, let me know when the next home inspection's coming up. I'll be here."

"Okay," she said.

He turned to the door, put his hand to the lock. Pausing there, he said, "I could've turned you in. Just remember that. When you're cursing me for leaving, you remember I could've told them what you did."

She said nothing. The denials had stopped long ago, but she had never admitted to anything either. No matter how hard he pressed.

It had taken him days to make the connection. The first news reports had drawn little reaction from him. It was only when the authorities linked the dead man and the injured woman to the incident in the community hospital in Superior, Pennsylvania, that things had changed. And then, ten days after the incident, an appeal went out across the news channels asking for clients of the Schaeffer-Holdt Clinic to come forward. He had become quiet and distant after that, and he had started drinking even more. Not to the point of losing control, he didn't want to derail the adoption, but it was there nonetheless. The stale odors, the bottles in the recycling box.

Then this morning, he had said, "I can't do it, Libby. I can't pretend this thing isn't hanging over us."

And so, he was gone.

He closed the door behind him, and Libby listened to him getting into the car, the engine starting, the car receding into the silence.

Only her and Ethan now.

And really, wasn't that all she needed?

54

MARIE PULLED UP OUTSIDE THE CHURCH, APPLIED THE PARKING brake, let the engine die. Anna shivered in the passenger seat, pain rolling around her body. The aches were always there, but the deeper pains were calling today. The one in her jaw kicked hardest, the hurt unwilling to be contained there, spreading up the side of her head and out through her neck and to her shoulders. She pulled her coat tight around her; Christ, it was cold, even though new green showed on the trees.

"Here we are," Marie said.

"Can I have my patch now?" Anna asked.

Marie sighed and shook her head.

"It hurts, goddammit."

Marie reached down into the footwell by Anna's feet and retrieved her purse. She dug inside and found a patch, sealed in a foil pouch. Anna snatched it from her fingers with one hand, undid her shirt with the other. She tore the foil with her remaining teeth, peeled away the paper backing from the clear plastic, and placed the patch high up on her chest, to the left side.

The hit came quick and smooth, but not strong. Not yet. It would be hours before that warmth enveloped her entirely. But this would do. The sharp edges of the world dulled enough not to cut her.

"Okay," she said, aware of the languor of her voice. "Thank you."

Marie opened the driver's door and climbed out. Anna felt the biting chill sweep in until she closed it again. She didn't move at first when Marie opened the passenger door.

"Come on," Marie said.

Anna considered protesting, saying she'd changed her mind, but she knew there was no avoiding it now. She had to go along, no matter how pointless it was. Climbing out, she realized she hadn't been here since their father's burial. How long ago was that? Almost twenty years?

She followed Marie through the open gates, taking the path to the western side of the cemetery, beneath the shadow of the building. Anna remembered Sunday mornings in there, the commands to be quiet and still, the compulsion to giggle and fidget. A memory sparked in her mind, one that had not surfaced in decades.

Anna had been twelve, maybe thirteen, a couple of years at least past her confirmation. She had been doing homework at the kitchen table while Marie cleaned. Their mother had been at work. There was a knock on the door, and Anna had gone to answer it. It was Father Turlington, and he said he wanted to take Anna back to the church for some special instruction. Before she could answer, Marie had appeared at her side and asked Father Turlington if it was the same kind of instruction he'd given her?

Perhaps another time, Father Turlington had said, and he wished them a good day before leaving the step and retreating along the path.

Never go anywhere with that man, Marie had said, and Anna had accepted the advice without question. The episode hadn't crossed her mind for the best part of two decades, and now here it was, bright and solid as the world all around.

They navigated the paths between the graves, heading for the cluster of cherry trees at the far end of the cemetery. Anna slowed her pace as they approached the family plot, and Marie looked back, told her to come on, keep up.

Soon, they stood at the foot of a large square grave. Two

headstones at the top, three generations of names carved into the marble. All of them familiar, but only two conjured a face to go with them: Grandpa Henry—Henry Joy McKracken Lenihan—who had seemed planted in the corner of the living room when she was a child, always in his chair with a blanket over his knees, always with a quarter to find behind her ear. He died when she was six, but she had images of him burned into her memory. The smell of him, warm like fresh bread, and the glass of Guinness he had before supper every evening. And her father, who was buried here six years later. Oddly, her recollections of him were less clear than those of her grandfather.

And now a new name, down below the men's. Except it wasn't really a name at all, was it?

LITTLE BUTTERFLY, L'IL B,
TAKEN AT JUST DAYS OLD.

"We didn't know the birthday," Marie said. "Father Murtagh christened him at the hospital before they called it, so he's, you know . . ."

"Not in Limbo," Anna said.

"Yeah," Marie said. "It was important to Mom."

They stood in silence for a while before Marie said, "Do you understand now? That he's gone?"

Anna shook her head. "It's just words on a stone."

Marie turned to face her. "What do you mean?"

"Show me his bones," Anna said.

"What?"

"You dig him up and show me the bones of him," Anna said. "Until you do, it's just words on a stone."

Marie's open hand struck her hard on the right side of her face, and she felt sickly heavy pain in her nose and eye. She tasted blood as heat coursed over her lip.

"I want to go home now," Anna said.

SHE AWOKE WITH a start, suddenly aware and tingling all over. The fentanyl had pulled her under at some point in the late afternoon and held her there until now. She rolled over onto her side and peered at the clock by the bed. A quarter after one. Somewhere along the hall, she heard the chatter of one of the late-night talk shows in her mother's room. Philomena would be deep asleep on her bed, entirely unaware.

Anna stretched, savoring the smooth ride of the fentanyl. Two days of numbness from this little plastic film that adhered to her chest. It seemed a small miracle. But she had no time to wallow in it now, as tempting as it might be.

She had fallen asleep in the same clothes she'd worn to the cemetery that morning, including the coat. Hadn't even kicked off her shoes. She eased herself off the bed and went to the closet. The bag lay on the floor, already packed, save for one thing.

Anna descended the stairs, wary of every creak of wood, each whisper of fabric. At the bottom, she made for the kitchen. The drugs were kept in the top cabinet, above the fridge, had been since she was a kid. But now it was sealed with a small padlock on a latch.

She rummaged through drawers until she found a stout-bladed screwdriver. A few seconds of prying, and the latch and the padlock fell to the floor. She opened the cabinet door and reached inside. Her fingers found the old tin tea caddy, and she lifted it down, set it on the table. Inside, a bundle of foil pouches, held together by a rubber band. She counted twenty-three and wondered for a moment where Marie had gotten these from. No legitimate source, Anna was sure of that. Didn't matter. She grabbed the bundle and stuffed it into her bag.

Outside, under the pale streetlights, she pulled the tarpaulin from her car in the driveway. At least five months it had been standing here. God knew if it would start. Anna unlocked the driver's door, tossed the bag over to the passenger seat, then lowered herself in. She inserted the key in the ignition and turned.

The engine barked a series of hacking, jerking coughs and splutters before it finally caught. She pressed the accelerator pedal, felt the car vibrate with the revving of the engine.

"Thank God," she said.

What now?

She had no idea where she might go. All her money was gone. Marie and her mother would be saddled with the hospital bills for years to come. She might have felt guilt over that, but there were a great many things vying for that particular emotion.

Only one objective stood clearly in Anna's mind: find the woman who took her boy. Find her and take him back. Didn't matter how long it took. She had years.

That decided, she put the car in reverse and backed out of the driveway. She paused for a moment on the street, looking up at the house that she was leaving for the second time with no expectation to return.

Then she put the car in gear and drove away, thinking only of her destination, no matter how far away it might be.

55

I T TOOK THREE YEARS TO FIND HIM. ANNA HAD BEEN TO HELL AND back in that time. There were long gaps in her memory, periods of haze when the fentanyl dragged her as low as a human being could go and still claim that title. Looking back, there were periods during which she couldn't even recall where she lived. She had vague images of sleeping in hallways, doorways, the floors of abandoned apartments. She supposed those had been the colder times; others, when she didn't risk freezing to death, she slept in her car, which she still owned. It was the only thing of value she had left.

It was a church-run shelter that finally helped her get straight after two years without a home. They sponsored her detox, then gave her a place to live while she straightened out. As soon as she was able, they had her working again. A coffee shop run by the same church, employing homeless people to help them get back on their feet. After six months, she had her own place again, as wretched as it was. She had an address, a bed of her own, and something resembling a life.

But she never forgot L'il B or the woman who took him from her. There was only one reason in the world to get herself straight, to have a place of her own, and that was to get him back. If not for him, she would gladly have given up on living. So as soon as she had the money, she bought a secondhand laptop from a pawnshop, and got herself an Internet connection. She lost days and weeks to searching through social-media sites, looking for a woman called Libby with a son of around the right age.

In the end, it was a dumb little Facebook app that made the connection. The app could take one photograph and scan through all the many millions on social media and find people who looked alike. Looking back, Anna couldn't clearly remember the other woman's features, only the idea that she looked like her. So she tried the app, uploading a photograph of herself.

The first two matches were women who were either too old or too young, and neither of them called Libby.

The third hit was a Liz Moore, from Albany, New York. The photograph was a professional portrait, taken in a studio. And it was not a personal Facebook account, but rather a publisher's page, highlighting a book that was to come out in the fall. Liz Moore was the author. Liz, as in Elizabeth.

Libby was also short for Elizabeth, wasn't it?

Anna had sat quietly in her one-room apartment for some time before entering the name Liz Moore into Facebook's search box. A lot of hits, but none of them matching this woman. She tried Libby Moore with similar results, then Elizabeth Moore. Nothing even close.

Next, she opened Google and entered: Liz Moore author.

There, first result, Official Website of Author Liz Moore. She clicked on the link and saw a site that consisted of a single page. That portrait again, and the cover of the book, along with a few lines describing the story. And there, at the bottom, in a font size so small she almost missed it, a Twitter handle: @LizMooreAuthor.

Anna clicked on the link to open the Twitter profile. Like the website, it gave almost nothing away. There were perhaps a dozen tweets going back over a few months, all promoting the book. Nothing personal. Nothing about children.

She looked at the follower numbers: less than three hundred, and Liz Moore followed only a few more. Did that mean she was in the habit of following back whoever followed her? Anna had her own Twitter account that she had recently created but never used.

An idea occurred to her. A stupid one, maybe, but worth trying.

She went to the Edit Profile page on her account and changed the bio section, which she'd left blank, to say: Aspiring author.

Then she went back to the Liz Moore profile and clicked the Follow button.

Within an hour, Liz Moore had followed her back.

Anna felt frozen in place. Could this be her? Could this be the woman who stole her baby? And if it was, what would she do?

She clicked on the Message button, and a dialog box appeared with a blinking cursor. A deep breath, then she typed:

Hi—You don't know me, and sorry to get in touch out of the blue like this, but I'd love to know more about how you got your publishing deal. Yours, a fellow writer.

Anna hadn't ever written anything more than a few notes on a scrap of paper, but the lie came easy enough. She didn't expect a reply, so she needed to think about another approach. But a reply came, almost instantly.

Hi, thanks for getting in touch. I got my deal the old-fashioned way—over the transom—by querying agents. I got taken on by a great one who then subbed the book around New York. Not very exciting, but it worked!

Anna read the words and thought, Is it you?

That's awesome. Would you mind if I picked your brains sometime about all this? I'm just starting out and could use some advice.

Less than a minute before the next reply.

Of course, though there's a lot of advice online already, most of which I followed. But sure, drop me a note. Always happy to help another writer.

"Is it you?" Anna asked aloud.

She held back, replied with a simple thanks, and let it lie for a week. While she waited tables at the coffee shop, wiped down counters, took out the trash, she thought hard about what to do. The possibility remained that she could be mistaken, that this could be some other woman with a resemblance to her, but she had a feeling in her gut that said otherwise. And she had to tread softly, not rush things. In the meantime, she created a fake Facebook account and added a handful of photographs she'd stolen from someone else's profile. Called herself Marie Douglas, from North Carolina, created a life for herself out on the Internet with a husband and a daughter.

After the week of silence had passed, she sent another message, asking about Liz Moore's book, what it was about, what her inspiration was. Liz Moore, if that was her name, replied quickly, and almost seemed glad of the conversation. They exchanged messages on and off for a few days, then Anna sent one more:

Hey Liz, I've just joined Facebook. Are you on there? I looked for your name so I could send a friend request, but I couldn't find you. I'm Marie Douglas, if you want to search for me.

Two and a half hours passed, and Anna feared she had gone too far, that she might have spooked her. Then two emails came, one after the other. The first said she'd received a friend request from a Libby Reese, the second that Liz Moore had sent her a message via Twitter.

Hey—I sent you a friend request. It's from Libby Reese, my real name. I use my pen name because I like to hang on to my privacy. My Facebook account isn't public, so you wouldn't have been able to find it. L.

"It's her," Anna said. "It's really her."

She felt a mix of joy and rage as she opened Facebook on her laptop and clicked on the Friends notification. There she was, Libby Reese. Anna clicked on the Confirm button, then through to her profile.

It was her, no doubt. Only a small number of friends. But

looking at the photographs, Anna was convinced this was the woman she remembered from that morning when everything was stolen from her. She scrolled down through the posts, and there, there he was.

"Oh God," Anna said.

She let out a shrill giggle that bubbled up from her stomach to her throat, then turned to hitching tears. One hand went to her mouth, the other to the screen, her fingertips touching his image. Three years old now, and so beautiful. Libby had called him Ethan.

"Hey, Little Butterfly," she whispered.

ANNA DIDN'T SLEEP for three days. Every time she lay down, her mind turned to her L'il B and how she was going to get him back. Every time, she opened her laptop and looked at the few photographs of him on Libby Reese's Facebook page. She had posted none of them herself. They were all from friends. Libby didn't seem to use the site much, and she gave little of herself away. Like she had something to hide.

On the fourth day, Anna called her sister.

"Hello?" Marie answered.

"Hey," Anna said. "It's me."

Quiet for a few moments, then, "Anna?"

"Yeah."

"Jesus, Anna, where are you? I've been looking for you. My God, we were so worried when you disappeared, we didn't know if you were alive or dead, and it broke Mom's heart, it really—"

"I found him," Anna said.

"What?"

"I found L'il B," Anna said. "She has him. The woman who shot me. I found them both. They're in Albany."

"Anna, no. Not this. Your baby died. Whoever you've found, it's not him. Please, Anna, come home."

"Will you help me?"

"Of course, I'll help you. If you come home, we can get you a therapist, whatever you need, but—"

"That's not what I meant. Will you help me get him back? If I go to the police on my own, they'll say it's not him. I need you to go to the cops with me, tell them L'il B's alive, that he's in Albany. Will you do that? Marie? Are you there?"

Anna closed her eyes and listened to her sister's breathing through the static.

"No, I won't," Marie said at last, her voice trembling. "I will get you all the help you need, but I won't do that because I know it's not true."

"Then fuck you," Anna said, spitting the words.

"Anna, I have to tell you, Mom's sick, she has canc—"

Anna hung up and threw the phone against the wall.

WEEKS TURNED TO months as Anna held back, biding her time, waiting for her opportunity. She noted the few posts that Libby Reese made on Facebook, and every post her friends made to her wall. Anna remained in the background, kept quiet, didn't post or comment, watching.

Then, one afternoon, someone called Nadine posted a link to a TripAdvisor review for a resort in Naples, Florida.

Ooh, look at it! I'm so jealous! This time next week, you'll be soaking in that infinity pool while I'm still stuck behind a desk in freaking Albany! Enjoy, you two, you deserve it! xxx

Anna clicked on the link to the resort. She had to admit, it did look wonderful, and she felt the bite of jealousy with which she had grown deeply familiar. Going back to the Facebook page, she stared at it in confusion for a few seconds before she realized what had happened.

Libby had deleted her friend's post.

56

TONIGHT

ANNA HAD ARRIVED THE DAY BEFORE LIBBY DID AND SPENT HER time walking the grounds, trying not to be noticed. On the afternoon of Anna's second day, she saw them, Libby and Ethan—no, L'il B—playing in the pool. Anna had stood in the shadows of the trees, watching, watching, watching. Biding her time. This was not the moment, but the moment would surely come. There would be a time when Libby's back was turned and Anna could take what was hers.

That moment had come tonight.

Anna had watched her getting drunk and dancing with that man while his partner looked after L'il B. Then she had followed them inside and observed as her boy entered the elevator unseen. Before the doors had even closed, Anna was on her way up the stairs, racing the elevator.

She couldn't remember what floor it was that L'il B had finally emerged onto. Only that she had stood at the stairs, watching along the hallway, as he wandered first one way then the other. And when she saw his distress, she could wait no longer, she had to go to him.

Anna ran to the boy, hunkered down in front of him.

"Hey, L'il B, what's up?"

He stared at her, then past her, his shoulders hitching as he bordered on panic.

"Where's my mommy?" he asked.

Anna took his hands in hers and said, "I know where she is, and I'm going to take you to her right now. I'm an old friend of hers. I've known you since you were born. But I bet you don't remember me, do you?"

He shook his head.

"Come on," she said, and she stood upright and led him back to the stairs.

She needed to figure out which floor she was on, then get him back to her room. She checked the signs for the room numbers outside the elevators: fifth floor. Pulling L'il B by the hand, she made her way back to the stairs. As she reached them, a man climbed the last steps. He froze, staring at her.

"Charles!" L'il B shouted.

She recognized him then, the man who'd been with Libby when the boy ran into the elevator. His face broke into a toothy smile.

"Hey, little guy!" he said. He looked to Anna. "Thank God you found him. We've been looking all over. His mother's down-stairs in the lobby. We can take the elevator."

"No," Anna said.

"I'm sorry?" His face creased with confusion. "His mother's absolutely distraught. I'd really like to take him straight to her."

"You've got him mixed up," Anna said. "He's my son. Excuse me."

"What are you talking about? That's Ethan. His mom's name is Libby, and I'm going to take him to her now. Okay, Ethan? You want to go find Mommy?"

"Yeah, find Mommy!"

He pulled at Anna's hand, trying to run to the man on the stairs. She allowed him to drag her to the top step.

"This is my son and you're not taking him anywhere," Anna said.

The man reached for L'il B, and without any conscious

295

thought, Anna extended her free hand. She didn't push. Not really. She simply took his balance and watched him fall. Heard the snap of bone, the hollow thud of his head on the steps.

L'il B cried out, but Anna whisked him away, up the next flight of steps, and the next, until they reached the sixth floor. The last step clipped the toe of her sandal, and she almost fell as the shoe bounced back down the stairs. She righted herself and led L'il B down the hallway to her room, limping, fishing in her pocket for the key as she went.

The busybody from across the hall emerged from her room, watched Anna and her boy approach.

"Well, who's this?" she asked.

Anna didn't answer. She unlocked her own door and pulled L'il B inside, then kicked off the remaining shoe.

"I want Mommy," he said as she lifted him onto the bed. "Charles fell down. He banged his head."

"Yeah," Anna said. "I'm sure he's fine. It's all going to be fine. We'll go find Mommy soon, okay? You wanna watch cartoons?"

He didn't answer, so she grabbed the remote control and turned the television on, and flipped through the channels until she found some brightly colored dogs in uniforms.

"*Paw Patrol!*" L'il B shouted.

Anna told him shush, and paced the room, trying to get her mind straight. She hadn't thought any of this through. What had she imagined would happen? That she'd just be able to waltz out through the doors with her boy? Of course they'd be looking for him. Probably hotel security would be watching the exits and the gates. She didn't even know how many exits there were.

"What do I do?" she asked the air.

L'il B had become quiet, transfixed by the moving images.

"What do I do?"

She sat down on the bed, her hands pressed to her temples, willing herself to think. Time passed, one episode of the cartoon was followed by another, and still she had no idea what course of action to take.

The wailing of sirens from outside stirred her.

Anna went to the sliding door that led out onto the balcony. Her room faced the main entrance gate with the fountain down below. She pulled the door open and stepped out onto the balcony. Looking down, she saw three police cars pull up.

"Oh no," she said.

Anna stepped back inside the room and pulled the sliding door over, then closed the curtains. She walked in a circle once, twice, three times, fear breaking through, ready to rob her of all reason.

Go to them, she thought. Take L'il B downstairs to the police and the security guards and explain, tell them what that woman had done, what she had taken from her. Tell the truth, because nothing is better than the truth. The truth has no regrets, didn't she always say that? Yes, she did.

But they wouldn't believe her. Just like back in the hospital, they'd think she was crazy. They'd take her boy and give him back to the woman who had stolen him.

"What do I do? What do I do?"

L'il B looked up at her now, worry on his face.

"Go find Mommy now," he said.

"Soon, baby," she said.

"Go now," he said, his voice rising.

Anna went to the bed, kneeled down beside it, and took his hands in hers.

"Baby, I want you to listen to me now. Are you listening?"

His gaze went back to the television. She reached for the remote control and turned it off.

"L'il B," she said. "Ethan. I don't know if you can ever understand this, but you're supposed to be with me. Something happened when you were a tiny baby, only a few weeks old, and you were taken from me. You're mine. Do you understand?"

He stared at her for a moment, then pulled his hands away. Then he scrambled off the bed and ran for the door. She ran after him, around the bed, reached the door at the same time, held it closed with her hand as he pulled on the handle.

Anna hunkered down and wrapped her arms around him.

"I won't ever let you go again," she whispered as he writhed in her embrace. "Never, ever. I promise."

"Let go," he shouted, his voice high and piercing in her ear. "I want my mommy."

"She's not . . ."

Anna stopped herself from saying it. How could he understand?

"Go find Mommy," he squealed.

"All right," Anna said. "All right. We'll go, but you have to be quiet. Can you do that for me? Can you be quiet?"

He nodded, calm now. She opened the door and led him out into the hallway. For time immeasurable, she wandered around the floor, from south to north and back again, certain only that if she stopped, she would lose her mind.

Eventually, she heard voices from below. Urgent footsteps.

Anna found a plain door with a sign that said it was for emergencies only. She pushed it open and found herself on a small landing, a narrow concrete stairway leading up and down. A harsh light blinked on overhead. Climbing seemed the only way, so she hoisted L'il B up into her arms and ascended one flight of stairs after another, cold on her bare feet, until she found herself looking up at the exit onto the roof.

Part of her felt a pull toward it, as if it were the only place left in the world. Another part of her dreaded it, knowing it would be the end of her.

She froze, locked there, until Libby Reese stepped onto the landing below.

57

RAYMOND VILLALOBOS SAID, "WHAT DO YOU MEAN, YOU'RE his mother?"

"Just what I said."

She glared at him with wild eyes. He'd seen crazy enough times to know it on sight, but this was more. This was dangerous.

"Don't come any closer," Anna Lenihan said. "Please don't. I don't want to hurt anybody."

He remained at Libby's side, Anna above them. He counted the steps between here and there, tried to calculate how quickly he could climb them. Two, three seconds, maybe. Not quick enough. She could do a lot of damage in three seconds.

"I'm staying right here," Villalobos said. "But there are cops coming. When they get here, I want you to stay calm, don't do anything stupid."

"Keep them away from me," Anna said.

"I'll try," he said. "Now, tell me what you want. Make me understand."

"I just want my baby," Anna said. "I just want him back. That's all."

"He's not yours," Libby said.

Villalobos put a hand on her arm to silence her, but she ignored him.

"He's adopted. I have all the documents. He was born in New York to an addict. The state took him into care, and we adopted him."

"That's a lie," Anna said, climbing a step higher. "You stole him from me."

"It's the truth, Anna, I swear on my life. Please let him go."

She climbed higher still, almost to the top, and the door leading out onto the roof.

Villalobos reached a hand up. "Don't go any further," he said. "Stay and talk to me."

"I found you," Anna said to Libby, a grin cracking her face. "It took me three years, but I did it. You couldn't hide forever. Not from me. I found you and I'm taking him back."

From below, the sound of a door opening and slamming into a wall. Heavy footsteps resonating up through the stairwell.

Villalobos looked up, saw Anna's eyes widen at the noise before she ascended the last two steps and shouldered her way through the exit. The door swung closed again.

"No!" Libby called after her.

"Goddammit," Villalobos said, then he set off at a run, taking two steps at a time, a band of pain tightening around his chest.

He emerged onto the roof, breathing hard, his shoes crunching on the gravel that covered the surface. At first, he saw no sign of her, then he heard the child cry somewhere off to his right. He turned in that direction and felt a chill deep in his gut.

Anna Lenihan stood before the low wall that bordered the roof, the boy in her arms. She stared out across the resort grounds, toward the sea. He knew the layout of the place well enough; the tiled terrace was seven stories straight down. Part of him wished he had found the boy in the pool earlier.

Libby staggered out onto the roof, and she turned to follow his gaze, then screamed. She was ready to sprint toward her son, but Villalobos grabbed her arm, told her to wait.

"Don't give her a reason to do it," he said. "Just hold back."

He heard the footsteps and the voices below, how many he couldn't tell, but it was too many. He went back to the door, saw Cole leading a half dozen cops up the final flight of stairs. He raised a hand to silence them, and Cole signaled at his people to be quiet. They kept coming, but slowly. Villalobos held the door for them as they emerged into the night.

"Shit," Cole said when he saw. He turned to the nearest uniform. "Radio in. Tell them we got a jumper and we need a negotiator here like now."

"I don't think we have time," Villalobos said.

"Me neither," Cole said. He glanced at Villalobos. "You all right, man?"

Villalobos swallowed and said, "I'm fine."

Cole signaled to the others, ordered them to spread out on either side of where Anna stood.

Villalobos tested the gravel with his shoe, listened to the deafening crunch of it. He cursed and began to move forward, stepping as gently as he could. Cole walked at his side.

"I talk, you grab," Villalobos said.

"Yeah," Cole said.

"Go low," Villalobos said.

"If I go low, and she drops the kid . . ."

"If you go high, she'll take you with her."

"Yeah," Cole said. "We've got to get her before she gets up on that wall."

But it was too late. Anna climbed up onto the wall. Libby wailed.

Villalobos kept walking, veering out to Anna's left, while Cole held back.

God help me, he thought.

58

NOW

ANNA TESTS THE AIR WITH ONE FOOT, LETTING IT HANG OVER the edge, balancing on the other. It would be so easy to bring it all to an end. No more nightmares. No more waking in the dark, panicking, reaching for her baby and remembering he's gone. Grieving for him anew, every time. The wound that never heals.

The fall will heal it. Once and for all, for ever and ever.

But does she have the courage? She doesn't know. Her foot comes back to the wall, and she shifts her weight, hoists Ethan up.

"That's it," the security guard says. "Just come back a little more. You're scaring me, you know? I'm not a young man any-more, I can't take the—"

Something stops the words from leaving his mouth. Anna sees him wave at somebody, his teeth bared. He's telling them to stay back, stay back, stay back.

"Let me talk to her," Libby Reese says.

Anna turns her head. "Why would I talk to you?"

"You don't have to. Just listen."

She draws closer. Anna wraps her arms tight around Ethan.

"There's not a word you could say that I'd want to hear."

Libby stops ten feet away, her hands up, as if surrendering. She trembles. Anna can smell the fear. Taste it. It brings her a savage pleasure.

Libby gets down on her knees, hands still raised, her surrender near complete. "I think you need to hear me say it. Please, just listen."

"You took everything from me," Anna says, spitting the words, feeling them raw in her throat. "You took it just because you could, because you had the money and you thought you could buy anything you wanted. Even my son."

"He's not your son," Libby says. "I told you. That is not your child. Ethan was taken from a couple in New York, meth addicts, and my husband and I adopted him. He is not your child, Anna, I swear to God, please don't take him from me."

Anna turns toward her, feels the edge of the wall as she does so, people gasp all around.

"Take him from you? He was never yours. You stole him from me."

Libby clasps her hands together as if in prayer. She closes her eyes, her face contorting as if in terrible pain. A high whine comes from her, then a gasping inhalation.

"I killed your baby," Libby says.

The words pierce Anna's consciousness and she becomes quite still.

"I killed your baby," Libby says again, her eyes opening. "In the trailer. When I shot at you I hit him. I killed him. He's gone. It was me. It was always me. Don't take Ethan. He doesn't deserve to die for what I did. Look at him. Please, look at him. Look how beautiful he is. Please don't take him."

Anna looks down at the child in her arms. He is very still and quiet, his eyes distant, as if his soul has left his body. But he is beautiful, just like her L'il B was. She feels something tear inside of her, something comes loose, and she cries out, deep sobs that burst from the center of her.

"I wish I could take it back," Libby says. "I wish I could go back to that morning and pull the gun out of my hand. I wish I could give you back your baby. But I can't. There's nothing I can

303

do to put it right, I know that. But please, don't take Ethan. He didn't do anything. Please let him go."

"Why couldn't you let me have him?" Anna shouts, her voice scorching her throat.

"I'm sorry," Libby says.

"Why didn't you just walk away? You saw me there with him. You saw he was mine. Why couldn't you walk away and let me have him?"

Libby has no reply. She slumps down, weighted by her sins, her eyes fixed on Anna's.

"Goddamn you to hell," Anna says.

She opens her arms and lets Ethan fall to the gravel roof. He lands hard but doesn't make a sound, his soul still absent. A policeman dives in, grabs the child, whisks him away.

"I'm coming, L'il B," Anna says.

She leans back, sees heaven and all its wonders.

Gravity takes her.

59

SOMEDAY

ETHAN PLAYS ON THE RUG ON THE LIVING-ROOM FLOOR, BUT he isn't really thinking about the building blocks and cars all around him. He is too excited. Tomorrow is his birthday. There won't be a party tomorrow. Daddy and Tanya will have a party with him today instead with a cake and presents and everything. There won't be a party tomorrow because tomorrow Daddy and Ethan are going to wake up early and get on an airplane and fly away. When they land, they will go to a special place and visit Mommy. Ethan hasn't seen Mommy for a long time.

Daddy has warned Ethan that he might not like the place where Mommy lives now, but he shouldn't be scared. Ethan doesn't care about that. He just wants to see Mommy. Ethan likes living with Daddy and Tanya, but he misses Mommy. Sometimes he misses her so bad that it makes him hurt inside and he cries.

Tanya has a baby in her belly. Ethan is going to be a big brother. Tanya showed him a picture. It was all fuzzy and it didn't look like a baby at all.

A few days ago, Ethan called Tanya Mommy by mistake. That made Ethan feel bad, and he hid under the kitchen table and cried. He told Dr. Sarah about it yesterday. Daddy takes Ethan to see Dr. Sarah sometimes. They sit on the floor and play with toys while they talk. Dr. Sarah said it was okay to call Tanya Mommy, even if she wasn't his real mommy. It wouldn't mean he stopped loving his real mommy. Ethan likes Dr. Sarah even though they sometimes talk about things that make him sad. Daddy says it's good to talk about those things.

Yesterday, they talked about the night Ethan got lost. He doesn't remember it very well. He remembers being scared, and the strange lady who took his hand and brought him to the room to watch cartoons. The lady fell. Ethan remembers that. He remembers the sound of it.

Sometimes Ethan has a dream. In his dream, he is way up high in the sky. It is nighttime and the sky is dark and there are stars. He is flying in the sky and he can see the moon, big and bright and fat. It hangs over the sea, reflected on the waves, and the sea stretches on and on. Ethan is so high up it makes him dizzy.

But Ethan never falls.

He never, ever falls.

AUTHOR'S NOTE

Lost You is a work of fiction. It should not in any way be perceived as an attack on the idea of surrogacy. While the story presents some questions about the commercial exploitation of women and those people who have no other path to parenthood, and the legal uncertainty they often face, the author fully recognizes the good done by surrogate mothers around the world.

ACKNOWLEDGMENTS

As ever, I owe my gratitude to a number of people who have helped get this book over the finish line.

Nat Sobel, my agent for the last decade, has steered me through some stormy waters, along with Judith Weber, and everyone at Sobel Weber. Likewise, Caspian Dennis and everyone at Abner Stein.

Nate Roberson, Molly Stern, and everyone at Crown; Jade Chandler, Geoff Mulligan, Liz Foley, Faye Brewster, and everyone at Harvill Secker; thank you for your patience and understanding.

I owe Joe Long thanks for his expertise in the workings of elevators, but also for his continued friendship, support, advocacy, and occasional care packages. Joe, I owe you a beer. Maybe two.

I continue to depend on the friendship of too many fellow crime writers to list here, but you know who you are, and I thank you.

And Jo, Issy, and Ezra, who make it all worthwhile.

ABOUT THE AUTHOR

HAYLEN BECK is the pen name of internationally prize-winning crime writer Stuart Neville. Writing under his own name, Stuart won the LA Times Book Prize for his debut novel and received critical acclaim for his Belfast-set detective series starring Serena Flanagan. His Haylen Beck novels are set in the US and are inspired by his love of American crime writing.

www.haylenbeck.com